INVOLUNTARY ADMISSIONS

A Novel by

D. R. Markham

INVOLUNTARY ADMISSIONS

PROLOGUE

Amy Bunton was exhausted. Making her fourth set of hourly nursing rounds for her fifth night shift in a row, she carried a tray of plastic syringes, 25 gauge needles and vials filled with brightly colored fluids. While double checking the medication administration record for Room 212, Amy cringed. She detested rousing a sleeping patient to give him a sedating medicine, but this particular doctor insisted. She was not about to cross him.

Shane jolted awake. A cold shiver ran through his body. Something was very wrong. His head felt funny. No, deeper. Inside his head. His brain. His brain felt funny. Shane tried to reach his hand to his head. He could barely move his right arm. It felt as though a hundred-pound weight were attached to it. He couldn't move his left arm at all. He struggled valiantly for what felt like an hour and finally he was able to bring his right hand to his face. Shane touched his sweaty forehead and gasped as he felt wires there. He could now sense them all over his head. While trying to pry one loose from his temple, his hand became damp with a sticky, cool gel. Seconds later, his hand felt nothing. His fingertips grew numb. His whole body went numb. His brain went numb.

Then, the trembling began. At first, Shane thought he was shaking out of fear but the tremors grew worse. He couldn't stop them. In a sort of detached haze, he realized he needed immediate help. In the grim darkness, he squinted his eyes to search for someone, anyone. What he saw was an empty, sanitized room, dimly lit by equipment panels. A hospital room. His confused mind tried to concoct a plan. His right hand slowly crept along the side of his bed. He felt nothing. He tried the same with his left side but his arm still would not budge. He tried to shift his body and reach over with his right hand but found his whole torso was immobile. It was a struggle to lift the stiff muscles in his neck but he managed and looked down at his legs. Leather straps. His legs were tied down with thick, leather straps. His left arm, too. There were even wider straps wrapped around his hips and chest, binding him tightly to the bed. Why was his right arm free though? It didn't really matter. He could barely move it anyway.

Shane yelled for help. He suddenly realized if he was in a hospital surely there was a nurse or doctor who could hear him. Unless...they were the ones who put him in these straps. Whatever he did, he had to act fast. The tremors were becoming violent and a blackness was threatening to overwhelm him. As he opened his mouth a second time, an eerie, strangle cry escaped his lips.

Amy looked at Room 212's patient electronic medical record on her computer on wheels, or COW as they called them. Room 212 was Shame Reynolds, a teenage male who was in restraints and having an overnight EEG. He had been sleep deprived the requisite 24 hours, but was allowed to doze through the procedure. She hated to wake the poor boy. It would only remind him he was tethered to his bed with electrodes attached to his scalp measuring his brain's electrical activity. She had left one of his hand free after injecting his midnight dose of the experimental medication. Shane had been cooperative then, and he had been asleep on the hourly checks after that. If staffing was by the book, an aide should be sitting with him all the time, but budget cuts would never allow that. He wasn't violent anyway. He didn't need such inhumane interventions. He didn't need restraints or a sitter. Amy had thought about releasing his other three limbs but the doctor wanted the six-point restraints on Shane all night. He wanted the medication given exactly per protocol, exactly on time. But she had gotten side tracked with another patient and it was already 3:15 a.m. Even though she was clearly within the half hour grace period nurses have for giving scheduled meds, she was worried. She knew there was no logical way the doctor would be able to tell that the boy's medicine was 15 minutes later than its timed dose. Especially since she'd already overridden the rules and signed it out in the computer at precisely 3:00 a.m. However, with Dr. Aiken, even ridiculously remote possibilities were reason for concern.

Amy tiptoed into room 212. She turned up the dimmer switch and looked over at Shane Reynolds. Her eyes flew wide open. The medication tray fell to the floor, vials smashed and the liquids mixed together to create a blood red pool at her feet. Within seconds, two other nurses on duty, alerted by the clatter, were by her side. All three of them stood there, frozen, watching Shane writhing in a grotesque seizure. His arm and leg muscles tightened violently. Foamy saliva, tinged with blood, oozed from his mouth. A clear fluid trickled out of his ears. His muscles relaxed after two whole minutes. Then, he started convulsing all over again.

Amy took a step forward. She had to help Shane. At least comfort him. One of her colleagues held her back. Dr. Aiken had left specific instructions if this should happen. They were to do nothing to save the boy.

CHAPTER 1

Kendra's tears stained the white, cotton sheets as she pulled her memory foam pillow down around her head, pressing it tightly against her ears. She could still hear that voice. It wasn't going away. Kendra felt the pillow being pulled being pulled from her clutches but she stayed there, lying face down, hoping her tormentor would give up.

"You have to get up for school," Mother said, sitting down beside her. "You can't lie in bed all day."

"Yes, I actually can." Kendra rolled onto her side. "I'm 15 and I can do what I want."

"Not in my house." Mother frowned. "I know I sound just like my own mother sounded to me at your age but honey, I'm worried about you." She stroked her daughter's long, golden hair.

Kendra pushed Mother's hand away. She used to love that, Mother petting her hair. Her hair used to be her pride and joy. Back when she still cared. She looked up at Mother. Auburn hair framed her kind face with a soft fringe. Her green eyes were full of concern. Kendra felt like such a disappointment to her. She had always known that Mary was the favorite. She wondered why she still cared what Mother thought. Kendra leaned over, taking a cigarette and lighter from her nightstand.

"Give me those!" Mother grabbed them out ofher daughter's

hand. She snapped the Marlboro Light in half and pocketed the lighter.

It didn't matter. What Kendra really wanted was the joint stashed in her jewelry box. It was a good thing Mother didn't know about that given the reaction she'd just had to a measly cigarette.

"You're not even listening to me," Mother said, apparently already having launched into another lecture. "There's something wrong with you."

"Thanks," Kendra said, sitting up. "That's nice to hear coming from your own mother."

"I didn't mean it that way." Mother took a deep breath. "It's not normal for a smart, pretty, teenaged girl to hide in her room every day. You never see your friends. You've missed so much school this term, I'm afraid it will set you back a year."

"I don't care." Her voice was flat.

"I know you don't. That's what worries me. You used to care." There was a long pause while Mother smoothed out the imaginary wrinkles in her crisp, navy slacks. "I've made an appointment for us later this morning with Dr. Park. She's a psychologist."

"I'm not crazy, Mother." Kendra rolled her eyes.

"Of course you're not, but there is something wrong, and it's beyond any help I can give you."

"I'm not going to a shrink." Kendra got up and stared out of her window. "Besides, I thought I had to go to school."

"You weren't planning on going anyway. Dr. Park is a psychologist who works out of her home in Chestnut Hill." Another awkward pause. "Doesn't that sound nice?" She sighed. "I'll let you in on a secret, honey. I've been to counseling before myself. You might find it helpful. I did."

"Just because you're a freak, doesn't mean I am." Kendra sat back down on her bed, hugging her knees to her chest. “I’m not going.”

Kendra Ann Sibley, you’re acting like a child.” Mother stood up, putting her hands on her hips. “We’re going and that’s final.”

Kendra started to cry. “I don’t want to. I’m too tired. Just leave me alone.”

Sitting back down, Mother blinked at the tears forming in her own eyes. “If you won’t do it for me, do it for your father. He called this morning. He’s flying down from Maine next weekend to see you. Mary will be coming the day after him for a quick visit. The whole family is worried about you.”

“Family...ha! That’s a laugh. We haven’t been a real family in years.”

“I know but I can’t change that.”

“Then you can’t help me and neither can your stupid psychologist.”

“Honey, honestly, I’m afraid I’m going to come home from work one day and find you...I can’t even say it.” Mother put her face in her hands.

Kendra watched Mother cry. She hated to admit it but maybe she did need some help. She felt awful. Suicide was looking better and better every day. “All right. Don’t cry about it Mother. I’ll go to the appointment. For Daddy.”

Dr. Aiken closed Shane Reynold’s eyelids and pulled the sheet over the boy’s head. “What was the exact time of death?”

“It was 0322 hours,” Amy Bunton said, her voice shaky. “What a tragedy.”

The doctor glared at her. “It is unfortunate but this is one of the few failures in my program.”

“It doesn’t make it any less painful,” Amy said, wiping at her tears. She was exhausted, not having slept since before her shift last night. Being detained for this painful inquiry was stressing her out.

"Amy," Dr. Aiken looked right at her. "Are you not keeping a healthy, professional distance from your patients?" He moved to the head of the gurney. "This is an exemplary situation of why personal emotions associated with a test subject are inadvisable. He began pushing the gurney. "Open the unit door for me."

Amy did as she was told. She watched Dr. Aiken wheel out the dead teenager. "Sure you don't need any help?" she called after him, fearing maltreatment of the boy's remains.

The unit door slammed shut in response. Amy went back to Shane's room and picked up a hospital gown strewn on the floor.

Marguerite, the hospital's Night Charge Nurse, entered the room and handed Amy a pair of gloves. "Be careful. There are traces of blood on that."

Amy dropped the gown and put the gloves on. "Do we have any biohazard bags at the nursing station?"

Marguerite didn't move. She stared at the floor. "No," she said quietly. "The psych aide just went to get some from the clean storage room." Looking back up at her coworker, she saw a pained expression on Amy's face.

"How can he be so cold about it?" Amy locked eyes with Marguerite.

"I guess he has keeping professional distance down to an art."

"He must be feeling something. He is human, right?"

"Well, that's up for debate."

Amy smiled faintly.

Marguerite averted her gaze again. "Maybe he feels a sense of failure for his new drug. That's about it."

"Sometimes I wonder if-"

"Don't! Don't go there. Shane already had a seizure disorder before starting the drug trial. Giving him an experimental medication that has a side effect of lowering the seizure threshold was dangerous. It's sad, but Shane knew the risks. He was desperate for treatment."

"He was only 16! He couldn't make a truly informed decision."

A psych aide came into the room with a bright red bag with biohazard markings on it. Amy took it and tossed the bloodied gown plus three soiled towels into it. She handed it back to the aide who kindly held it open as Amy peeled off her gloves and dropped them in.

"Please dispose of this in the biohazard bin, Kevin, and call housekeeping to do a basic decontamination cleaning of the room."

The aide nodded and solemnly left the room without a word.

Marguerite waited until he was out of earshot. "Shane was in state custody and the guardian approved the use of the drug because it was what Shane wanted. At 16 years old, this wasn't even necessary in the state of Pennsylvania. At age 14, a minor can consent to voluntary mental health treatment."

"It still seems wrong to me. Why did Dr. Aiken wait until 7 a.m. to come in and confirm his death? Shane's body was getting so stiff. He has no regard for human life. Or death." Going to the sink, Amy began to scrub her hands vigorously.

"Maybe in his years as a doctor he's become immune to it all. He doesn't see a death as an emergency. There's nothing for him to do immediately, so why rush?"

"He could at least respect the dignity of the patient."

"The staff too," Marguerite said. "It was kind of gruesome

having the body on the unit for almost four hours."

"Irreverent is what it was." Amy dried her hands with three paper towels. "I wish we were allowed to attend the funeral.

"Really? I think it's better that we can't. I know I couldn't handle it."

"He has no family," Amy said, trashing the paper towels. "Maybe I could arrange a memorial service."

"It's not your place."

"I just wish there was something I could do. We could have prevented this,"

"Don't start."

"If we'd just been equipped to have IV valium on site. Why aren't we prepared for emergencies?"

"As a free-standing psychiatric facility, we're not licensed for IV treatment, or even a true crash cart with advanced cardiac life-saving medications. I thought you knew this. Basic first aid, CPR, and calling the paramedics. That's it for us."

"Maybe if we had called 911..."

"They wouldn't have made it in time. We both know that. Besides, it's not in Dr. Aiken's protocol to call 911." Marguerite moved closer to Amy. She rested a firm hand on her shoulder. "Just leave it alone."

Dr. Aiken let the gurney roll to a stop. He unlocked the door to his office, pulled the body in, and shut the door behind him. Such menial labor was beneath him but it was the only way to ensure appropriate disposal of the bodies. He turned the bolt lock and tested the door. It was secure. Moving to the back of the room, he pushed one of his bookcases away from the wall, grunting as it finally gave way. His elevator was visible and he pushed the one button available. When the doors opened, he wheeled the gurney in. As the doors closed, Dr. Aiken pulled the sheet down just enough to expose the boy's face.

"You have disappointed me, Shane Reynolds."

The elevator doors reopened into an autopsy lab and morgue. Dr. Aiken left Shane's corpse at the entrance and headed to a computer terminal. Pulling up a list of names and number, he punched at the keys.

"Seems like we have a vacancy. Plot D-12"

By 10:30 that Friday morning, Kendra and Mother arrived at Dr. Park's house. It was one of those older homes, built in the early 1900's. Mother said it was charming. Kendra thought it was creepy. The interior was more modern and the psychologist had an office area just off her living room. Kendra assumed it was once a dining room because of the old fashioned chandelier. Now, it was a stylish but subdued shrink shop with black and grey furnishings.

Dr. Park called Mother by her first name, Helen. She called Kendra Miss Sibley. Kendra liked that. The doctor asked Mother to wait in an alcove just outside of her office. Kendra liked that, too.

The psychologist invited her to sit anywhere she wanted, so Kendra picked a black, leather recliner. She pushed a button on the side of the chair which eased it back until she was almost lying down. Dr. Park sat opposite her on a grey love seat, curling her short legs underneath her. The psychologist's jet black bangs fell into her eyes as she read some papers on her lap. On the drive over, Mother had told Kendra that the doctor was Korean but had lived in the United States since she was 15 years old. As if any of that mattered. Mother could suck information out of people before they knew what hit them. But Kendra wondered how Dr. Park felt at 15 years old, moving to a new place, nothing ever being the same again. She wondered if Mother remembered what it was to be 15? Had Mother ever been 15? She was probably born an adult. It was different back then anyway. Mother could never know how a 15-year-old girl today felt. She didn't understand. No one really did. Maybe Daddy, a little. But he was a guy and he wasn't around anymore anyway.

Dr. Park got right to the point. "Your mother tells me it's just you and her at home. Your older sister lives in Connecticut and your father left when you were five. Do you have much contact with him?"

Kendra stared at the plush, black carpeting. "We visit every couple of months. Didn't Mother tell you that?" She closed her eyes and put her hands behind her head.

"Sometimes mothers and daughters have different stories to tell. I want your version. I want to know what you think. So your mother never remarried?"

"No. A few guys have come and gone. Nothing serious. They're all jerks."

"What about you? Any boyfriends? Anyone special?"

Kendra said nothing. Better to let Dr. Park assume the worst even though the opposite was true. Why wasn't she boy crazy like the rest of her friends? She'd never even had sex. Not that she'd tell any of her friends that. She just wasn't interested. Not even in Tyson. He'd been inviting her to hang out at Pastorius Park but she just kept putting him off. He probably thought she was playing hard to get. More like impossible to get. Maybe she was gay. Nah. That didn't interest her either.

Dr. Park looked at her notes again. "Your mother also said that you've been depressed for the past year, especially in the last three months. Is that correct?"

"Uh-huh." Kendra didn't open her eyes, though she was tempted.

"She tells me that you've been having what she calls temper tantrums. Is that what you'd call them?"

"Temper tantrums?! I don't think so. Mother makes me sound like I'm a 3-year-old or something. So I get pissed off. Big deal. That's normal."

Kendra was mad when they'd first arrived here and she wanted to stay mad but that feeling was going away. She felt sad, really. She felt like crying. It was hard not to look at Dr. Park. She was nice. She was calm. She spoke like she was talking to an adult, not a child. Kendra knew it was rude not to look at her or answer properly. Besides, the doctor was waiting her out and the silence was irritating. Usually, Kendra played that game out. And this time it was even on Mother's tab.

"Okay, I get angry and it's hard to control my temper."

"What do you do when you get angry?"

"Yell and throw something. Then, I cry."

"Are you angry right now?"

"A little," Kendra tried to conceal a smile.

"Do you want to yell and throw something right now?"

"No." Kendra laughed for the first time in months.

Dr. Park laughed too. "Good because most of my stuff is breakable. Can we talk about your depression in more detail now?" She caught Kendra's gaze for the first time in the conversation. "I have all your outward symptoms listed here from the screening form. Sleeping about 14 to 16 hours a day, no appetite, weight loss of 10 pounds, crying spells, temper flare ups, lack of attention to grooming and skipping school. Would you agree with those?"

"Yeah. It's all true." Kendra blushed a little.

"Your mother also says she thinks you're smoking pot."

Kendra was impressed. Maybe Mother wasn't so dumb after all. She stayed silent though. Best not to confess this one.

Dr. Park said, "A lot of teens use alcohol and drugs to cope.

Adults too, for that matter. Maybe you're using it to cope with your depression?" She paused for a minute. "It's actually a good sign to me that you're seeking help. Perhaps just the wrong kind. There are much better treatments for your condition than marijuana. It can leave you more depressed and unmotivated. How much do you smoke?"

Again, Kendra said nothing.

"It's okay," Dr. Park said, "It's confidential. I can't tell the police and I won't tell your mother how much you use. I won't even write the amount down. Just so I can have an idea of how to help you. Here," she said, reaching her hand out. "You can even hold my pen."

Kendra smirked. "Usually just a couple joints a week. It depends how much money I have or if I can bum it off someone."

"Thank you," Dr. Park said. She put her notes down on the love seat. "Now can you tell me in more detail about your mood? In other words, how are you feeling?"

Kendra thought hard. "I can't describe it."

"Try. Just do your best. There's no right or wrong answer." Putting her feet back down on the floor, Dr. Park leaned forward, her head in her delicate hands, her elbows resting on her knees.

Kendra raised the back of the chair half way up so she could look at the woman. "I feel like I've been swallowed up into a big, black hole."

Dr. Park nodded. "Good description. Go on."

"I kind of like it there."

"Why?"

"I don't know. It's safe, I guess."

"No one can hurt you in there?"

"Yeah, kind of." Kendra sat straight up in the chair. "I'm also afraid that I'll never get out of it either. Does that make any sense?"

Dr. Park and Kendra talked about her thoughts and feelings for the next half hour. Kendra amazed herself with what she'd bottled up. Also, what she was willing to share with this woman she'd just met. Dr. Park had a way of drawing things out of her. She felt herself float into a daze while talking, the words came automatically and her conversation was peppered with comments like *tired, afraid* and *lonely.*

She was snapped back into full consciousness when Dr. Park asked, "Do you plan to kill yourself?"

No one had ever asked her that. Mother was too afraid. Daddy wouldn't know enough to ask. Mary had her own life. Besides, they were never that close.

"I've thought about it."

"Do you have a plan of how to kill yourself?"

"I thought about taking an overdose of Mother's medicine. She pops stress pills."

"Do you know what her pills are called?"

"The bottle says alprazolam." She doubted she was pronouncing it right but Dr. Park was nodding.

"Have you ever actually tried to kill yourself?"

Kendra thought for a moment. "I was close once. About two weeks ago. I stayed home from school. Mother was at work and she had a class after that so I knew I'd have lots of time. I had a handful of pills in my hand.""

"What stopped you?"

"I was afraid it wouldn't work. That I'd still be alive somehow. End up a vegetable or something. I saw a show about that. There were these losers who screwed up at killing themselves and ended up in wheelchairs having to be spoon-fed and stuff like that. That would really suck. Knowing me, that would be my luck."

"That is a frightening possibility. Do you think that will stop you the next time you feel suicidal?"

"No," Kendra said, looking at the floor again. "I've been doing research online. I know how to do it right now."

Dr. Park nodded. "It's time to bring your mother back in now." She went to the door, opened it and waved her in. Both women sat on the love seat.

"Helen, Kendra, I think we need to look at more intensive treatment than I can provide for you at the moment."

"What does that mean?" Kendra asked, leaning forward.

"Your mother and I discussed this as a possible option before you came in. I was hoping we could do this on an outpatient basis but I'm afraid it's too risky at this moment in time."

"We need to get you some help before this gets any worse." Mother walked over to the recliner.

"What do you want to do? Lock me up somewhere?"

"No," Dr. Park said. "But we do want you to be safe."

No one said a word for a few minutes.

Then, Mother spoke up. "There's a place about 70 miles west of Philadelphia. They can help us with your problems. I think it's for the best."

"You think it's for the best! You think it's for the best to lock me up and throw away the key? No fucking way! I can't believe you're doing this to me! You tricked me. Both of you. I thought I could at least trust you Dr. Park. You ratted me out. Thanks a hell of lot for nothing, you bitch."

Kendra started toward the door but Dr. Park blocked her way.

"I'm sorry you feel betrayed," she said, "but I have to put your safety first. Suicidal thoughts, especially with a plan and access to that plan, need to be handled on an inpatient basis."

Kendra thought about pushing her way past this tiny, evil woman. She could easily shove her aside. She could probably take Mother too. But that might just make things worse. They might call the cops or something. Instead, Kendra turned away from Dr. Park.

"Please don't send me away, Mother. I'll be good. I'll go to school. I'll hang with my friends. Whatever I'm supposed to do, I'll do it. I swear." She was trying for sad and sincere but she knew she just sounded desperate.

Do you think you can honestly make good on that promise right now?" Mother said, not falling for the act.

"Can't I just go live with Daddy?"

Mother sighed. "We have this discussion all the time. The answer is, and always will be, no."

"The intent," Dr. Park said, "is not to lock you up because you've been bad. You haven't been bad. You have an illness. It's called Major Depressive Disorder. That's where your behavior and anger are coming from."

Kendra stared at her feet. She could feel her palms getting hot, her fists clenching.

"You are angry about a lot of things," she continued. "Some of the anger is coming out in your rages. Some of it, you are turning inward toward yourself. That's where the suicidal feelings are coming from."

"It's an illness," Mother said. "Your brain chemistry isn't working right."

"You think I'm brain damaged?" Kendra wiped her runny nose on her sleeve. "You think I'm crazy?"

"No one called you that," Mother said, "but you do have something wrong with you. Something that can be treated."

"Right. As long as it's not *your* fault. As long as you can pin it on *me*, then you're happy."

"We need to get you some help. Despite what you think, I *do* love you and I *don't* want to lose you."

"Yeah, sure," Kendra said, muscles tensing. "That's why you want to send me away." Choking back sobs, she stalked over to a small, black, lacquered table behind the love seat. She felt her anger well up and screamed as she picked up a pile of papers and threw them in the air. Swiping at the remaining sheets of paper on the desk, she scattered them to the floor. Then she flipped the table over on its side.

Dr. Park patted her arm reassuringly as Mother, at first hesitantly, then with more confidence, approached Kendra who was now just standing still and screaming. Mother encircled her daughter in her arms. Kendra didn't pull away. She just let her arms hang to her side as her screams changed to sobs and she let her head fall onto Mother's shoulder. Finally, they were both softly crying, hugging each other.

Mother pulled back and looked Kendra straight in the eye. "I can't handle this anymore. You have to get help. We have to go there. We have to go there right now."

"I know," Kendra said, accepting the tissues Dr. Park was handing out. "I hate when I get like this but I can't help it. It just takes me over. I don't blame you for hating me."

Mother took Kendra's face in her hands. "I don't hate you. I love you. More than I can ever tell you. That's why I'm doing this."

Kendra pulled away, bent down and stared at the overturned table. "Sorry Dr. Park. I didn't mean to do that. I don't think I broke it or damaged it, did I?"

"Don't worry about it. I understand that you're upset. I'm more concerned about you than my table."

Both of them lifted the lightweight piece of furniture and turned it back upright. They stared at the mess of papers on the floor.

"Can I help you pick those up?"

"No. They are all confidential documents. I do appreciate the offer though. I'll tell you what you can do. Promise me that once you're finished with your inpatient treatment that you'll come back and see me for outpatient sessions."

"You mean you'd still talk to me?"

"Of course."

Kendra took a long look at the doctor. She didn't look angry. She didn't look upset at all. *If someone had treated me that way and did that to my stuff, I'd be majorly pissed,* Kendra thought.

"How long do I have to stay in this stupid hospital?"

"There's no set time frame. It's based on how much time you need to get better. Maybe a week or two?"

"Two weeks?! That's insane!"

Mother spoke up quickly. "Maybe, she said. Maybe less. We'll see what they have to say once we get there."

"It better be less. What's this place like anyway?" Kendra asked.

"It's very nice," Dr. Park said. "It's done up like a hotel, out in Lancaster County. Once you settle in, I think you'll enjoy the relaxing country setting."

"I doubt it." Kendra sighed. "What's it called?"

Dr. Park smiled and said, "It's called Aiken's Haven."

CHAPTER 2

Kendra was overwhelmed. She didn't want to sign any more papers. She didn't want to answer any more questions. She just wanted to go home. When they had first entered Aiken's Haven, Kendra had calmed down. The place looked like the resort hotel they had gone on vacation to the year before the divorce. On the tour of this hospital, Kendra saw a fancy dining room, a pool and they even had a game arcade in the recreation room with several X Boxes, PlayStations, a Wii and some old timey games, too. She was almost looking forward to a weekend at this place. Almost. *Strange. No one was swimming or gaming,* she thought.

Then, back in the Admissions Office, she'd been interrogated by several different people, all asking the same questions that Dr. Park had already covered. Mother had been reviewing and signing legal forms for most of the afternoon. They had spent a lot of time sitting and waiting for the next person to throw questions and documents at them. Now, as they watched a young medical resident, Dr. Williams, finish typing rapidly on a laptop, they were sitting and waiting again. It was close to dinner time. Kendra was hungry, tired and irritated.

"Don't leave me here," she said, gripping Mother's hand.

From behind the desk, Dr. Williams handed Mother a slip of paper and wrote an X by the signature line. Mother extracted herself from Kendra's grasp and signed the form without reviewing its contents. Her brain was too full to input any more information. She set the pen down on the office desk and turned to Kendra.

"I know you're scared. I am too."

"What the hell? If you're scared, then let's get out of here, like right now."

"I'm not scared exactly. Just apprehensive. You've never been in a hospital overnight, that's all. How about you try it for tonight and we'll see how it goes in the morning?"

Dr. Williams stood up. "Actually, you'll have to give it 72 hours."

"Seventy-two hours?" both Kendra and Mother asked in unison.

Dr. Aiken asked me to admit Kendra on an involuntary commitment status.

Mother asked, "Why did I sign admission forms? Why wasn't this explained to me?"

"I apologize if it wasn't," the doctor said. "Your daughter is suicidal and while we want your consent and cooperation to treat her, for the sake of safety, in case you change your mind, she's being admitted to the hospital regardless, for evaluation."

Now it was Mother's turn to stand. "I didn't understand that at all. I thought I was bringing her in voluntarily. This was our choice."

Dr. Williams sat back down and motioned for Mother to do so. "After the 72 hours are up, depending on how she is doing, that will be an option open to you."

"What are the other options?" Kendra asked.

"If Dr. Aiken feels you're ready to go home after his assessment and your mother agrees, then you'll go home."

"And if he doesn't?"

"If he feels your daughter is still an imminent danger to herself or to others, he could extend the commitment to a longer period of time."

"It's up to him? What if I disagree with him?"

"It's actually up to a Mental Health judge and the doctor. And you can be part of this hearing."

"A hearing? My daughter doesn't need to go to court. She hasn't done anything wrong. She needs help."

"No, of course not. It's just called that because all people who have been remanded to a mental health facility against their will get a mental health hearing and have an attorney there so that they can be sure that they are being fairly held in treatment or directed into the proper level of care."

"Oh my God, Mother! What have you gotten me into?"

"I'm not quite sure. I don't like it at all that I have no control over my daughter's treatment."

Kendra sat up straighter in her plastic chair. Maybe Mother was going to change her mind. "I don't like it, either. I'm with you Mother. Come on. Let's bolt!"

Dr. Williams folded his hands together, resting his chin atop them. "I'm very sorry but that's not a choice you have at this time. You are staying with us for at least the next three days."

Mother shook her head. "Can I call a lawyer?"

"You most certainly can," Dr. Williams said, "but it's after business hours on a Friday. The courts are closed. He wouldn't be able to do anything until Monday. Even then, he couldn't violate the Mental Health laws."

"How can this be happening?" Mother had tears of fury in her eyes. "I just wanted to get some help for my girl."

"I know," he said. "And that's exactly what you're doing. Believe me, this is in the best interest of your daughter. It guarantees an adequate period of time so that we can keep her safe, assess her and plan a course of treatment."

"Why are you talking about me as if I'm not here?" Kendra asked. She looked over at her mother and folded her arms firmly across her chest. "You're going to cave, aren't you? I'm stuck here."

Mother put an arm around her. "Well, we did come here to get you help. Besides, it doesn't look like we have any other option."

Madison Blythe pushed the print icon on her computer and sat back in her leather swivel chair. Soon the machine next to her was spitting out page after page of printed material.

"Another exciting Friday night, isn't it Winston?" She patted her English bulldog on top of his head. "It's just you and me, buddy."

The dog snorted and drool ran out of the side of his mouth onto the hardwood floor.

"I couldn't ask for a better date," she said. "Are you up for a walk? Want to go for a walk,

Winston?"

The bulldog slowly lugged his stout body toward the door while Madison attached his leather leash to his studded collar.

"Can I get a bit more enthusiasm than that?"

Winston grunted twice.

"That's better."

Closing the door to her apartment, they descended the two flights of stairs to the street. Crossing it, they went into the tiny park. It was deserted. Madison turned up the collar of her coat and let Winston off his leash.

"Go do your business, boy."

Madison sat on a bench and tried to clear her thoughts of the article she'd been writing. *How to Be Your Own Best Friend.* Hadn't that been done to death? Besides, she was sick of spending time with herself. What she really wanted to write was *How to Get a Life.* Still, she was grateful for the work that the women's magazine offered her. With all the self-help articles she'd written in the past year, she could probably compile them into a book. That would at least bring more income.

"That's a good boy, Winston." She patted her pooch on the head. "Do you want to walk some more or head back home?"

The dog sat on its haunches, staring up at her. He let out a lackluster bark.

"I'll take that to mean we're going home." She reattached the leash and went towards her building. "You're as lazy as I am today."

Once inside, Madison slid out of her coat and back into her chair. Winston started sniffing papers lying around on the floor.

"Don't eat those," Madison said, picking them up and placing them on her desk. "My writing is what keeps you in dog food and treats."

She scooped a rawhide bone from the sofa cushion and held it out to Winston who began chomping on it immediately. Walking over to his favorite floor pillow, the dog carried his bone like a cigar in his mouth. He circled around three times, plopped down on the pillow, then resumed chewing on his prize.

With her bulldog pacified, she picked up the pages that had come off the printer and plopped herself down on the sofa. Reading the same passage three times, she gave up and tossed them onto the old steamer trunk that served as her coffee table.

"Give it up, Maddie," she said aloud. "You're in no mood to edit tonight."

Grabbing the remote off the trunk, she flipped on the TV.

"How about popcorn and a movie tonight, Winston? Or in your case, a bacon treat and a movie?"

The bulldog waddled over to the couch, pulled himself up and lounged beside Madison, resting his massive head on her leg. Within seconds, he was snoring. Within minutes, so was she.

"Look at this," Dr. Victor Aiken said as he dropped a thick journal on the counter in the hospital laboratory. "What do you think?"

Jesse folded the newspaper pages he'd been looking at and tucked them in his lab coat pocket. He picked up the journal. Another medical magazine with another article about Victor. In the beginning, he was annoyed that his own name was never mentioned in any of these publications. Lately, he was feeling grateful for that fact. He pretended to read the article.

"A well written piece," he said.

"That it is." Victor sat on one of the lab stools. "Did you see that wonderfully accurate description of Aiken's Haven? '*On the leading edge of adolescent and child mental health treatment*'?"

"I saw," Jesse said, passing the journal back to Victor.

"What is this?" Victor asked, stooping down to pick up the folded newsprint that fell out of Jesse's pocket.

Jesse snatched the pages away from Victor, stuffing them into the chest pocket of his lab coat. "Nothing. Just a story I'm following."

"I hope you are not keeping secrets from me, Jesse."

"No, Victor. This isn't related to our work."

Victor nodded and left the lab. Jesse retrieved the newspaper articles out of his pocket. He unfolded the top one, reading it for the tenth time. The third paragraph jumped out at him, just as it had on first reading it.

The body had been in the lake for at least six months,
the coroner said. It was identified by dental records
to be the corpse of James Henry Torrence, an unemployed
male originally from Philadelphia.....

Jesse certainly hoped the murder case had nothing to do with their work.

In the front of the hospital, Kendra was sobbing. "Don't go, Mother. I'm really, seriously scared now." She wiped at her dripping nose with her sleeve.

"Believe me," Mother said, "I wish I could stay here with you."

Dr. Williams put an arm under Kendra's elbow. "It's time to say goodbye."

Mother put a protective hand on her daughter's shoulder. "Can't I at least go to her room with her and get her settled in?

It's not advisable," he said. "It's best for both of you if you part ways here." Dr. Williams took a few steps away from them and looked behind a series of filing cabinets. "Olivia? Could you come out here please?"

A large, morose woman came out from behind the files. "Yes? What can I do for you?"

"I'm going to escort Kendra to her unit now. Could you please show Mrs. Sibley to the front door? She'll be going home now."

"Certainly," Olivia said.

Making clucking sounds that Kendra couldn't quite make out, Olivia guided Mother by the elbow toward the reception area. Kendra couldn't believe Mother was going with the woman. Then, to her joy, she saw Mother pull her arm away from Olivia and rush back to where Kendra and the doctor were.

"I'm just not comfortable with this," Mother said. "I'm not leaving."

"Okay," Dr. Williams said. "You are welcome to sit in our reception area as long as you need. I will be taking Kendra to her room though."

The doctor placed his hands on Kendra's shoulders and forcefully whirled her around. Kendra tried to pull out of his clutches with no success. He was in control as he strongly moved her down the hallway toward a door. Kendra thought about fighting, maybe kicking or hitting, but she was frozen with fear. Fear of what would happen if she did fight.

Mother started after them but Olivia copied the actions of Dr. Williams, almost pushing her in the opposite direction and directed her to leave.

Mother looked back at her terrified daughter just as she was being pushed through a set of double doors.

"Don't worry, Kendra! I will get you out of here somehow."

Olivia placed a firm hand on the back of Mother's head, turning her away from Kendra.

While Olivia continued to try to usher her out of the building, Kendra was being lead further into the hospital. It sure didn't seem like a resort anymore.

CHAPTER 3

Mother walked into the Visiting Lounge and Kendra waved her over to the secluded section of armchairs near the unlit, stone fireplace that she had saved for them. Most of the other kids' parents had already arrived for the 7:00 p.m. visitation hour and Kendra had been worried Mother wasn't going to make it in time. She breathed a sigh of relief as Mother sat down in the wing back chair beside her, leaning over to take her hand. They both had tears in their eyes.

It had been 24 hours since they had seen each other and Kendra had never been away from home overnight before except to stay at Daddy's. Not even slumber parties as a kid or hanging with friends. She hated those kind of things. She'd certainly never been in a place like this. She was terrified and she couldn't even fake it.

Although Dr. Park had been right about the place being designed more like a hotel than a hospital at first glance, it sure didn't feel that way. She didn't like the people. The staff or the other patients. She'd hardly slept and her eyes felt heavy.

"How are you doing?" Mother asked, squeezing her hand.

"I'm really scared. I want to come home."

"You will come home but not today." Mother looked into the empty fireplace. "I had a long talk with Dr. Aiken on the phone this morning and I just met with him before coming to see you. It was a really good talk. I understand things a lot better now."

"You talked to the doctor without me?" Kendra pulled her hand out of her mother's grip.

"He said you'll probably need to stay here for about a month to get the best treatment."

"A month! I can't stay here that long. I'll die!" Kendra folded her arms across her chest. "Daddy would take me out."

"He doesn't have custody of you so he can't legally do that," Mother said, sighing.

"He would if he were here and he knew I was locked up with a bunch of psychos."

"Well, he's not here, is he? And even when he was, he was hardly around." Mother closed her eyes and cringed. "I'm sorry. That wasn't fair. But it's not fair of you to pit us against each other that way."

"I'm only telling the truth."

"You're only being manipulative."

"You just say stuff like that when I disagree with you. Everything has to be your way."

"When it comes to doing what's best for you, yes. Dr. Aiken is a very well-known and respected psychiatrist. I researched him. We're lucky to have him as your physician. I think it's wise we listen to his recommendations and advice."

"Dr. Aiken has barely talked to me," Kendra said. "How can he know how long I need to stay or what treatment I need? He doesn't even know me."

"He explained to me that he has other attending doctors and medical residents working under him. Plus there are social workers and nurses. They all work together and discuss your care in a meeting called Treatment Team. Besides, he said it takes time to determine and implement the proper course of treatment."

“You sound like you’re just repeating what he said to you. And why don’t I get to be at that Treatment meeting thing? Since it’s about me, I should be there to defend myself, don’t you think?”

Mother looked straight at Kendra. “I’m sure Dr. Aiken knows what he’s doing.”

“Whatever. I still don’t like him. He’d cold. It’s like he has no feelings.” Kendra paused to get Mother’s full attention. “And those eyes. They’re creepy.”

“Kendra!” Mother glanced at the other families and lowered her voice to a whisper. “He can’t help it if he was born with different colored eyes. It has nothing to do with his skill as a doctor.”

“Can he even see properly? Isn’t that a sign of brain damage?”

“You’re stretching it now.”

“It’s not just him. It’s the other kids here, too. They’re weird. Way worse than me. A lot of them are into hard core drugs and one guy sets fires. They’re a bad influence on me.”

A faint smile came to Mother’s lips. “Is this another not so subtle way of building a case for getting you out of here?”

Kendra returned a sheepish smile. “Yes, but everything I said is true.”

“I’m sure it is, but you and I both know you’ve already started down the wrong road all by yourself.”

“Just weed,” Kendra said, “nothing major.”

“To me, marijuana is major,” Mother said.

“That’s a good one coming from you.”

“Exactly what do you mean by that?”

“I may be cutting school but I can still add.”

“What are you trying to imply?”

"It means that you weren't an angel, either. Let's see. You got married six months before I was born. Mary lived with Grandma until she was five. And you think pot is major."

"It is. I never said I was perfect. Maybe I just want my daughter to avoid the mistakes I made."

"Oh, so now I'm a mistake."

"I didn't say that, Kendra."

"Is that why you want to get rid of me? Put me away? Lock me up for a month?"

"No! The exact opposite. I want to keep you around. That's why I'm trying to get you help."

"If that's true then you better get me out of here fast. They do strange experiments here. They did one on me last night."

"What are you talking about?" Mother sounded concerned.

"They gave me a pill that made me all dizzy and sleepy. Then, they put gel in my hair and attached a bunch of wires all over my head. I was too buzzed from the pill to fight them. I fell asleep. When I woke up it was all over but my hair was still sticky."

"Kendra Ann Sibley, are you telling me the absolute truth?"

"Yes. I wouldn't lie to you about something like that."

"I would hope not," Mother said. "Perhaps I do need to have another talk with Dr. Aiken. From the sounds of things, I'd better do it tonight."

As the Visiting Lounge was clearing out, Mother approached Jack, one of the staff psych aides, and asked to talk with Dr. Aiken. She was told he wasn't available but that one of his residents could meet with her. Jack pulled a cell phone from his pocket, contacted someone and stayed in the Lounge. They waited in the chairs by the doorway until Dr. Dushkriti came in.

He was the resident who had taken over admitting Kendra

from Dr. Aiken as soon as Mother had left. He spoke so quickly, in his East Indian accent, that Kendra had only caught about half of what he was saying. He had gotten irritated if he was asked to repeat himself. She had found that out quickly. She wondered if Mother would fare any better with him.

Mother stood up and extended her hand to him. "I'm Helen Sibley. Kendra's mother."

"Dr. Dushkriti," he said, nodding and giving her hand a quick shake. "What can I do for you?" He was tapping a pen on the stethoscope around his neck.

"My daughter tells me you did some sort of experiment on her last night. Something about pills, gel, and wires on her head."

"Yes, yes. An EEG." He turned to go.

"Wait!" Mother said loudly. Then more even toned, she asked, "What is the EEG for?"

"Measures electrical activity in the brain," Dr. Dushkriti said.

"I know what an EEG does." Mother was able to clearly understand his rapid speech. "I want to know why no one told me why one was being done on my daughter."

"It was included in the consent forms you signed on admission," he said, starting to walk away again.

She followed him. "I don't recall signing forms for this. Doctor, why are you doing these test on my child? I just want a simple explanation." Her face was reddening.

He sighed. "We are looking for changes in her brain waves during sleep."

"But why?"

He sighed again. "One of many tests we are doing." He was going to stop there and clearly thought better of it. "Sleeping and waking EEGs will be done to rule out any convulsive disorders or cerebral lesions. We're looking for differences in her brain circuitry from that of normal adolescents."

"You think I'm not normal?" Kendra asked.

Dr. Dushkriti did not answer.

"Well?" Mother asked.

"I think you should discuss any results with your daughter's attending physician, ma'am."

"That's what I was trying to do in the first place. Can you get Dr. Aiken for me, please?" She spoke through tight lips.

"He'll be here in the morning. You can talk to him then."

"I have to return to the city. I work on Sunday mornings. I need to see him tonight."

"Why don't you call him in the morning?" Dr. Dushkriti said, whirling around and leaving the room before Mother could reply.

Back in her room, Kendra rested on the double bed, the thick, down comforter providing her little comfort. Jack had insisted that she needed to be back in her room. Mother had hugged her tightly and assured her she would track down Dr. Aiken tonight. Kendra knew she meant it but she doubted Mother could do it.

A nurse came into her room shortly after she'd returned. The name *Amy B., RN* was embroidered onto her scrubs. She had a strong Canadian accent and she was the nicest of all the staff, so Kendra wasn't afraid when she saw her. That quickly changed when she saw a shot in Amy's hand.

"Who's that for?" Kendra sat upright in her bed.

"It's for you," Amy said. "Dr. Aiken wants you to have this medication and he wants us to do another test tonight. An EEG."

Kendra looked at the pale liquid in the syringe. "Forget it. No shots for me."

"Kendra, you must. The doctor ordered it for you. It's part of your treatment."

"What part of Canada are you from?"

"That obvious, eh?" Amy said. "Nova Scotia. Now are you ready?"

"How come you moved to Pennsylvania?"

Amy laughed. "All right, I'll tell you. Then you take the injection. No other stalling tactics. Agreed?"

Kendra nodded as she scooted to the edge of the bed.

Amy sat down beside her. "There are very few jobs for nurses in Canada right now. A lot of us move to the Sates, especially new graduates."

"How come there's no jobs in Canada?"

"There are too many nurses and not enough positions."

"That sounds dumb. I thought the government runs the hospitals there. Can't they fix it?"

"I'm not getting into a political discussion over the Canadian health care system with you. It will bore you and irritate me." Amy smiled. "Besides, you're not really interested. You need to take this medicine."

"No. Mother told Dr. Dushkriti tonight that she didn't want me taking any medication at all."

"I checked. Your mother has signed all the permission forms. She must want you to have it. I'm sure she wants you to get better. I'm sure you want to get better, don't you?" Amy smiled with her mouth but her eyes looked sad.

"What if I refuse the shot?"

"You're only 15 years old, not technically at the age of consent yet so, unfortunately, it doesn't really matter if you refuse.

Only your mother can. I'm sorry."

"Maybe you should call her."

"Please, Kendra. Don't turn this into a big deal." Amy looked around. "It'll be worse if you refuse. You don't want me to call extra staff to hold you down. I'd hate to see that happen. I promise I'll be as gentle as I can."

Kendra knew Amy meant what she was saying about being gentle, but she was still afraid. Something wasn't right. She knew that Amy knew it too.

Kendra ran to the adjoining bathroom, pulled the door shut and realized, too late, that there was no lock. She leaned on the porcelain counter top, with her head in her hands.

"Kendra," Amy said softly through the door. "Please come back out."

"Just a minute." Turning on the gold-colored faucet, Kendra filled the shell shaped sink with cold water and splashed some on her face. She patted it dry on the plush towel. Releasing the stopper, she watched the water drain out.

When she opened the bathroom door, Amy was standing by the night table, the syringe still in her hand.

"Ready?" she asked, reaching out to hold the girl's hand.

Kendra put her hand in Amy's and let herself be led back to bed. "I guess I have no choice, do I?" Her face was wrenched into a pout.

"Not really," Amy said, taking the cap off the needle.

Helen Sibley slammed the car keys on her kitchen counter, picked them up and slammed them down again. The long drive home hadn't helped to calm her nerves. Tears filled her eyes as she paced the room.

"What do I do?" she said aloud. "If I take Kendra out of that place, she might kill herself. If I leave her there, God knows what they'll do to her. I don't know the answer." She paced. "Great! Now I'm talking to myself like a crazy person!"

Helen sat down on the couch and fished her cell phone out of her purse.

"Aiken's Haven. Can I help you?" The operator's voice carried a strong New York accent that grated on Helen's nerves. It reminded her of an employee she'd once had to fire. Abrasive as sand paper.

"I need to speak with Dr. Aiken," Helen said.

"You'll have to call back tomorrow morning."

"This can't wait. I need to speak to him tonight."

"I'm sorry but he's not here, ma'am. You need to call back in the morning."

"This is urgent. Can you page him or something?"

"No ma'am. He's not on call this weekend. Although he does do rounds every weekend. Would you like to speak to Dr. Dushkriti? He's the physician on call?"

"I tried that already. I want to speak to Dr. Aiken and only Dr. Aiken."

"That's not possible ma'am. Call back in the morning."

"He's a doctor isn't he? It's urgent. There must be a way to reach him."

"No ma,am," the operator said. "I have other lines to answer. "Good bye."

A dial tone buzzed in Helen's ear. She stared at her phone. "Unbelievable!"

She jumped up from the couch and went to the study. Getting a business card from her desk drawer, she tapped Jake O'Roarke's number onto her cell phone keypad. He probably wasn't in his office but it was worth a try. After listening to four rings, his voicemail picked up.

"You have reached the law offices of Barran, Crowley and Riordan. To leave a message, please listen to the directory of names and press the corresponding number. For Arthur Barran, press 1, for William Crowley, press 2..."

Helen disconnected, unable to wait until Jake's name came up. Of course he wouldn't be there at this hour. He checked his messages regularly but she needed someone to talk to right now. Who else could she call? She thought of her ex-husband but decided that might just make matters worse. Paul would want to haul Kendra out of that place, no questions asked. He wasn't a stupid man. He just couldn't think in the abstract terms of mental illness. Helen dialed her older daughter's number but hung up after one ring. What could Mary do from Connecticut tonight? Both of them would be in town soon enough anyway. Soon enough to criticize her decision.

Helen went back to the living room and dropped face up onto the couch, touching the back of her hand to her forehead. She closed her eyes, hoping for a solution to come to her. It did. She could talk to Maddie. Maddie wouldn't judge her and Maddie might have an idea. Helen smiled as she thought of the two college years spent with her best friend. She felt a sense of melancholy wash over her, grateful that they had remained close ever since those difficult years.

Madison sprinted to the ringing landline. Switching off the fax function on her all-in-one printer, she picked up the phone's handset, pushed the talk button, and answered it as she headed back to her computer.

"Hello?" she said, leaning back in her chair, swinging her legs up on the desk.

"Hi, it's Helen. Sorry to be calling so late."

"That's okay. I'm up anyway. Editing an article. The joys of freelancing. I thought I'd finished pulling all-nighters after our college days. How can you still stand to be taking classes?"

"Because one day I want to finally earn that degree I promised myself."

"You're already a success. You have your own bookstore. Who needs a degree?"

"Let's discuss that later. Right now I have a problem and I thought you might be able to help me. In fact, there might even be a story in it for you in the end."

"Helen, I'm your best friend. You don't have to bribe me to do you a favor, but you've certainly got my interest. How can I help?"

"I know you're unrelenting when it comes to doing research for your work. If anyone can find out something, it's you."

"Enough flattery," Maddie said. "What do you need?"

"It's about your Goddaughter."

"Kendra? What's going on with her now? Still depressed?"

"Yes," Helen said. "In fact, it's gotten worse. Worse to the point where Dr. Park, that psychologist I told you about, felt that Kendra might...well, that she might try to kill herself."

Maddie's heart sank. "That's awful. Tell me what I can do. Anything for Kendra."

"I put her in a hospital. Aiken's Haven."

"I've heard of the place," Maddie said. "That's where they treat teenagers for mental illness and behavior problems, right? I interviewed one of the doctors, several nurses and a few of the patients there when I wrote that article on homeless teens last spring.

"Oh, thank God you know the place already. That will make it easier."

"Make what easier?"

Helen explained the situation to Maddie.

"I hated to leave Kendra tonight but I have to open the bookstore in the morning. Sundays are one of my best days. My insurance only covers fifty percent of Kendra's hospitalization. I can't afford to close up the store, even for a day." She sighed deeply. "I don't know. Maybe this is just my daughter's overactive imagination at work."

"Do you really think so?"

"Honestly, no. I believe her this time. I want to get her help but I'm starting to get a bad feeling about the place myself."

"So you really can't just sign her out of the hospital? You're her mother."

"I might be able to in a day or so. Since Kendra is suicidal, the doctor had her involuntarily committed to the hospital against her will. Technically against my will, for that matter. Even though I signed admission papers, it didn't matter, she was being admitted whether I agreed or not. Apparently, they can keep her longer if they feel she's unsafe. If she's not still thinking about killing herself, I may be able to take her home Monday, but I'm afraid."

"Afraid of what specifically?"

"Everything. Afraid of leaving her in a place I don't fully trust. Afraid of bringing her home and risking that she still may be thinking of hurting herself." Helen started to cry. "There's no good answer.

"Legally, can you get her out of there and get her transferred somewhere else? Have you called your lawyer?"

"Couldn't reach him. Besides, this commitment thing is legally binding. Even if I could reach Jake, we couldn't start to fight this until Monday when the courts are back in session."

"This is unbelievable. I'm so sorry, Helen."

Helen took a big, deep breath. "Do you think you could find

out exactly what is going on there, Maddie?" Helen asked. "You could pretend you're doing a follow up story on the homeless youth."

"I doubt they'd go for it. Although I did the interviews, they weren't too keen on me being there the first time. They had a hospital representative, a Risk Manager he was called, who sat in on every interview I did. Apparently, I was a risk that needed to be managed."

"I'm terrified for Kendra. I've even thought of going to the police."

"That won't help," Maddie said. "You don't really have any specific complaint. You actually signed admission papers. And these type of institutions are protected by strict confidentiality laws that even the cops can't mess with. It practically took an Act of Congress for me to get in there to do those interviews. There were so many forms, I think I signed away my first born child and any retirement pensions to them."

"Then what?" Helen asked. "How can we find out what the hell is really going on in there? How can I protect my daughter?"

"The only way to know what's going on in such a protected facility is to actually be in there."

"I tried that tonight. I got nowhere."

"That's because you're a parent. A visitor."

"What do you mean?"

"I mean that suddenly my mental health isn't quite up to par."

"Maddie, what are you thinking?"

"They still have an adult wing there, don't they?"

"Yes," Helen said. "I don't think I like where this is going."

"November has always been a depressing time of year for me," Maddie said. "I think I need to be admitted to a psychiatric hospital."

"I cannot let you do that! What if they give you drugs and do experiments on you?"

"I can hide pills under my tongue and spit them out later. The kids I interviewed taught me that. I just didn't put it in the article."

"What if they commit you?"

"I won't say anything that will make that happen. I'll make it seem like I need help but that I'm safe. How did you say the doctor worded it?"

"Imminent danger to self and others."

"Okay then, I'm depressed with occasional thoughts of suicide, but I won't ever hurt myself or anyone else because my religious beliefs are that suicide and homicide are sins. That will keep me there on my own free will, don't you think?"

"I don't know. They're tricky. All those confusing documents."

"I promise I'll carefully read any paper work I sign. Even the ridiculously long pages that no one reads. I'll refuse to sign anything even remotely suspicious. Don't worry. I can make sure Kendra's all right and blow the roof off the place if something sinister is going on."

"No, Maddie. It's too much to ask. It's too much of a risk."

"You didn't ask. I offered. And I've already been branded as a risk in the past." She laughed. "You still have my spare key, right? Just make sure you come over here twice a day to feed, water and walk Winston. He can have the run of the place while I'm gone."

"What if someone recognizes you?"

"Doubtful that anyone would remember me from my last visit. The article was pretty benign and Aiken's Haven was just one of many references. Also, it put them in a good light. Even if someone does remember me, aren't we writers prone to depression anyway? I can just say that I remembered it as being a good place to seek help."

"I can't let you do this."

"Helen, I couldn't love Kendra any more if she were my own daughter. I'm her Godmother. I've been there since her birth."

"You've been a wonderful godmother and a terrific friend but this is a crazy idea. I would never have called if I thought you were going to suggest putting yourself in danger. There must be another way."

"Can you think of any other way?"

"Well, no. But I can't let you do this. I have to say no."

"Too bad," Maddie said. "I packed a bag while we were talking. I'm already on my way."

CHAPTER 4

It was going to be a long drive. Maddie hadn't slept well last night and tonight wasn't looking any better. She turned on the radio in her car. *The Oldies*. Funny how they didn't seem that old to her. A favorite song from her college days came on and she cranked up the volume. What year was that tune from? Oh yeah, her pre-med days. As the darkening scenery whipped by her windshield, Maddie thought back to that rough year.

Madison had stared at the body part. It looked like a slice of an arm. No bones were exposed to give her a clue. She could see the median nerve and the brachial artery above it. The dead meat on top looked somewhat like the biceps. That was it. She was looking at a medial view of the arm.

Ding! Time for the next body segment. This one was easy. She jotted down abdominal aorta and its branches and waited for the bell to ring, not needing the full three minutes.

"Earth to Maddie," said Kyle, the student behind her, as he gave her a light shove.

She looked back as he pointed ahead to the X-ray series. She hadn't heard the bell go off. As she moved forward, she let out a big yawn, not sure if she was genuinely tired or just plain bored. Maybe both.

Finally, the anatomy lab exam was over. Grabbing her coat and books from the floor in the back of the classroom, she hurried out the door.

"Maddie, wait up," Kyle said, flying down the cement stairs of *Cadaver Hall.*

"I'm glad that's over," she said. "I hate bell ringers."

"I know. A sit down exam would be easier. How did you do?" Kyle asked.

"Fine. Wasn't that hard."

"For you, maybe," he said. "It's not fair. You get the A's and I'm the one who really wants them."

"You can have mine." Maddie said.

"Thanks. Want to get a bite to eat at the pub?"

"Actually, I'm not feeling that well. Can I take a rain check?"

Kyle said, "You just name the time and place, and I'm there."

"You don't give up easily, do you?" she said, laughing.

"I figure that eventually you'll get so tired of me asking you out, that you'll say yes just to get me off your back."

"Kyle, you're sweet, and I like you. I told you that I'm just not dating anyone right now."

"It's your loss," he said, grinning.

"It probably is. I'm sure when I come to my senses, you'll be with some other girl."

"No way. I'll wait for you. You'll come around."

She chuckled. "I'm going home to take a nap. I'll see you tomorrow in physiology class."

"See you then, beautiful."

Turning the corner, Maddie pulled her knapsack off her right shoulder and let the load fall fully onto her left one. It was difficult to lug the textbooks on only one side, but the sharp, muscular pains were getting to be too much on her right side. It was probably just stress. Or bad posture. She walked up the front stairs to the dormitory, feeling the strain in her thighs and calves. Maybe she needed to work out more. Who was she kidding? Maybe she needed to work out period. She had no energy though. In the front lobby, she looked back out behind her. It was cold, gray and it was drizzling a freezing rain. She hated November.

Maddie passed by a group of giggling girls, surrounding the television, in the common room. One of the soap operas was on. She used to watch it but got bored with the storylines over the last month. In the stairwell, she had trouble taking the steps. Her chest felt heavy and she got dizzy for a moment. She sat on one of the steps, almost passing out right there.

In her dorm room, Meghan was doing sit-ups. She was in shorts and a tee that showed off her athletic figure. Her thighs looked big but there wasn't an ounce of fat on them. Mattie's roomie was all muscle. The only flaw she could find on Meghan was her skin. It was so pale you could see her veins through it.

Maddie dropped her knapsack on the floor, untucked her tee from her jeans and flopped down on her bed. She needed a serious nap before she tried to tackle any homework.

"198...199...200." Meghan let out a groan. "Hey Maddie. What's up?"

"Nothing. Going to catch some Z's then tackle anatomy. You?"

"I've got a ton of homework and basketball practice at 6:00." She went to her dresser and pulled out some jeans. "I'm going to an early dinner at the cafeteria. Want to join me?"

"Thanks. I'm not really hungry though."

Meghan walked to the door. "You have to eat something."

"I just can't seem to choke anything down. I don't know what it is."

"I guess you just have to try," Meghan said, shrugging her

shoulders. "I know Whitney is going to dinner at 6:00. Maybe you can go with her." She stood at the door for a few minutes.

"Okay," Maddie said. "I'll go with her." She had no intention of it.

Meghan left the room, headed for the noisy cafeteria, in search of a healthy meal option.

Maddie closed her eyes and tried to stop the thoughts spinning through her head. It was no use. Her homework, her night class at 7:00 and the thought of going home for Thanksgiving next week were overwhelming her. She tightly shut her eyelids and pulled the pillow over her head. She let herself drift off to sleep.

"Knock, knock," Whitney said, as she walked into the room. "Do you want to grab a bite with me, Maddie?"

Maddie opened her eyes slowly and sat up on her bed. "What time is it?"

"Sorry, did I wake you? It's almost 6:00."

"It's okay. I was just grabbing a short nap. I've got a lot of studying to do tonight."

"Let's go eat that cafeteria crap first. They've got spaghetti and garlic bread."

"I'm not going to eat tonight."

"Are you watching your weight?" Whitney asked. "You don't need to. You're skinny enough already."

"It's not that. I just don't have an appetite."

"Sure." Whitney sat down beside her on the bed. "You don't have an appetite or you don't want to eat?"

Maddie shrugged. "Both, I guess."

"I'll let you in on a secret. You can eat all you want and still be thin. That's what I do."

"How do you do that?"

"It's easy. I just vomit after each meal."

"Gross!"

Whitney laughed. "It is gross but it works. Vince thinks I look great."

"You do look great," Maddie said. "I'll bet Vince hasn't seen you leaning over the toilet bowl, though."

"He caught me a few times," Whitney said, "but I told him I'd been drinking too much. He's the last person who can get on my case about that."

"I don't think I could make myself throw up even if I wanted to."

"No problem. I have a back-up plan."

"Somehow I knew you would. What is it? Just curious."

"Laxatives."

"Laxatives. You're kidding."

"No. It really works. If I can't throw up enough, then I just take a triple dose. Your stomach hurts for a day or two after, but it's worth it."

"Whitney, you know this is dangerous. You can throw your system out of whack. Not to mention what your vomiting does to your body."

"I know, I know. Problems with heart, teeth, stomach, throat. I've heard it all, but I feel fine. It's not going to happen to me. I can handle it. Well, I'm off to pig out on spaghetti. Are you coming?"

"No. I really couldn't eat a thing."

"I wish I had your problem," Whitney said. "I'll come by after dinner and we can walk to psych class together."

"I'm going to skip tonight's lecture," Maddie said. "I already read the chapter and it'll just be a review for me."

"You're the only one I know who reads the chapters before the lecture. I'm lucky if I get to them at all. There's just not enough time in the day. Well, catch you later."

Once Whitney left, Maddie looked longingly at the candy bar on Meghan's desk. She got up and pulled the scale out from under her bed. She still weighed too much to eat anything.

The next morning, Whitney and her roommate, Helen, came to meet Maddie and Meghan. Maddie had really liked Helen right from their first meeting.

"Breakfast time," Helen said. "Are you two ready?"

"Almost," Meghan said. "Just let me finish putting on my eye shadow.

Maddie hadn't bothered with make up in weeks. Helen was done up in subtle shades of brown that complimented her green eyes nicely. Whitney didn't even need make-up. Her chocolate colored complexion was so smooth and even but she accented it with gold toned shadow anyway. They could all be models. Maddie sighed and buried herself in an old, Icelandic sweater and baggy jeans. She let her bangs fall over her face.

"I heard they're serving pancakes and waffles today," Whitney said. "I'm having both. I bet I can eat more than anyone." She winked at Maddie.

They walked downstairs to the dormitory basement which housed the cafeteria. Whitney and Meghan debated the merits of volleyball versus basketball. Whitney and Helen were both volleyball players.

"You really should join one of the sports," Helen said. "I know I've mentioned it before, but it would be good for you. Give you more energy. Besides, if you like volleyball, we need more good players on our team."

“I don’t think volleyball is my game.”

“Leave her alone,” Whitney said. “She’s aiming for med school. She doesn’t have time to waste. Right Maddie?”

“If that will get Helen off my back then you’re right,” Maddie said, laughing.

They all laughed as they took their places in line and selected food from the service bins. Seated at one of the long dining tables, the four of them started eating. Rather, three of them started eating. Maddie picked at her food and pushed it around on her plate, the pancakes getting mushy in the thick syrup.

“Aren’t you going to eat?” Helen asked her.

“I am eating.”

“It’s delicious,” Whitney said, syrup running down her chin.

Meghan nodded. Her mouth was full.

Maddie cut a small piece out of a pancake and swished it around in the syrup. She brought the fork to her lips, opened her mouth and put the food inside. Pulling the fork out through clenched teeth, she made sure it didn’t touch her lips. Then she started to chew. Feeling nauseous and dizzy, she spat the pancake into her napkin and left the table. Helen followed her.

“Maddie, I think you have a major problem.”

“I’m fine, Helen, really.”

“You’re not fine. You’re way too thin, you’re always tired and you’re not the fun, sarcastic girl I met at the start of this semester. I miss that. I didn’t want to say anything but I think it’s seriously affecting your health.”

“I guess I know something is wrong. I’m just not quite sure what it is yet.”

“I know how you can find out,” Helen said. “I was having a tough time a few weeks back.” She paused. “I’ve never told anyone this before...”

"You can trust me," Maddie said. "What is it?"

"Okay. I'm...I'm pregnant."

"Oh my God!"

"I know. I had the same reaction."

"When did you find out?"

"I'm two and a half months."

"What are you and Paul going to do?"

"Wait. It gets worse."

"Tell me."

"I can trust you, right? I mean, I feel like I can really trust you."

"Of course you can trust me."

"You know that Paul and I have been together since ninth grade?"

"Yeah and I'm jealous."

"This isn't the first time this has happened."

"Helen? You've been pregnant before?"

"We have a five-year-old daughter. Mary. She's with Paul's mom right now."

"I can't believe it. You're a mother. Twice now."

"At 19 years old. Pretty sad, isn't it?"

"No. I mean, if you're happy about it..."

"Fifty-fifty, to be honest."

"Well, you do have options."

"I know. That's why I went to the student health center to talk to a counselor."

"And..."

"And if it's a boy, Kevin. If it's a girl, Kendra."

"Those are great names. So what about school?"

"Paul and I will both finish out the year. He's got a friend with a landscaping business. He'll start full time right after spring exams."

"What about you?"

"I think it's time for me to be a real mommy and have Mary with us full time, too. I'll have two years of college behind me. I can always go back later."

"Can't you do both somehow?"

"Paul's mom is getting tired of raising Mary. She's pretty much done. My mother won't help. Hell, she'll barely speak to me."

"What about your father?"

"He sides with her. It's easier for him that way."

"Day care?"

"We can't afford that and Paul's family isn't really in a position to help us out."

"Okay, last idea – night school?"

"I doubt I can handle raising Mary, a new baby and college. I don't think I'm going to have a lot of time to go to classes and do homework. Plus, who would watch the kids?"

"Good point. So what about you and Paul? Your relationship?"

"It's good. We're getting married over Christmas break. We would've gotten married someday. This is just a little sooner than we planned."

"Can I be-"

"Maid of Honor? Of course. We've become so close over the past few months, I can't imagine asking anyone else."

The girls hugged.

"Helen, I can't believe everything you've been through. I'm so glad you told me about it."

"Me, too. You're one of the few people I can really trust. In fact, since you are the first to know about my baby, I think you'd make a great godmother to Kevin or Kendra."

"Oh, I'd be honored."

More hugging.

"Good. Now that I'm all taken care of, we have to take care of you."

"Meaning?"

"The student health center. You'll have to have your head on straight and be in the best of health if you're going to be there to help me out over the next year."

Maddie chuckled. "I'll think about it."

"Don't think about it. Do it. Right now. I'll go with you."

"Really?"

"Just let me tell Whitney and Meghan that we're leaving."

"Don't say anything about what's going on."

"I don't have to. We've all noticed it. But don't worry, I'll say we're going to the library. I'll be right back."

At the student health center, they had signed up and waited 45 minutes.

"I hate to do this to you," Helen said, "but I have to get to class. I didn't think it would take this long. I can cut if you want. Unless you promise you'll stay until someone sees you?"

"You can go. I'll give it 15 more minutes."

Helen went to the receptionist and then came back saying, "You're next on the list. I'll meet you back at your room later and you can tell me how it went."

A few minutes after Helen left, the receptionist called Maddie's name and took her into an exam room. She hopped up on the exam table. Feeling dizzy, she had trouble focusing on the nurse who came in to talk to her.

"Hello, Madison," she said, smoothing her crisp, white uniform. "What seems to be the problem? Is it the flu? Everyone's getting the flu this week."

"It's not the flu."

"Then what's wrong?" The nurse wrapped a BP cuff on Maddie's arm.

"I'm having trouble eating."

"That can be part of the flu."

"No, I'm not sick. I just can't bring myself to eat."

"Let me check your temperature, just I case." She stuck a thermometer in Maddie's mouth as she finished reading the blood pressure result. "Are all your vaccines up to date?"

Maddie sighed. She wanted to just leave but decided it was easier to just give in.

After 5 more minutes of questions and examinations, the nurse was finally reassured that she did not have the flu.

"I'm embarrassed to say this," Maddie finally told her, "but I think the problem is more emotional."

"Oh. Well then, do you need to talk with a counselor or a psychiatrist?"

A sense of shame washed over her. "Yes. I think that's exactly what I need."

"I'll be right back."

Maddie sat alone for what seemed like forever, feeling like a complete loser.

The nurse returned in 3 minutes, according to the clock.

"Let's get you right over to see Dr. McLaren. He's got a free half hour now."

Dr. McLaren's office was dark. The curtains were drawn and only one lamp lit the room. Maddie sat in an old arm chair. He was in a pseudo-leather office chair at his desk, reading the nurse's notes. He swiveled to face her.

"Hello, Madison. I'm Dr. McLaren. So, you're having trouble eating?" he said, in a thick Scottish brogue. "Tell me about that."

"What do you want to know?"

"Anything you care to tell me," he said, stroking his salt and pepper beard.

The man looked just like she'd pictured a psychiatrist would look. Maybe he could help her. "I don't know where to start."

"It seems like you also have trouble making decisions."

"Sometimes," Maddie admitted.

"You look like you feel depressed."

"I don't feel great."

"Have you ever been diagnosed with depression before?"

"No. I've never seen a psychiatrist before."

"Poor appetite, indecisiveness, and low mood can all be indicators of depression. Especially in absence of any physical illness. Why don't we try you on an antidepressant and see if it helps?"

"Do I really need that?" Maddie felt a little uneasy about the hasty diagnosis.

"Let's give it a try. Trust me."

She was ushered out of Dr. McLaren's office with a bottle of pills and told to return in a week or call if any problems came up.

Two days later, Maddie was back at the student health

center. She had decided to take the medicine but it was already causing problems. Dr. McLaren wasn't available but one of the interns from the medical school was taking walk-ins under his supervision.

After only a few minutes' wait, she was brought into an examining room. She breathed a sigh of relief as a young, blond man came into the room. She wasn't sure she would've stayed if another McLaren type had walked through that door.

"Hi, Madison. How are you today?"

"Not so great, Dr. Heik..." She tried in vain to read his name-tag.

"Heikkinen. It's Finnish. No one can pronounce it right, so just call me Joe."

"Okay, Joe." Maddie laughed.

"I read through the notes in your chart. There's not much in there, so I'll need you to tell me what's going on."

"I came back because the medication is making me really dizzy. My eyes are blurry and I have a permanently dry mouth."

Joe went to the sink, filled a paper cup with water and gave it to her. "Imipramine, the antidepressant you're on, is an older drug. It's causing all of those side effects. In fact, you're on a high dose for an initial prescription. What did you think of your session with Dr. McLaren?"

"Honestly?" Maddie waited for a nod. "He spent very little time with me. It wasn't very helpful."

"I've got an idea," Joe said. "Let's go to the snack bar in back and talk about what's bothering you. I'll even spring for a soda and a muffin."

While Maddie picked at the muffin and sipped a diet soda, Joe asked her all sort of questions. Questions about school, home, family and friends. He was easy to talk to and she learned a lot about him, too. It felt a bit like a date until Joe brought up the subject of food. Maddie clammed up.

"I thought we were getting along so well," Joe said.

She nodded. "We are."

"Then why the silent treatment?" He grinned.

"I'm not sure."

"Can I take a guess?"

She laughed. "Go right ahead."

"I think that you don't want to talk about food because you're on the verge of developing an eating disorder. Have you heard of anorexia nervosa?"

"Sure. Everyone has."

"So you know it's about control issues more than it is about food or weight?"

"Maybe you could explain that part in more depth. I've been skipping my Abnormal Psych lectures lately."

Joe gave her a detailed description of the disease. Some of it, she already knew. Some of it was news to her. She could see how she was fitting into the profile. Why hadn't she figured it out herself?

"Denial," Joe said.

"What?"

"You're in denial. You could recognize an eating disorder in one of your friends but you have the exact same problem and you can't admit it to yourself."

"I wasn't aware I'd asked that out loud."

"You didn't. I could read it in your expression."

"You're good."

Joe laughed. "I think we can head this this thing off from becoming full blown, if that's what you want."

"Definitely."

"Let's forget the medication. I think we need to talk more about what part of your life is making you feel out of control."

They talked for another hour until they were interrupted by the receptionist. She told Joe that another walk-in patient had arrived. Joe told Maddie to set an appointment with him for his next rotation day. As he left, she looked down at the table. Half of her muffin was gone.

CHAPTER 5

It took two hours for Maddie to navigate the rain soaked streets. It was coming up on 1:00 a.m. when she arrived at the facility. She walked up to the large, oak doors, took a deep breath and paused.

"Aiken's Haven," Maddie said aloud. "A psychiatric hospital. Do I really want to do this?"

Thinking of Kendra, Helen's panic and the possibility of a career-advancing scoop, Maddie walked up the steps, hoping no one would recognize her from her last visit. She had to do it for Kendra. Maybe it would end up being a really big story too and help her make the leap from freelancer to staff writer at one of the major newspapers or magazines. Or even an online publication. She pushed her way through the front doors only to see the upheld palm of a security guard. He was so old and frail that he probably couldn't have stopped anyone if he needed to. She made it easy on him and followed his orders.

"What are you doing here, ma'am?" he grumbled.

Ma'am. She hated that term, especially when it was uttered by people older than her. Maybe it was time to do something about those tiny wrinkles forming at the corners of her eyes.

"Excuse me, ma'am? What can I do for you?" The old voice crackled with the nasty rasp that came from too many years of smoking too many cigarettes.

Maddie decided not to take offence. After all, this fellow was older than dirt. One strong gust of wind and his bones would probably crumble into dust. She decided that he called every woman *ma'am* and left it at that.

"I need to see someone about checking myself in," she said.

"Just a minute." The security guard left the lobby, unlocked a door and went into what looked like an office.

Maddie admired the opulent décor while she waited. She tried to peek into some other rooms but every door was locked.

Ten minutes later, a large woman, with a nametag reading *Olivia*, came to greet her.

"What can I do for you?" Olivia said, a clipboard gripped in one hand.

"I need to be admitted," Maddie replied.

"We don't usually admit people off the street. Did someone refer you here?"

"Yes. Dr. Park. She's a psychologist in the city."

"Yes, we know her. It's odd that she didn't call ahead."

"It was quite a while ago that I saw her. She told me to consider treatment here if things got really bad."

"You should have called her first."

"I didn't think of it. This is kind of an emergency. This is a hospital, right?"

"Well, all right. We can call her in the morning."

"I doubt she'll remember me. I used a different name. I was embarrassed."

"Humph."

"So can you help me?"

"I suppose we can assess you. Follow me."

Maddie dutifully followed.

They entered a large office where the walls were painted in a relaxing shade of mint. Mahogany was the wood of choice. Olivia sat behind a majestic desk.

"You can sit there," she said, pointing to a hunter green loveseat with matching ottoman.

Olivia pulled over a laptop. "Name?"

"Maddie. Madison Bl...Blankenship," she said, thankful that her ex-boyfriend's surname came quickly to her mind, but sad that he himself came to mind. It still hurt. Even after a year.

John Blankenship. His name still gave Maddie that familiar tingle. She'd loved him with such a passionate intensity that it was almost painful at times. Through their three years together, she knew he didn't feel quite the same. She'd lied to herself. Convinced herself that her powerful feelings were enough to change him. That he would grow to love her the same way. In her mind, the wedding was planned. The two kids – a boy and a girl. A house in the country. Hell, she may as well have thrown in a white picket fence. She felt her face flush recalling how she had felt like a teenager, swept up in his intoxicating sensuality. If she was honest with herself, there was a part of her heart that would always have a place for him. The overwhelming obsession with him had finally faded, but he'd always be with her. She smiled with a mix of relief and grief at the loss.

"Excuse me," Olivia said. "I asked you a question."

"I'm sorry. What did you say?" Maddie shook her head. She was prone to distraction when she was tired.

"You're going to have to cooperate if you want our assistance."

"Sorry. My concentration's been off lately."

"Obviously. Now, as I was saying, do you have insurance?"

Wow. This woman was brimming with compassion. Maddie wanted to say something sarcastic but she bit her tongue.

Instead, she said, "Yes, I have my card here."

"This says you last name is Blythe."

"That's my maiden name. I haven't changed it on the card yet." The lies were coming easily. "The insurance is still good." She couldn't afford to pay for this stay out of pocket.

"We'll see."

Olivia went to the small office next door. Her assistant kept a messy desk and Olivia swiped the papers onto the floor to make room for herself. As she picked up the phone receiver to call the insurance company's 24 hour benefits' verification line, she paused. She didn't like this Blythe woman. Or was it Blankenship? Whatever her last name was. What was up with using an alias for Dr. Park? None of this sounded right. Maybe she should call Dr. Aiken on this one.

Olivia's features softened as she thought of Dr. Victor Aiken. Maybe someday it could happen for them. She chuckled, recalling how she had met him when he was just a boy. She had been 20 years old then, just staring out in this business at a run-down boys' ranch. He was a 12-year-old punk. She had hated him on first sight. Maybe it had been fear of her instant, inappropriate attraction to him. She gave him a hard time throughout the years he stayed at that facility, but she'd also admired his tenacity and keen intelligence. She was surprised he survived so well. By the time he left there, he was becoming a handsome young man and her love-hate feelings for him were mostly love. She couldn't let him know that, though. After all, she was eight years older and, at the time, he was still a teenager.

Having kept tabs on him over the years, she had felt a certain pride when Victor's medical career began. Once he became a psychiatric resident, she knew they were meant to be together. The older they got, the less the age discrepancy mattered. It was only a matter of time and patience on her part. He would come around soon, just like he did with the job. When she'd called him up to apply to work at his new hospital, Victor had laughed at her. Said he never wanted to hear from her again. It tore at her heart. She had begged and pleaded, claiming she wanted to work with the best. She sent him emails and left voicemails, pouring out her feelings of respect and admiration. It was the ranch he hated, not her. Several weeks later, Victor had reconsidered. He called her back and hired her. Now she was indispensable to him.

After a few minutes alone, Maddie started to get worried. Maybe this woman was on to her. She stood and walked to the office door, carefully trying the knob. It was locked. Olivia had locked her in! Maddie felt a jolt of panic run through her.

"Get a grip!" she told herself. This was probably standard procedure in a psychiatric hospital.

Pacing around the office, Maddie pulled a desk drawer open. Highlighters, pens, paperclips. Nothing of interest. She tried all the other drawers but they were all locked.

Hearing the door click open, Maddie sat back down as Olivia returned behind her desk, an odd smile on her face.

"Okay, your insurance is valid. Now, why do you need our help?"

I certainly don't need your help, Maddie thought. Instead, she said, "I'm having problems with depression." She blinked her eyes to make them watery. They were already bloodshot from being up so late.

"Are you suicidal?" Olivia asked.

Was that a hopeful tone in her voice? Maddie wondered. "Um, yes." Maddie wring her hands.

"What is your plan?"

"My plan?" Maddie looked up at Olivia, then quickly looked away.

"Your suicide plan," Olivia said, ready at the keyboard.

"Oh. I thought about taking pills."

"Do you have any pills on your person or at home that you could overdose on?"

And if I don't are you going to offer me some? Maddie thought. Instead, she nodded her head and lightly bit her lip.

"Is that a yes?" Olivia demanded. "What type of pills"

"Heart pills."

"Do you have a heart condition?"

"My mother does. She lives with me." Maddie was thankful that neither one of these statements were true.

"Are the pills in your purse?"

"No. At home."

"Have you actually attempted suicide?"

Maddie stared at Olivia. "Do you have to hold a dagger to your jugular to get some help around here?" She immediately regretted the outburst.

Olivia stared at her with a blank expression.

"Sorry, I'm so irritable lately," Maddie said. "I had some pills in my mouth tonight but I spit them out." Maddie hoped she was giving the right answers. Just enough to get admitted but avoiding any need for medical procedures, like pumping her stomach.

"What specific type of cardiac drugs were they?"

"Does it really matter? I spit them out."

"I see." Olivia rose from her swivel chair. "I guess you don't want to answer my questions. That's fine. I'll call Dr. Rutger to talk to you."

Maddie was left alone in the locked office again. Olivia had left the laptop open on the desk. Maddie took a peek at it. Her name and insurance carrier were listed at the top. Under the section, *Notes*, the word *suicidal* was written with three exclamation points. Maddie suddenly realized that this would become a part of her permanent medical record. It wasn't a complete charade, she reasoned. After all, she had felt suicidal back in college and still did get depressed from time to time. Maddie hoped her act was convincing enough to get admitted voluntarily. She did not want to get committed. And being charged with insurance fraud was not something she wanted to risk, either. Maybe Helen had been right. This wasn't such a bright idea. Though if Kendra was in danger, she needed to do this, no questions asked. And if this story turned out to be as good as she thought it would be, even that itself might be worth taking the chance. She loved writing but freelancing certainly wasn't keeping her in good financial shape. She was still renting, still living paycheck to paycheck. If things didn't improve soon, she would have to cave in and look for something nine to five and give up her dream. Unless she was serving a prison sentence for insurance scam. Then, she'd be well taken care of courtesy of the state. Or was this a federal issue? *Don't worry about it,* she told herself. She'd be fine. A court couldn't prove she wasn't suicidal or depressed. Bending the law was certainly worth Kendra's safety. Maddie smiled at the motherly instincts she'd always felt for the girl. Someday she would have one of her own. Of course, first, she had to find a husband. Helen swore it would work better that way when she thought about doing it on her own. But she was getting way ahead of herself again. First, she had to go out on a date. Her year long dry spell was getting old.

Maddie refocused and looked at the sheets of paper clipped to a clipboard on the desk. They were all blank, legal forms.

"You shouldn't be looking at those."

A strikingly tall, middle-aged man with thinning, blond hair and blue eyes enter the room.

"I was just..."

The man shook a finger at Maddie, but smiled. "Tsk, tsk. Though I can't blame a person for being curious."

Maddie couldn't place his subtle accent. Norwegian? Swedish, maybe? She had a fondness for Scandinavians.

He held out his large hand to her. "I'm Dr. Lars Rutger." He enclosed Maddie's tiny hand in his and clasped it with the other hand, shaking it firmly.

"I understand you are feeling depressed and that you made a suicidal gesture tonight."

Maddie rescued her hand from his grip. "That's right," she said, remembering to look down at the floor, intentionally keeping her voice quiet. She sat down, slouching in the chair and continued to avoid eye contact. The last one was difficult since this man was a stunning specimen. Still, she had to play the role of depressed patient as best she could. "I think I also have a problem with food." Perhaps including some real life past experiences would help her be more convincing.

"Have you ever been diagnosed with an eating disorder?"

"In college, I had anorexia nervosa."

"Hmm. I believe we can help you here. We have an Adult Acute Care Unit and Long Term Unit. I would admit you to the A.A.C.U. first for observation."

"How long will I stay in the hospital?"

"That all depends on how your treatment goes."

"Can you give me an estimate?" Maddie asked.

"You'll probably be in the A.A.C.U. about a week."

"Do I automatically go to a Long Term Unit after that?"

"We'll see how things go. Some people need more treatment and go to the L.T.U. Some people step down to outpatient level of care. Let's get you admitted first and see how this first part goes. I'm glad you're willing to get help voluntarily. That makes things easier."

He started toward the door, but Maddie stayed in her seat.

"I was wondering," she said, "since I've heard such great things about Dr. Aiken, is it possible to have him as my doctor?" Having the same primary doctor as Kendra would certainly be beneficial.

Dr. Rutger's smile tightened. "Dr. Aiken supervises all of the physicians here. In effect, he is part of all patient treatment. I'd be happy to admit you and have both of us handle your case."

"Yes, okay," Maddie said, trying to keep her voice low and calm. Now that she'd offended this man, she wasn't sure she should be under his care. It didn't really sound like Dr. Aiken would be around much. Supervising usually meant hands off, but it was much too late to back out now. Mattie was caring less about getting a story anymore. *Just think about Kendra,* she told herself.

"I need you to sign some documents with Olivia. Then, we can get you settled in." Dr. Rutger turned the doorknob. "I'll do a medical and psychiatric history with you once you're on the unit."

"Medical and psychiatric history?"

"Just questions about your health up until now. Don't worry. It won't hurt a bit."

Dr. Rutger opened the door, but hesitated. "Mrs. Blankenship? Do you want us to call your husband for you?"

"No," Maddie lied about her imaginary husband. "We're separated."

"I see," he said, and left the room.

Olivia immediately entered. She sat back at her desk, adjusting a bronze name plate that read, *Olivia Garvin, Chief Admitting Officer.*

"We have some paper work to do," she said, releasing the legal forms from her clipboard and placing them on the desk in front of Maddie.

Maddie leaned forward and reached for the top sheet, which would sign her into Aiken's Haven as a voluntary patient. It was straightforward. No legalese to wade through. She took a breath, crossed the fingers of her left hand, and signed her name with her right. She started to reach for the second page.

Olivia yanked the first page from her grip and grasped it tightly. Then she nodded, apparently giving Maddie permission to take the next page. This form asked for her address, phone numbers, that sort of thing.

Wanting to put as little as possible in writing, Maddie said, "I'm so tired. Do I need to fill this out now?"

"I can type in the information from your insurance company forms. They're faxing them to me now." Olivia said, suddenly agreeable. "Just sign it on the bottom there. Press hard. There are several copies it has to go through."

It seemed harmless, so Maddie signed her name. She repeated this on the next few forms that again asked for demographic information. Olivia snatched up each triplicate form as soon as Maddie finished her signature.

"We'll give you copies later, when they're fully filled out. I'm just going to scan a copy of your driver's license into my computer and then we'll be done."

Maddie was hesitant about this but she really had no choice. Besides, they already had her insurance information and all her personal contact data. What difference did a driver's license make at this point? She handed it over.

The phone on the desk rang, startling Maddie. Olivia answered it and jumped into a heated conversation.

"This will just take a minute," Olivia said to Maddie, then lowered her voice as she returned to the caller. "I told you what I wanted and I expect my orders followed," she hissed into the receiver.

Maddie couldn't figure out exactly what the argument was about. She watched Olivia stand and move toward the window. Olivia's face was reddening and she spoke in a harsh whisper as she cranked open the jalousie windows, fanning her face with her hand.

As a cold breeze blew into the room, Maddie watched the legal forms fan out on Olivia's clipboard. She looked again. Holding the papers down, she flipped through the first few. To her horror, she saw that the forms beneath the ones she signed were not exact copies of what she signed. They were completely different than the top forms. Maddie grabbed the clipboard. The line for the signature was in the same location on all of the underlying two sheets, but the contents were different on every one. Maddie looked at the second page underneath the first demographic form she'd signed. *Authorization for Experimental Treatment*, it said at the top. She examined the dark imprint of her signature from the previous page. Desperately trying to think of a way out of the mess she was now mired in, Maddie felt sick to her stomach.

"I'll take that," Olivia said, grabbing the clipboard, while slamming down the handset of the phone. She hugged the papers close to her chest and picked up the phone again.

"I'll call a psych aide to take you to the unit."

"Fine," Maddie replied, her voice quivering.

Once the patient had left, Olivia smiled. She liked working the night shift. It gave her a chance to get things in order without all the interruptions of the regular work day. Besides, she knew Victor trusted her to run things in his absence. Going to her laptop, she went online to one of her favorite sites. It was how she found out everything about everyone. There was a cost but it was worth it. The cursor was blinking at her, waiting for her command. She typed *Blythe, Madison.*

The Adult Acute Care Unit consisted of a circular nursing station surrounded by eight patient rooms. Everything was painted in various shades of blue. Maddie felt like she was engulfed by the sky. The psych aide walked her to her room and motioned for her to sit on the bed. It was not too soft and not too hard, a rare find in a hospital. Covering it was a thick, baby blue, patchwork comforter. Maddie looked around the room. There was no door. Only a large opening between two, thick, Plexiglass walls at the front. The staff at the nursing station could look right into her room, along with the seven other rooms encircling them. The other three walls in the room were robin's egg blue with puffy clouds painted on them. It was pretty and calming, though sparsely furnished. A false sense of security rested in her.

"Hi, Madison," a woman said as she entered the room. "I'm Amy. I'll be your nurse tonight."

When Maddie said nothing, the nurse asked, "Can I get you anything?"

Maddie looked down at her hands.

"I know it can be scary coming into a place like this, but I really am here to help you." Amy paused. When she got no type of acknowledgement, she said, "Aiken's Haven is primarily a facility for adolescents, but this one area is reserved for adults so the place can be helpful to anyone who needs it. We specialize in care for all ages."

Feeling inconsiderate not replying, Maddie nodded.

"Can you look at me, Madison?"

Maddie looked up. Amy was medium height with brown hair and a smooth, white complexion. She had caring, hazel eyes and a quirky accent. Was everyone here foreign? Was that a good sign or a bad sign? Maybe this nurse was genuinely one of the good guys.

"Do you have any questions that I can answer?" Amy asked.

"No," Maddie said. "I'm just really tired."

Dr. Rutger entered the room and the peaceful aura vanished. Amy left and he grilled Maddie for 20 minutes with a barrage of questions. Maddie stuck as close to the truth as possible.

"You said you are childless and currently separated," Dr. Rutger stated. "Any plans for reconciliation?"

"No. He's gone for good," Maddie said. "No need to include him in therapy." Better to nip that one in the bud.

"Your parents?"

"They're retired. Down in Florida," Maddie lied. She didn't want any of her family dragged into this. She prayed no one would investigate her answers.

"Siblings?"

"A brother in New York. A sister in California." That much was true.

"You don't have any close family members living here?" This seemed to please him.

"There's no one I'm very close to."

He nodded and finished up the interrogation.

"I'd like to get you started on some medication tonight," Dr. Rutger said.

"I'm feeling much safer now being in this hospital. I don't think I'll need anything."

He waved Amy back into the room and continued typing into his laptop. "If we want to treat your suicidal depression aggressively, we need to use medication. I can prescribe it p.o. for tonight."

Maddie looked to Amy for help since her pre-med courses in college didn't include pharmacology.

"A pill. By mouth," Amy explained. "It's Latin. *Per os*."

"Aren't there a lot of dangerous side effects to psychiatric drugs?"

"Psychotropic drugs. Yes," Dr. Rutger replied, "but not as dangerous as attempting suicide. Besides, I'm sure Olivia in Admitting reviewed them with you before you signed the consent forms for them. That's our standard procedure."

"I don't remember signing anything like that."

"Well, you did. Here it is." He turned the laptop to show Maddie a scanned document.

The top of the page said something about *Discussion of Side Effects of Psychotropic Medications*. At the bottom, it was her signature all right. Maddie leaned a little closer. Was this one of those hidden forms? Or was this a computerized trick? Maddie wondered how many other forms were signed on her behalf without her knowledge. She felt a chill run down her spine.

Dr. Rutger interrupted her thoughts. "Amy can go over the side effects with you again. It should be a nurse explaining this material anyway. I don't know why Dr. Aiken insists on having Olivia and her team distribute it."

"I don't mean to be difficult," Maddie said, "but I really don't want to take anything."

"I don't believe you're in sound mind at the moment to make that judgment call," Dr. Rutger said. "If needed, we can give you an injection."

"No! I don't want a shot!" Maddie moved to the other side of the bed.

"Nurse," Dr. Rutger said. "Give her 100 mg IM of Protocol

Drug #8." He left the room.

Maddie stared wide-eyed at Amy.

"I know you're frightened," Amy said. "These medications are serious drugs, not to be taken lightly, but if the doctor has prescribed it for you, he feels it's in the best interest of your mental health."

"I still don't want to take it."

"I understand how you feel. Is there anything I can do to make you feel more comfortable with this?"

"What does this Protocol Drug #8 do? How does it work?" Maddie asked.

"To be honest, I don't exactly know." Amy shrugged her shoulders and sat down on the bed beside Maddie.

"How can you give a patient a medicine when you don't know what you're giving them? How long have you been a nurse?"

Amy smiled kindly. "Don't worry. I've only been practicing for six months, but I promise, I got straight A's in nursing school. Some of the psychiatric medications we've been using for years have actions in the brain that aren't entirely understood yet. The basic physiological action, yes, but not all the microscopic details. The research has shown them to be effective against psychiatric symptoms, though. Through usage of them, we study and learn more about their physiological effects. We improve them and develop better ones with less side effects. But the brain is so complicated. So yes, it's not ideal, there are unpleasant and even dangerous though rare side effects, but these medicines have been scientifically proven to help. They give people a higher quality of life and even save lives in some situations."

"But isn't that taking quite a risk?"

"I guess it's a trade ff. Improved mental health through these medications or avoiding the meds but staying sick. It's a tough choice for people with these illnesses. Honestly, I don't know what I'd choose if I had to make a decision like that."

"If you *had* to choose?"

Amy looked at the ceiling for a few seconds. "If the alternative was the deterioration of my mental health and possibly thinking about suicide, I would opt to do anything to reverse that. So if I had to choose, I suppose I would take the medication."

"What if a bad reaction happens?"

"In here, all nurses are to immediately notify the attending doctor and Dr. Aiken if any side effects arise."

"What if they can't handle what comes up? What if it's a fatal side effect?"

Amy took a moment before replying. "Well, I suppose I have to be honest and say that it could be a possibility that fatal reactions could occur."

"That's not too reassuring. I don't like the thought of taking any medication, especially not a mystery medication."

"Maybe I've presented this badly," Amy said. "There is a lot *known* about these drugs, too. With the med you've been ordered, I know it affects the brain's neurotransmitters, I just don't know specifically how, or its future intended purpose."

"You don't even know why you're using it."

"Again, I've misspoken. For example, there is one medication, desyrel, that was originally designed as a sleep agent. It was then discovered to have an antidepressant effect. With the development of newer and better antidepressants, it's been relegated back to the role of helping with long term sleep problems, and it works quite effectively that way. No one uses it as an antidepressant much anymore. As time goes on, new uses for medications can be discovered. Right now, Protocol Drug #8 is designed to help with impulsiveness, aggression and behavioral control. It's still in the R&D stages. Research and development."

"I don't want an experimental drug."

"I understand your concerns, but I have seen this medication help other patients. The data collected so far says that most of the adverse effects seem to occur in adolescents and children, so you should probably be fine." Amy looked weary.

"It's not even for depression," Maddie said. "Why is he giving it to me?"

"Well, they are testing it for a variety of uses." Amy sighed. "You did sign the consent for it. Even if you've changed your mind, the doctor has ordered that it be given with or without your permission."

"Can he do that?"

"I'm sorry, but if he feels you're in impending danger, yes, he can order it that way. And if he changes your status to an involuntary patient based on your refusal, he can pursue legal action to force medication on a regular basis. But we're getting ahead of ourselves."

"He can do that because I'm suicidal, right? He would do it, wouldn't he?"

Amy nodded. "You should just take it." She lightly patted Maddie's hand. "If not, we will have to call in the psych aides to hold you down, so I can give the shot to you. We may even be required to restrain you to the bed." Amy lowered her voice to a whisper. "I'd hate to be ordered to do that."

"Aren't restraints for people who are out of control?"

"Yes, or considered a danger to themselves." Amy gently held both of Maddie's hands in hers. "Again, Dr. Rutger would say you are a danger because of your suicidal thoughts.

"It's like a horrible game, isn't it? And one I can't win, can I?"

Amy shook her head. "I'll be right back."

Amy Bunton went to the medication room to prepare the injection. She kept one eye on her patient while drawing it up in the syringe. Once again, she felt very uncomfortable. She didn't like the games that were played in the American healthcare system. Not that the government regulated system back home in Canada was perfect. Hell, she couldn't even get a job. But at least, she didn't feel like she was walking an ethical tightrope all the time when she was in nursing school there. She missed the simplicity of life in the Maritimes. She missed the ocean. She missed her parents. Adjusting to the differences in the two countries was more difficult than she thought it would be. Americans seemed more aggressive, more opinionated. Sort of in your face. She felt intimidated. They called her passive. She'd yet to make a good friend here. Give it time, she told herself. It takes time to assimilate, to stop being homesick. Maybe she'd fly back for Christmas if she could get the time off. If there were any job openings, she'd move back home in a minute. For now, she was trapped in the one-year contract she'd signed with Aiken's Haven. After all, they did pay for her to take the U.S. nursing boards and her state license. They paid her flight down and gave her money toward other moving expenses. They even found her an apartment and paid the security deposit. She did owe them the full year. She was stuck.

Maddie watched the nurse return. She raised her hands, shaking her head in genuine fear.

"Can't I just take the pill form?"

"Once the doctor changes his mind, there's no going back. Sorry. He wrote the order for an IM injection." Amy said, "I know you're scared, but agreeing to take the injection calmly is much better than the alternative. I promise I'll keep a close eye on you for the rest of the night."

“All right,” Maddie said, believing that Amy would keep her word. Besides, she couldn’t think of any other way to get out of the situation. One dose probably wouldn’t hurt, she told herself. She had to do it for Kendra.

After giving the injection, Amy got Maddie tucked into bed. She unpacked the few clothes from Maddie’s small suitcase and put them into cubbyholes built into the wall.

As Maddie watched Amy take her purse, her vision started to blur. Her head felt funny. Blackness enveloped her.

CHAPTER 6

Maddie woke up to see Amy sitting on her bedside.

"What...time...is it?" Maddie asked, yawning.

"It's only 7:00 in the morning. Sunday morning," Amy whispered. "You've only been asleep about three and a half hours. I told you I'd watch over you. I wanted to check on you one last time before I go off shift."

"Don't worry," Amy held her hand up. "I'll be back at 7:00 tonight. I've asked my boss if I can be on this unit again. We float to different units, but I want to be back here tonight."

Maddie nodded, trying to keep her heavy eyelids open.

"You look tired," Amy said, standing and straightening the comforter. "Go back to sleep for a while. I'll ask the day staff to wake you for breakfast."

Maddie tried to sit up but Amy eased her back down.

"You need rest."

"But...feel...better." Maddie's jaw wouldn't move properly. It was stiff and her words came out slurred.

Amy smiled. "I'm glad you're feeling better but you still need to rest."

"Not suicid-" Maddie could barely speak now.

"Not suicidal anymore?" Amy asked.

Maddie tried to nod but her head wouldn't move. Couldn't

Amy see this, she wondered?

"You still look and sound very groggy from the medication. I'm going to leave now and let you get some more sleep. I'll see you when I come back on shift tonight."

Maddie didn't answer. She couldn't move her mouth anymore. Or any of her muscles. The blackness washed over her.

Kendra glanced at the large unit clock that hung above the nursing station. It was 8:30 a.m. In half an hour, she and another patient, Adam, were going to sit in on a group therapy session on one of the long term units. No one told her why she and Adam were picked to go, or why the other six patients from her unit weren't going. She wasn't even allowed to talk to Adam to find out what he knew. Kendra could feel herself trembling as she shed her hospital gown and dressed in the uniform of sweats she was issues for the daytime.

The nurse entered while she was still pulling up her elasticized pants. "Time to go."

Kendra blushed. "Just give me a minute to get dressed." She couldn't remember the nurse's name and the woman wasn't wearing a name badge to help Kendra out. "I thought we were going at 9:00."

"Schedule's been changed. Hurry up."

Kendra fumed inside. If she wasn't so frightened of what they'd do to her, she would complain about the way the staff treated her. Well, except for Amy. Amy was nice.

Kendra joined the nurse and Adam. The trio left their unit in silence. In the hallways, both teens looked through the shatterproof glass windows at the pristine swimming pool and then the empty Recreation Room. A dip in the pool sounded like a great idea to Kendra. She hadn't been allowed to use it though. Or any of the games. She'd been stuck in her room for almost two days and now she was getting out only to go to another unit, with staff and patients that she didn't know, to attend a group on a topic that she also didn't know. She would never forgive Mother for this. As soon as her imprisonment was up, Mother better get her out of here. Kendra felt a nudge to her elbow and turned to look at Adam.

"How long are you stuck in here?" he asked in a barely audible whisper.

"Only one more day. What about you?"

"I've been here two weeks. They're going to transfer me to a long term unit soon. That's why I'm going to their group therapy today instead of our unit's."

"Why am I going then?" Kendra asked, panic in her voice. "I won't be transferring."

"Don't be too sure," Adam said. "I thought I was coming in for a couple of days, too."

"Can't your parents get you out?"

"I only have foster parents." Adam looked at the floor. "They suck. I don't want to go back there."

"It can't be worse than here."

"It's about the same. My foster mom doesn't care about me or any of the kids in the house."

"Then why did she take you in?"

Just then, the nurse escorting them stopped in her tracks. Kendra, wrapped up in Adam's story, walked right into her.

"Sorry," she said, cringing.

The nurse glared at her. "Wait here," she said to the teenagers. "I'm going to see if they're ready for you." She opened the door to a unit labeled *Adolescent Long Term #3* and disappeared.

Kendra stared at Adam intently. "We're alone! This is our chance!"

Adam shook his head. "Already tried that. Believe me, it's not worth it. It was brutal when I was caught." He shook. "You can't get out of this prison anyway."

"I will tomorrow."

"Maybe. At least you have parents who care, right?"

Kendra thought about this for a moment. "Yeah, I guess I do." She felt sheepish. "So you never said why your foster mother took you in."

"They get a certain amount of money from the government for each kid they take in. She has as many as they let her keep."

"I bet she doesn't get on your case."

"Only if I get in her way. Besides, her old man takes care of that." He lifted his sweatshirt and showed her some bruises in various stages of healing.

"That sucks."

"See, I told you. You're lucky."

The door to the unit opened and Kendra and Adam were ushered inside. The unit was a lot bigger than their current one but overall, it looked the same. They were led into a room with at least 20 other teenagers in it. Adam took a seat and Kendra sat beside him, moving her plastic chair a little bit closer to his.

"I'm scared," she whispered to him.

"It's okay," Adam said. "We'll stick together." He looked around the room. In a hushed tone he said, "Look around. No one's staring at us."

Kendra scanned the crowd cautiously. Adam was right. None of the patients were paying any attention to them. In fact, she wasn't even sure they were aware that the two of them had come into the room.

"They look like zombies," she said. "What's wrong with them?"

"Too much medicine, I guess. Another guy who used to be here, Shane, told me that he'd never go to a long term unit. He said these are the units where they experiment on people."

"That sounds like something out of a movie." Kendra said.

"Where do you think they get the plots for those movies/" Adam replied.

Another teen entered the room and came toward the two newcomers. He looked perfectly normal.

"Hey, I'm Clarence. You guys come from one of the acute units?"

"Yeah. I'm Adam. This is Kendra. Are you a patient in here?"

"I know, I know. I don't look like the rest of these broccoli-heads. I guess I'm lucky. They're discharging me next week."

"See," Kendra said to Adam. "It's not as bad as you're making it out to be."

"Oh, it's bad here all right," Clarence said. "I just seem to have a better reaction to the medicine than most of the kids. Dr. Aiken keeps calling me his star patient."

"Dr. Aiken's creepy." Adam said.

The three teenagers nodded in unison.

"I'm just glad I'm on his good side," Clarence said.

"How do you get on his good side?" Kendra asked.

"Beats me. If you react well to his medicine, he likes you. That's all I've figured out."

"Can you control that?" Adam asked.

"I don't think so. I heard a couple of the nurses talking about me. They said that it's nice to see a success once in a while. One of them said something like it makes a difference when the patient actually *needs* the medicine."

"What the hell does that mean?" Kendra asked.

"It means I was a freak." Clarence laughed. "No, it means that we all get the drug whether we need it or not. Apparently, I needed it."

Kendra leaned forward in her chair. "Why did you need it?"

Clarence looked down at the floor. "I went kind of crazy before I got here. I was hearing voices in my head. They kept telling me to do stuff, like tear up my room and things. I even hit my little brother." He bit his lip. "I'd never hurt him. I love the little butt wipe. It was like I was a different person. I was just totally angry all the time. So the medicine fixed that and I can go home again."

"I just wanted to be left alone," Kendra said. "I didn't hurt anyone. Why would Dr. Aiken give me the medicine?"

"Duh," Adam piped in. "He just said everyone gets it."

"Then I'm going to be a zombie too. Mother better get me out of here tomorrow."

"Don't hold your breath," Adam said.

Kendra was about to argue, when a tall, pale man entered the room. He closed the door and looked around at all the faces, making eye contact with each one of them, even if he had to bend way down to do it. He cleared his throat loudly.

"Today, our group is going to center around anger management. We will look at positive and negative ways of dealing with this powerful emotion. At the end of the meeting, I want each of you to list at least one anger management tool that you can use during the rest of the day. Before we get started, there are two new guests with us today. Adam, Kendra, my name is Simon. I'm the Social Worker on this unit. Now I want to go around the room and have everyone introduce themselves to our visitors.

Kendra and Adam watched in shock as each patient took a turn listing their name. *Cassandra...Karen...Allie...Josh...Brenden.* Only the name was uttered and each teen spoke in the exact same tone of voice. A dead voice.

Kendra turned to Clarence. “Help us out here, okay?

“Don’t worry,” he answered. “I’ll get you through this.”

Sunday was Olivia’s regular day off but she had been in the Admissions Office for hours already. Her investigation of Madison Blythe had turned up all sorts of interesting facts. She wanted to print out and compile everything she’d found so she could present it to Victor in a comprehensive, but succinct way. Maybe he would be so impressed that he’d finally come to see her in a new light. Not just a devoted employee, but a loyal and resourceful woman with his best interests at heart.

Olivia began weeding through her stack of incriminating evidence when she held up one sheet of paper. It was a printout of an old newspaper column. One of those small local papers. It was titled, *Homeless Teens: A Growing Epidemic.* The byline listed Madison Blythe as the author. Victor would certainly be interested to know that this supposed patient had already written a story that featured Aiken’s Haven.

Olivia reread the article and set it down on the desk, puzzled. “I don’t get it,” she said aloud. The article was not completely flattering to the mental health care industry, nor the legal system, but the excerpts about Aiken’s Haven were mostly innocuous, if not positive. Could it be that this woman really did need psychiatric help and thought this was a good place to seek it?

“Not a chance,” Olivia muttered. “Too much of a coincidence.” Remembering all the lies she discovered in her research, she concluded that Madison Blythe was up to no good. She had lied about her parents’ whereabouts. Even her name and marital status. A person doesn’t lie unless they are trying to hide something or misrepresent themselves. Olivia knew all about such motivations.

Picking up the phone, sje began to dial Victor's home number. She hung up and dialed again. After the first ring, she hung up. She couldn't wait to tell him her information but he would probably be annoyed that she interrupted him on a Sunday. Of course, he'd probably look at his caller ID and know she had started to call him. Damn it. She began to sweat as she awaited an angry return call.

Dr. Victor Aiken did not pick up his home phone. He never heard it ring. Just down the hall from Olivia, he was seated behind his desk in his office, attacking his keyboard with punishing strokes. As he answered a buzz from the receptionist, he saved and closed the file he'd been working on. The A.W.O.L. list disappeared from sight and a screen filled with calming clouds and dozens of icons filled the monitor.

"What is it, Jane?"

"There's a woman up here to see you. Her name is Helen Sibley. Did you have an appointment with her?"

"No," Victor said. "What does she want?"

"Just a minute." There was a long pause. "She wants to discuss her daughter's discharge.

Victor rolled his eyes. "Did you already tell her that I am in the building?"

"I'm sorry, sir." Jane's voice quivered.

"The damage is done." He said sharply. "Send her in, but have security escort her."

"Yes, sir. Right away."

A few minutes later, a loud knock sounded on the door.

"Come in," Victor barked, not getting up from his chair.

A man dressed in uniform ushered Helen into the office. "Helen Sibley to see you Dr. Aiken."

Helen took a tentative step forward.

"Sit down." Victor pointed to a cushioned chair in front of his desk. He nodded to the security guard who remained at the door.

Helen obeyed the command and took a seat. "I'm here to discuss my daughter, Kendra Sibley."

"Yes. What can I do for you?"

"I was willing to sign her in but they had her come in on an involuntary commitment. It should be up tomorrow. I want to take her home and I was hoping I could do that now."

"There is still another day left to her commitment."

"I realize that. I thought a few more hours really wouldn't make a difference"

"I would say that it makes a significant difference."

Helen sighed. "I don't see how."

"Your daughter's condition is tenuous. I need those hours to assess her level of safety."

"I don't think that's reasonable."

"It is a fact that cannot, and will not, be changed." Victor's eyes bored into hers.

"But you could discharge her."

"The courts are not open until tomorrow, even if I wanted to."

"But I was reading about designating examinations, where a doctor can discharge-"

"Ah, Wikepedia. You have the term and your information incorrect. When two designated examiners determine that a patient can be released from involuntary status, it still must be approved of by a mental health judge. Again, court is not in session today."

Helen shook her head. "Can I at least see her? The receptionist said she wouldn't let me visit."

"Visiting hours are at 7:00 p.m."

"This is ridiculous." Helen stood up. "I haven't been allowed to speak to her since last evening's visit. I want to know how my daughter is doing."

Victor stood also. "Your daughter is depressed and suicidal. That is why you brought her here. She is a danger to herself. She is now in a safe place receiving the treatment that she needs."

"That may be your opinion," Helen said. "I think Kendra will be better off coming home. I am her mother and that is my decision."

"I am afraid I must override your decision," Victor said. "I do not think Kendra would be better off being free to act on her suicidal impulses. Are you willing to risk your daughter's life?"

"Dr. Aiken, to be perfectly honest, I feel that I'm risking her safety by having her stay in here. You may be doing great work. You may be helping other people. But I no longer think this is the place for my daughter to be."

"I am sorry you feel that way," Victor said, sitting back down in his chair. "I do not foresee Kendra being ready for discharge tomorrow. He motioned for Helen to sit.

She remained standing. "She's coming home with me tomorrow."

"No, she is not. I am going to have her commitment extended. A 90-day length of stay is what comes next. Again, it involves the mental health court, mandating her to stay here, with or without your consent. I see no problem getting the judge to agree with my diagnosis and treatment recommendations."

Helen placed both hands on the desktop and leaned toward the doctor's face. "I'll have you know I've been in touch with my lawyer."

"That is good to hear," Victor said, leaning forward in his chair. "Your lawyer is welcome to attend the commitment hearing."

Helen shrunk back a bit, still standing. "Will that be held tomorrow?"

Victor laughed. "The system does not move that quickly. Perhaps in a week or two. You will be notified of the date and time of the hearing."

"A week or two! That's unacceptable!"

"I agree with you. But whether you accept it or not, that is the case." Victor came out from behind his desk. He tried to pat Helen on the shoulder but she shrugged away. He went toward his office door. "If you will excuse me, I have a lot of work to do."

Helen stared at him. "I'm not done."

"You are done here. Do you want to leave of your own accord or does this security officer need to assist you out?"

Helen had barely noticed the uniformed officer at the door. "I'll find my own way out," she said. Seething, she marched back to the reception area, the security guard trailing her the entire way.

She approached the reception desk. "I forgot my cell phone. Do you have a phone I could use?"

Jane smiled wanly. "There's a telephone at the far end of the lobby." She pointed in the direction of a nicely furnished sitting area. "Dial 9 first to get out. If it's long distance, I'm afraid you'll have to call collect."

"It's not," Helen said, walking quickly away.

She sat on one of the suede-like microfiber couches, out of earshot of the receptionist. Picking up the phone, she dialed the number to the hospital.

Jane came on the line. "Aiken's Haven. Can I help you?"

"Adolescent Acute Care Unit #3, please," Helen whispered in a disguised voice.

"One moment. I'll connect you."

"Adolescent A.C.U. #3. This is Leslie. Can I help you?"

"Yes," Helen said hurriedly. "I'd like to speak to my daughter, Kendra."

"She's in an individual session with the doctor right now."

"Can you interrupt them? It's very important." Helen glanced furtively back at Jane. The receptionist didn't seem to be catching on. She was busy answering other lines.

"I'm sorry, we don't interrupt therapy for phone calls. Why don't you call back during phone hours?"

"Phone hours? For the love of God, when are they?"

"Four and eight o'clock on Sundays. You should have been told this on admission."

"Thanks for nothing," Helen said, hanging up. She sat back, letting the couch engulf her. Setting her purse firmly on her lap, she set her mouth in a hard straight line. She didn't close the bookstore early for nothing.

"I'm going to sit here until I can talk face to face with Kendra," she said, not loud enough for Jane to hear, "or until I come up with a plan."

It took two minutes for her to pick up the phone again. Doing the same thing, she got herself connected to the Adult Unit.

"Can I speak to one of your patients, please? Her name is Maddie?"

"I'm sorry, we don't accept incoming calls."

"I'm sure she'll take my call. My name is Helen Sibley."

"One moment. Yes, you are on her approved call list. However, she's asleep right now."

"Could you wake her up?" Helen asked. "It's very important."

"I can't do that. Why don't you call back during regular phone hours?"

"Of course? Why don't I do that?" Helen slammed the phone down.

Jane looked up from her reception desk. Raising her voice to be heard across the room, she asked, "Can I help you Mrs. Sibley?"

"No," Helen said back, loudly. "Just an upsetting call."

Jane stared at her. "Going home now?" she prompted.

Helen shouted back, "No! I won't be going home. I'm staying put until I have my daughter back!"

Jane shrugged and went back to her ringing phone lines.

Kendra sat cross-legged on the bed in her room. She was surprisingly glad to be back on her regular unit but she was annoyed that Dr. Dushkriti was drilling questions at her. He sat on a stool he had wheeled into the room, typing notes into his laptop, and nodding in the most infuriating manner.

It was none of his business how she felt about her parents' divorce or how often she saw her father. She didn't want to talk about it. She didn't even want to think about it. Sometimes, it crept into her thoughts though. Now, with it being shoved in her face, she found herself being jettisoned back ten years.

Mother had been yelling again. She yelled a lot then. Cried a lot, too. She wanted to be called *Mother* instead of *Mommy.* Daddy was still *Daddy.* He wasn't yelling. He wasn't saying anything.

Kendra had gone out into the backyard to finish the tunnels she had been digging in the sandbox. Daddy came out with his hoe and headed for his vegetable garden. She smiled at him. He waved and smile back. They were having a good time in the back yard, Kendra with her tunnels and Daddy with his vegetables. Then, Mary had to ruin it all.

"Kendra, come and play skipping with me and Kelly. We need a third person." Mary stood with her hands on her hips, a jump rope in hand, best friend by her side.

"I don't want to." Kendra told her older sister, starting on a new tunnel.

"You have to," Mary said. "We need you to turn the rope."

"No!" Kendra picked up a handful of sand and threw it at her.

It only hit Mary's legs and sprinkled to the ground but she ran into the house yelling, "I'm telling Mother!"

Within seconds, Mother was standing beside the sandbox, with her hand on her hips and Mary at her heels.

"Do not throw sand at your sister. Go play with Mary and Kelly."

"I want to stay here." Kendra poured water from her red bucket into one of the sandy holes to create a nice, muddy texture.

"Give me that!" Mother grabbed the bucket out of her hands. "You're getting all dirty."

Daddy stopped his work in the garden and came over to see what was going on,

"Paul, this is your fault," Mother said to him. "She follows your example. She never plays with other children. It's not normal. My psychology professor says that a five-year-old should be relating with other children her own age." She threw her hand up in the air. "You're both a couple of hermits!"

"What's wrong with a little girl playing in a sandbox, Helen?" Paul leaned against the hoe, his shoulders hunched forward. "Do your college classes cover that?"

"We won't discuss this in front of the girls. Mary go play with your friend. Kendra, I want you to go to your room and think about what's wrong with your behavior."

Mary scowled as she ran off to the front yard. Kendra went into the house and upstairs to her bedroom. She wasn't sure what Mother expected her to do but she had some pictures in her new coloring book that needed work so she got her crayons out.

By the third picture, Daddy came in with a plate of chocolate chip cookies and an orange soda, the old-timey kind, that comes in a bottle. He winked at Kendra. She waved at him, took a sip of soda and went back to drawing.

While trying to decide if the princess should have a blue or purple gown, she heard Mother calling her for dinner. She went to the bathroom to wash her hands. She sang the Happy Birthday song, remembering to wash for two minutes.

During dinner, Mary talked about her dance class and the recital next Tuesday. Mother talked about her night classes at the college. Kendra and Daddy ate the ham and rice casserole. Kendra only picked at the green beans. She looked up at Mother to see if she noticed, but Mother wasn't looking at her plate or her green beans. Mother was looking at Daddy and her face was all pinched.

After dinner, Mother sent Daddy out of the room and told the girls to help her clear the table. She took Kendra's plate to the sink, even though there were still beans on it. Mary tried to tell on her, but it was ignored this one time.

When the dishes were done, the three of them sat back down at the kitchen table.

"I have some bad news to tell you two. Your father and I are getting a divorce." Mother looked first at Mary, then at Kendra. Neither one of them said anything.

"Do you know what a divorce is?" she asked. "It means that your father and I are not going to be married anymore, and your father is going to live somewhere else."

Again, Kendra and Mary just stared.

"It doesn't mean that we don't love you. We love you both, but your father and I just can't get along with each other. Do you understand?"

Mary began to cry. "But Kelly's parent's aren't divorced. None of my friends' parents are divorced."

Mother leaned over and put an arm around her. "That's because some of them never got married to begin with." She sighed heavily and rolled her eyes. "Doesn't that girl in your class, Chantal, live with just her mother?"

Mary wailed even louder at this. "That's because her dad is in the Army."

"That's part of it. But I talked to her mother at that last Parent-Teacher night. They've been separated for over a year now. So you're not going to be the only one in your class with unmarried parents."

Slipping out of her chair, Kendra headed for the back door. She wasn't quite sure what a divorce was but she was sad that Daddy wouldn't be allowed to live with them anymore. She wandered out to the backyard, heading for the sandbox. Daddy was sitting at the picnic bench, the one they had built together. It still looked a little crooked to her. Daddy said it was perfect. She went over and sat beside him, picking at a loose splinter of wood.

"We're getting a divorce," Kendra said.

"I know." His voice was quiet.

"I don't want it."

"Neither do I." He took a big breath and let it out slowly, making that whistling noise with his nose.

"Where do you have to go?"

"There's an apartment nearby."

Suddenly, the splinter Kendra was pulling at ripped free from the picnic table. The bare wood showed underneath.

"Oops! I'm sorry, Daddy. I wrecked it."

"It's all right. We can put some more stain on that spot and it will be as good as new." He took the splinter from her and stared at it. Turned it over and stared at the other side. "I guess we better do it now."

He got up and went to the garage. Kendra followed him. They returned with a small can of wood stain and two paintbrushes. Daddy stirred the stain. They painted the spot and it did look as good as new.

Afterward, they went into the garage to clean the brushes with turpentine.

"What did you do?" Kendra asked him, "to get in trouble with Mother?"

Daddy put his clean paintbrush on the workbench, then reached for hers. He rinsed it over the sink.

"It's what I didn't do." He looked at his girl and patted her head. "I guess I'm too much of a hermit."

"Like me!" Kendra said, excitedly. "Mother said I'm a hermit, too. Will I be sent to the apartment with you?"

"No," Daddy said. "I guess it's best if you stay here with your mother and your sister."

The next Saturday, Daddy was gone. Kendra went into his study. All the furniture was gone. She sat down in the middle of the room, picking at the balls of wool on the carpet.

"Don't do that!" Mother popped her head into the room. "You'll ruin the carpeting. What are you doing in here anyway?"

Kendra looked up at her. "Could I go and stay with Daddy at the apartment?"

Mother's hands went to her hips. A bad sign. "No. Your father can't take care of you properly. Besides, wouldn't you miss Mary? She and Kelly are out front. Why don't you go and play with them? It's a beautiful day outside."

Kendra shrugged her shoulders and went out to the backyard, heading for the sandbox. After a few minutes of shoveling, she went to the front porch. Mary and Kelly were sitting with their jump ropes.

"What are you doing?" she asked them.

"Want to play Double Dutch?" Mary asked.

Kelly nodded. "Can I go first?"

Kendra didn't know how to skip that way but she figured she could turn the ropes. "Sure, I'll play."

After a while, Kelly was called to her house for lunch and the sisters went into their house.

While Mother was preparing egg salad on whole wheat bagels, Kendra told her, "I played with Mary and Kelly. Skipping. Double Dutch."

Her effort netted her a bagel and a glass of skim milk.

Kendra waited, but Mother wasn't saying anything. "I'm not a hermit anymore."

"I'm glad to hear it."

"Can Daddy come back now?"

"Oh, Kendra." Mother sat in the chair beside her. "Your father is not going to be coming back but it's not your fault. You and Mary are going to see him tomorrow. You can visit him at his new place okay?"

"No! I want him to come home!" She ran into Daddy's study and threw herself on the floor, pounding and kicking. Once she stopped screaming, she wiped her eyes and runny nose on her sleeve. Mother came in the room. She tried to hug her but Kendra wouldn't let her.

"It'll be okay," Mother said. "Now I want you to get cleaned up because I'm going to take you and Mary shopping this afternoon. We're all going to the mall and we're going to meet a friend of mine there. Doesn't that sound like fun?"

"I don't want to go dumb old shopping!" Kendra beat her feet on the floor.

"Stop that right now and go to your room." Mother pointed to the staircase.

Kendra stomped up the stairs, slammed her door and plopped on the floor.

Mother came up a while later. She didn't have any cookies or soda. "Thanks to you, I've canceled the shopping trip, but my friend has dropped by to visit. I want you to be on your best behavior and come downstairs. Is that clear?" Mother reached out her hand.

Kendra nodded and got up but wouldn't hold her hand. They descended the stairs in silence. As they entered the living room, Mother scooted her daughter in front of a man sitting on their couch.

"Bob, this is Kendra." She turned back to her girl. "Bob's a friend of mine from the University of Pennsylvania."

"Hello there, little lady," Bob said, smiling. He had a bushy beard and he was dressed all in black. Kendra stared at him.

"Aren't you going to say hello to Bob?" Mother asked, her tone sharp?

"Hi," she said. "I'm a hermit. Just like my Daddy."

Bob chuckled, but Mother glared at her. Fortunately, they

were all quickly distracted by Mary, who came running into the room.

"I found them!" She ran up to Bob and put her girl scout badges on his lap. "I got this one for baking cupcakes for the bake sale. This one for changing my bicycle tire. This one is for swimming 10 lengths of the pool without stopping."

Leaving them to admire Mary's badges, Kendra went back up to her room. Putting her crayons back in their box, she took them, and two of her coloring books, and went back downstairs.

"I'm running away," she said.

No one heard her. They were still gushing over Mary who was showing off her latest dance moves.

Kendra went out the back door and took one last look at her sandbox. Then, she left.

Mary told her later that Mother had called Daddy as soon as she knew she was missing. Bob had gone home, and Mother and Daddy had searched the neighborhood, spotting Kendra in the school yard down the street.

She had seen them both walking toward her, but she kept on coloring. They stood there talking, close enough for her to overhear them.

"What should we do?" Mother had asked Daddy.

"I'll take care of it," he told her.

"No," Mother said. "I'm tired of being the bad guy. Maybe I did handle this one poorly. I think I should talk to her. It'll give me a chance to make it right."

Mother approached Kendra slowly. She sat on the cement staircase, one step below her girl.

Kendra waited for her to yell, to march her home to her room. Instead, Mother picked up one of the crayons, the purple one, and started coloring the castle Kendra was working on. *Mother never colors*, Kendra thought. They finished the picture.

It looked good. She smiled at Mother. She got a big smile from Mother in return.

"We did a good job together, didn't we?" Mother asked.

"Uh-huh." Kendra gathered up her crayons. "Hey, Daddy," she said, looking up at him. "Look at what Mother and I did?"

"Very nice," Daddy replied.

"Hey Daddy," Kendra said, looking up at him. "Can we build a new picnic bench when we visit you at the apartment tomorrow?"

"Sure." Daddy laughed. "We'll put it on the balcony. How about a sandbox, too?"

"Great." She looked over at Mother. "Can we go home now?"

Daddy took the crayons and coloring books. He held Kendra's hand. With a smile on her face and tears in her eyes, Mother held her other hand.

"Race you both to the house," Kendra said.

Daddy let her have a head start. She could hear him behind her. She looked around and saw that he was catching up. She ran faster. Looking back again, Daddy was still running and now Mother was running beside him. She was laughing. Kendra beat Daddy back to the house but when she touched the driveway, she saw that Mother was right beside her.

"We tied," Kendra told her.

"Yes," Mother said. "We did."

CHAPTER 7

Victor stared at his cell phone. Why was Olivia texting him? Why did she want him to come to the Admissions Office? He was not surprised that she was at work on her day off. She was one of his most loyal minions. What concerned him was that she knew *he* was here. He thought most of that stalking nonsense was behind them.

Reluctantly, he called her.

"This is Olivia." She practically sang the words and it set Victor's teeth on edge.

"Dr. Aiken here. I assume that with it being a Sunday, you are contacting me over an emergency that you cannot handle."

"Oh, I've handled it, all right," Olivia said, her mouth obviously too close to her phone.

Victor held his cell slightly away from his ear. "They why did you presume to bother me?"

"I've gathered some information that I know you're going to want to look at. I think the quicker we nip this in the bud, the more chance we have of preventing a disaster."

Victor looked at the ceiling, then closed his eyes and sighed. "What is it? Just tell me the situation."

"I'd rather show you," Olivia said, a desperate eagerness leaking into her voice.

Of course you would, Victor thought to himself. Anything

to get near me. He was seriously considering getting rid of her now, but she had become so useful to him, he was not ready to dispose of her just yet. When he moved on to his new facilities, he would definitely have to take care of her.

"All right. Come over to my office."

"I didn't know you were in the building," Olivia said, giggling. "I'll be right over."

"I can hardly wait," Victor said, after she had already disconnected.

The knock on his office door came quicker than expected. She must have run all the way. Victor shook his head. "Enter."

Olivia came into the office, a sheepish expression on her face. "I know you don't like to be bothered," she said, moving around to his side of the desk, "but this is something you absolutely need to know right away." She placed a black folder on his desktop.

He opened it and read the first page. *Report on Adult inpatient Madison Blythe (aka Blankenship).* Victor looked up at Olivia who was reading over his shoulder.

"Reading is a solitary activity."

Olivia backed up.

"Why don't you have a seat?" Victor motioned toward the chairs on the other side of his desk.

Olivia obeyed the suggestion. She didn't take her eyes off Victor while he read her entire 12-page report. Once he finished, he closed the folder and set it back down on the desk.

"You have certainly done your homework."

Olivia smiled. "Yes. Isn't is awful. I wonder what she's up to?"

"What makes you so certain that she is indeed up to something?"

"She's a freelance writer. She's looking for a story."

"Writers are not immune to mental illness," Victor said, sliding the report back toward Olivia. In fact, there are a long list of them with both psychiatric and substance abuse problems. Ernest Hemingway, Virginia Woolf, Sylvia Plath, Leo Tolstoy, Ezra Pound. Need I go on?"

"She only writes articles."

"Agreed, she is not in their company."

"So she could be faking her depression."

"That is certainly a possibility."

"So why don't you sound very concerned?" Olivia's face was scrunched up into an anguished look. "We need to do something about her."

"You have done your duty by reporting this to me. I will take over from here."

"But-"

"That will be all, Olivia. Why not go home and enjoy your day off now?"

Olivia stood, frowning. "If you're sure I can't do anything else for you."

"I am sure." He watched the woman dejectedly lumber toward the door. "By the way, good work."

Olivia craned her neck around and smiled brightly. "Thank you!"

After ten minutes, Victor cracked open his office door. Once he was sure that Olivia was gone, he emerged into the hallway. He strode with confidence and purpose to the Adult Acute Care Unit. It was time he reviewed the chart of one Madison Blythe.

When Maddie awoke, a man in a bright white lab coat was

standing over her. As her vision cleared, she stared at him. He was tall, with dark, slick hair and pale, white skin. Something was wrong with his eyes but she couldn't tell exactly what. He was typing into a platinum laptop.

"What time is it?" Maddie asked, in clear, easy speech.

"Hello, Madison. It is almost 3:00."

"In the morning?"

"No. It is Sunday afternoon. You have been sleeping all day." His tone was accusatory.

"Who are you?" Maddie asked, slowly sitting up in bed. Every muscle in her body ached.

"I am Dr. Victor Aiken, C.E.O. and Medical Director of this hospital."

"And you're checking on me?" Maddie lightly touched her sore jaw.

"Did you not specifically request me as your treating physician?" he asked.

"Yes," Maddie said. "I didn't think it had been arranged, though."

"It would have automatically occurred. I oversee all of the patient cases here."

"And the doctors? You oversee all over them, too?"

"Yes. Why do you ask?"

"I think the medicine Dr. Rutger gave me was too strong. My head feels sort of congested, my thoughts are all hazy, and it made me sleep for ages. More than 12 hours, I think, if I'm adding correctly."

"Those are just initial side effects," Dr. Aiken said. "They will wear off once your body gets accustomed to it."

Maddie struggle to think of another strategy. "Actually, other than that, I'm feeling much better mood-wise today.

Maybe I just needed a good rest. Perhaps some counseling? I don't think I need any more drugs." Still feeling stiff, Maddie shifted her position with difficulty.

"Counseling will help. We will conduct intensive individual therapy with you starting tomorrow. You will attend a group therapy session at 3:30 today."

Why did the word *brainwashing* come to her mind, Maddie wondered? Best not to argue if she was going to get out of taking that awful stuff. "That sounds good."

"Yes. It does. However, according to Dr. Rutger's notes, you are in a severe depressive state. Therapy alone will not work without the adjunct treatment of pharmaceuticals. Aiken's Haven is on the leading edge in that field. You are very lucky to be here." He remained standing, his posture perfect.

The fog in Maddie's brain was less dense now. She looked up at the psychiatrist. His smile looked prideful. Or was it conceit she read on his expression?

"Is that why I'm getting an experimental drug?" she asked.

"Protocol Drug #8? Yes. It is proving to be an excellent agent to relieve aggression."

"But, as you just said, I'm depressed."

There is always an underlying agitation and anger in Major Depression that needs addressing. An anger that one turns on themselves."

"Major Depression. Is that my diagnosis?" Maddie asked.

"Not officially," Dr. Aiken said. "We are still investigating your history and symptoms, so a final diagnosis is yet to be determined. It is one of several diagnoses that we are considering."

"What are the others?"

"It could be part of a Bipolar condition. We are also looking at an Axis II diagnosis. Borderline Personality Disorder." His tone was acerbic.

Maddie wasn't sure what an axis was or what the meaning of this last new disorder was but she didn't like the condescending expression on Dr. Aiken's face. She decided to change tracks.

"Back to the medicine. What does it do exactly?"

"Simply put, it is a behavior and emotion modifier. It controls aggressive feelings and actions, against others and oneself."

"How does it do that? Physically?"

"Physiologically. It alters the arrangement and distribution of the neurochemistry in your brain."

Maddie touched her hands to her temples. "Why doesn't the medicine have a name?"

"It does. Protocol Drug #8."

"A real name."

"You mean a generic and trade name? That is because I am still working on it. Perfecting it. It is still in the trial phase. Once that is completed, I will give it a beautiful name."

"I don't feel comfortable taking something not approved by the F.D.A."

Dr. Aiken looked taken aback. "I assure you, the F.D.A. is well informed of our practices here, as are all the appropriate governmental agencies regulating drug trials." He turned to leave.

"What if I refuse to take any further doses?" Maddie's fists were clenched now.

Dr. Aiken said, "Your suicidality is sufficient grounds to warrant forced administration. It is also cause for involuntary commitment if that is necessary."

"You mean you would keep me here against my will?"

"That can be arranged." His strange eyes glared at her.

"And give me shots against my will?"

"If that's what it takes to keep you safe." Dr. Aiken smiled.

Maddie reviewed her options. To refuse treatment could get her locked up involuntarily for who knew how long. And God only knew what they'd do to her brain in that time. She wasn't sure they could legally force the medicine on her, but if she was trapped in here, how could she stop them. And getting these shots could mean serious health problems. Short term and long term. Either way, she was getting the drug. Maybe pill form was better. Maybe less side effects. Better to be here voluntarily, on her own free will. Better to be taking a pill and at least have the chance to spit the pill out. Although, the way she was being watched like a hawk, the little time she'd been awake, that might not be possible. Hopefully, she wouldn't be here long enough to suffer any serious or long-lasting harm.

"Okay, Dr. Aiken. I'll stay here voluntarily. I'll take the medication. If that's what you and Dr. Rutger think is best."

"Wise choice, Madison."

As if she had one. Unsure what else to say, she merely nodded.

"I will see you tomorrow," Dr. Aiken said.

To Mattie that sounded less like a promise and more like a threat.

To the minute that Dr. Aiken had projected, Maddie found herself sitting in the group room. She surveyed the other participants and felt a lump in her throat. Everyone looked so troubled. She had no idea how to fake it in this environment.

A clean-cut woman nodded a greeting to each patient. Somehow, she looked well dressed, even though she was wearing the same scrubs as the other staff. When the woman spoke, Maddie felt more at ease.

"My name is Beth," she said. "I'm a social worker and I run the adult group therapy sessions here at Aiken's Haven." She looked at Maddie. "You're the new admission. You must be Madison."

"Maddie is fine." She felt her cheeks flush a little.

"I'll introduce the rest of the group," Beth said. "From your left, this is Mark, Sam, Ben, Stacy, Star, Julia and Charles. Today we are continuing our discussion on stress management. Who can tell me one unhealthy way they used to cope with stress in the past and one positive way the learned from yesterday's session?"

The thin girl named Stacy spoke up. "I learned that starving myself and throwing up after I do eat aren't very good ways for me to deal with my problems. It's better if I talk to people about what's bothering me."

Maddie found herself nodding.

"Excellent," Beth said. "You've come a long way in just a week."

"She's just telling you what you want to hear. She pukes every day." A pudgy, Italian named Sam went next. "I'm really going to stick to my changes. I won't get high anymore even though it's hard when all my friends do. Dr. Aiken says I should keep working on my poetry as a way to divert my attention."

Maddie had a feeling that this man was just spouting rhetoric, also telling the social worker what she wanted to hear. She stayed silent.

"That's a good plan, Sam," Beth said, "but don't be overconfident. Just as you said about Stacy, the urge to use, same as the urge to throw up, will keep haunting you, even though you know better. It's a positive step that you've admitted you have a drug problem, but that doesn't make the problem go away."

"I disagree with you," the young woman named Star said. "Pot and coke made me more creative. I write better songs. I play better."

"You're just hiding from yourself, Star," said the grey-haired man named Charles. "You're afraid you've got no real talent. It's better to face things honestly. I wasted my whole life pretending I wasn't a homosexual. I should have admitted it 30 years ago. I'm sure my ex-wife would agree."

Everyone laughed. Maddie didn't join them. This was bizarre. She wasn't sure what was wrong but it felt fake, forced. Now, she didn't know how to fake being fake. She shrunk in her seat when she saw Beth looking at her.

"Do you want to add anything, Maddie?"

She shook her head. She was at a complete loss for what to say.

"She's too good for us," the unkempt man named Mark said. "You're too fucking good to talk to us?" He stood up.

"Please sit down, Mark," Beth said. "Maddie's new. She'll talk when she's ready."

Mark glared at Maddie. "You think you're better than me?"

Maddie shook her head quickly.

"Yes, you do." Mark ran his hand through his disheveled hair. His eyes glazed over. "You're on their side. You're one of them."

Maddie looked pleadingly at Beth.

"Mark is suspicious of strangers," Beth said. "Perhaps if you told us something about yourself, he'd feel more comfortable."

Maddie stared at Beth. *How dare she put me on the spot,* Maddie thought. She didn't want to reveal anything about herself, true or false. She just wanted to get out of that room. She just shook her head.

Mark suddenly jumped up and lunged toward Maddie. Maddie screamed and covered her head with her hands. Beth told Stacy to get help and she, along with Charles and Sam, held Mark back before he could assault Maddie. Several psych aides rushed into the room within seconds and arm-escorted Mark out. Maddie felt her heart racing.

"I'm sorry," Beth said. "He's very paranoid and he targeted you as a threat."

"Is he coming back?" Maddie asked, still breathing hard.

"Not today. He'll be isolated from the rest of us. Don't worry. You're safe."

Apparently not, Maddie said to herself. She stood up and fled through the door. A moment later, Beth had an arm around her and was leading her to the nursing desk.

"I know you're scared, this being your first interaction with the other patients. Why don't you stay out here and talk to the nurse? You can join us again for group tomorrow."

The nurse, Nancy, came out from behind the nursing station counter. "Do you want to talk about what happened in there?"

"No. I just want to lie down."

"Okay," Nancy said. "I understand. Let me know if you change your mind or if you need anything."

"He isn't here, is he?"

"Mark? No. He won't be back on the unit until he has calmed down. Don't worry. You're safe."

Still not reassured, Maddie walked back to her room. *Why do they keep telling me that*?

Lying on her bed, staring at the serene ceiling, Maddie thought about her own coping skills. Impulsivity was a relatively new quality for her. Apparently, not one her better ones. Look where it got her this time. Careful, planned actions hadn't always worked for her in the past, however. She thought back to that autumn years ago when she'd finally broken free from that rigid, controlled person she'd modeled herself to be.

Maddie had pulled into the wide driveway and heard a loud crunch under the tires. Her car came to an abrupt halt. Great. Just what she needed. Not only was she dreading coming home to the house in Bethlehem for Thanksgiving, but now her get-away transportation was stuck in the snow. Massive snow in November. Why did winter have to start so unusually early this year? She didn't want to be stranded here a minute longer than she was obligated to stay. She wasn't being fair, though. Things has been better with Mum since she'd gone away to school. The phone calls were civil. Maybe Dad would be coming by, too. Besides, she was anxious to see Baxter and Chelsey.

"Madison? Is that you?" Mum yelled from the front stoop? "Madison?"

The wind was picking up, but it wasn't that hard to see through the blowing snow.

"Yes, it's me."

"Hurry up. It's cold out."

Silently thanking her for the news flash, Maddie abandoned her car, figuring she could dig it out later, and trudged up the stone steps to the front door. She stamped her feet on the frozen, straw welcome mat to shake the muck loose from her boots. As she walked through the doorway, a lump of fresh slush fell from the shoulder of her linen coat and soiled the parquet floor of the front hall.

"Look what you've done," Mum said. "I better clean that up before it leaves a stain."

As Maddie hung her coat on one of the wooden hangers in the closet, her mother dashed to the kitchen to get a rag and spray bottle. She returned to wipe the slush from the flooring and polish it to its original luster.

Standing up, Mum said, "It's good to see you," giving her

daughter an awkward hug.

Maddie returned the forced embrace. "Yes, you too.

"I can't believe it's been three months." She stood there with the spray bottle and damp rag in her hands.

"Yes, three months."

They stood there in the front hall, an uncomfortable silence settling over them. Mum's dark brown eyes bored into hers. They looked so much alike. The same eyes, the same ash blond hair, the same milky white complexion. It was like looking at herself 25 years into the future.

"How is school?" Mum asked.

"Fine." Maddie didn't want to tell her the truth. Yet.

"Can you be a bit more descriptive, Madison?"

"I'll give you the whole scoop at dinner, okay?" she said, waiting to be invited in. Though she had lived in this house since birth, it was Mum's house. Dad had bought it for her as a wedding present. Once you moved out, you couldn't just walk right back in.

Mum wasn't making any overtures, so Maddie said, "Can I come in?"

"Of course." Mum stepped out of the way. "You want to come in to my house. You just don't want to talk to me."

"I've been driving in this freak snowstorm for almost two hours. Can I just sit down for a minute?" Immediately, Maddie regretted her impatient tone.

"Fine. Your brother and sister are in the family room. Maybe you'll want to talk to them." Mum stalked off to the kitchen, dirty rag and spray bottle clenched tightly in her hands.

As instructed, Maddie went to the family room. Along with the rest of the house, it was immaculately furnished in the arts and crafts style that Mum cherished. Her older brother, Baxter was lying on the carpet, watching sports on television. His dirty blond hair was pulled up into a man bun, exposing a diamond stud in one earlobe. He wore black jeans and a black, silk shirt. Bet he had gotten an earful. Her younger sister, Chelsey, was sitting on one of the sofas, flipping through a magazine. She looked more like Dad. Her closely cropped hair, pale skin and lithe figure, clad in form fitting jeans, gave her the look of a runway model. Not for the first time, Maddie wished she was tall and stylish like her siblings. But she still looked good in her faded jeans and mohair sweater.

"Maddie!" Chelsey jumped up and gave her a real hug.

"Hey Maddie," Baxter said, getting up off the floor. "Good to see you." He gave her a real hug also, followed by a light punch to the arm.

The girls plopped down on the overstuffed sofas, one for each of them to stretch out on. Baxter returned to the carpet but her turned down the volume on the T.V.

"I made Mum mad," Maddie warned them.

"Already?" Baxter said. "You're good."

Chelsey threw a pillow at him. "Mum's been mad all day. Dad was going come over but he called and wanted to bring his new girlfriend to meet us all. Mum had a fit. I don't blame her. That was tacky."

"Now he's not coming at all," Baxter said. "He'll call you later, he said. We both talked to him already."

"Okay. I haven't seen Dad since the fourth of July picnic at his last girlfriend's house. What was her name?"

"Who knows?" Baxter said.

"I never see Dad, either," Chelsey said, "and I live in the same city as he does. He's just too caught up in his new life."

"It would be nice to see your own Dad once in a while," Baxter said. "I mean, I don't care that much, but it's important for a

Dad to see his daughters."

"It's rude of him not to come, especially since you came all the way from New York. When did you get here?" Maddie asked him.

"About two hours ago. I-"

Mum walked into the room. She was wiping her hands on a clean dishtowel.

Maddie decided to try and apologize for their tiff in the front hall. "Dinner smells great, Mum."

"Thank you," Mum said, curtly. She sat on the sofa that Chelsey was on, swatting the girl's feet off the cushions with the dishtowel. Maddie put her feet back on the floor, too.

"So what are my children talking about?"

"Nothing," Chelsey said, sitting up and glancing at some sketches strewn across the coffee table. She gathered them together and put them back on the table, face down.

Maddie picked up the sketches and examined them slowly. They were drawing of cocktail dresses and evening gowns. "Did you do these, Chelsey?"

"Yes. What do you think?" She moved over to Maddie's couch.

"I think they're beautiful. You have talent. Real talent. Where did you learn to do this?"

"In art class. We're doing a fashion design segment. In fact," she glanced at Mum, "I was thinking of applying to the Fashion Institute of New York. Or Drexel has a great program too. Of course, it's hard to get in. I'd go to Albright, too. I'll apply to as many schools as I can."

"That sounds great."

Suddenly, a palpable tension filled the room. Chelsey took the sketches from Maddie and put them face down on the coffee table.

"What's so great about drawing pictures for a living?" Mum said. "If you can make a living that way."

"Baxter *takes* pictures for a living," Maddie said, putting an arm around Chelsey. "What's the difference?"

"Your brother," she said, "is a successful photographer with his own New York studio. I see a big difference."

Maddie wanted to point out that Baxter hadn't started off that way but she knew there was no use in arguing further. Chelsey's light jab to her ribs told her she was correct.

Mum gazed out of the patio doors. "I don't understand why a smart girl like Chelsey can't go to college like her sister and take a pre-med program like her sister. Not that her sister will tell me anything about her courses." She stood up and went back into the kitchen.

"Something wrong at school?" Baxter asked.

"Why won't you talk about your classes?" Chelsey asked. "Is there a problem?"

"Oh no! Not you guys too," Maddie groaned. She put a throw pillow over her face.

They all burst into laughter. Maddie stopped laughing before the others.

Seated around the expansive dining room table, they waited while Mum fussed over last minute details in the kitchen.

"Don't sweat it," Baxter said to Chelsey. "I was a failure in her eyes to when I chose to go into photography." He laughed quietly. "It wasn't until I opened Blythe Studios that she finally got off my back."

"I'll try not to cave in to her before I have my own design house."

"What about you, Maddie?" Baxter asked. "There really is a problem at school, isn't there? Are you going to keep telling Mum everything's fine?"

"I think it's too late for that." She sighed heavily. "How do you tell Elyse Blythe that you-"

Mum entered the room. She put a bowl of steamed vegetables on a wooden trivet and set a basket of hot biscuits beside it.

"What are the three of you whispering about?"

They all answered together, "Nothing."

She returned to the kitchen and in quick succession came back with roasted potatoes, steaming gravy and a golden turkey.

"The meal looks great," Chelsey said.

"Yes. There's so much delicious food," Baxter said.

"Too bad Dad couldn't join us," Maddie said. "I mean, it's just..."

"I know," Mum said. "I wish Eric were here, too. It's been a year since the divorce so I guess we'll have to get used to not counting on him." She looked like she was about to cry. "That just gives me more time to focus on you children. So, Madison, tell us how your studies are going?"

"Why don't we eat first?" Maddie reached for the biscuits.

"Yeah," Baxter said, grabbing the potatoes.

"Wait!" Mum gave Maddie a sharp look. "No one eats until Madison tells me why she's avoiding my questions."

Maddie looked down at her empty plate. She looked over at her brother. He shrugged his shoulders. She looked at her sister. Her head was down, staring at her own empty plate.

Maddie felt like she was eight years old again. Like the time she had forgotten her new sweater, the one with the bright red cardinal embroidered on it that Mum had made for her birthday. She knew she had accidentally left it at school, but lied and told Mum some older kid at school had stolen it so Mum wouldn't yell at her for being forgetful. After Mum called the school and the sweater was located in the lost and found bin, Mum had gone on for hours, telling Maddie that she was an ungrateful child, how disappointed she was that her own daughter had lied. That had just been the first in a series of such lectures throughout her childhood. Maddie would have preferred a grounding or even a spanking.

"I guess I have to tell you sometime," Maddie said, looking up from her plate and looking Mum straight in the eye. "I dropped out."

"Whoa," Baxter said.

"I'm glad I'm not you," Chelsey said.

Maddie glance at Mum who was holding her hand to her heart.

"I just dropped out of my pre-med courses," she said. "I'm switching my major to English next semester."

"Are you failing?" Mum asked.

"No. In fact, I've been getting mostly A's."

"Then why on earth would you give up your dream?"

"I don't enjoy the classes. Biochemistry, Anatomy, Physiology, Organic Chemistry. They bore me. I don't want to spend my life doing something that bores me. Besides, there's no guarantee I would have been accepted into med school. It's pretty competitive."

"You barely gave it a chance!"

"I did. I gave it a chance. For you." Maddie heard her own voice quiver but she continued. "I'm not the one who chose this path. You are. You want me to be a doctor. I don't. It's not my dream."

Mum stood up and stalked into the kitchen.

"Good for you," Baxter said. "It's about time you stand up for yourself with Mum.

"You better go talk to her," Chelsey said.

"Yeah," Baxter added, "or we'll never eat."

Maddie was about to go to go to the kitchen when Mum suddenly rejoined them in the dining room.

"So what are you going to do with a degree in English? Read books for a living?"

"I want to be a writer. Books, stories, articles. I'm taking an elective in creative writing right now and I'm going to start applying to several journalism schools for next fall."

"You need talent to be a literary success."

"Thanks for the vote of confidence. I don't expect to win a Nobel Prize. I want to write articles for magazines and newspapers. I also like fiction. I've written some good short stores. Maybe I'll write mystery novels. My professor says I do have talent."

"Maybe so, but how can you support yourself that way?"

"I probably won't be rich, but I'll get by."

Mum sat down and looked at the ceiling. "I just want you children to be able to take care of yourselves so you don't end up like me. You don't want to end up alone, depending on someone who is not dependable.

"I realize how important that is to you. It's important to me, too. But don't you also want us to be happy at whatever careers we choose?"

"Of course, Madison. I want you all to be happy. But happiness is elusive. You can't support yourself on happiness. You have so many more opportunities than I did. I want you to get a solid education. I never did. Now my only means of income are alimony and some child support for your little sister. Even that ends next year."

"Be honest," Maddie said. "You're not exactly starving."

Baxter snickered. Chelsey smiled and threw a biscuit at her. Maddie laughed and threw it back.

Mum cleared her throat. She looked at each of them and shook her head. "Dinner's getting cold. Let's eat."

Without a word, they all dutifully filled their plates with the fragrant food.

Chelsey broke the silence. "Who's going to say the Thanksgiving blessing?"

"We'll just skip it this year," Mum said. "There's not much to be thankful for."

CHAPTER 8

Adam and Kendra were in an alcove on the Adolescent A.C.U. #3, called the *Livingroom.* The other six patients on the unit were in their rooms, sleeping off their medications.

"What did you think of the long term unit?" Kendra asked.

"I think it's creepy," Adam said, flipping through a booklet on depression.

Kendra was glancing at a second copy of the same material. "Don't they have anything better to read?"

Adam made his voice deep and monotone to imitate the staff. "All activities in this hospital will be therapeutic and aimed at your recovery."

"I don't see how flipping through *Teen Vogue* or *Twist* will hurt me. At least I wouldn't be bored."

"I'll take bored over what's going to happen tomorrow."

"Is there any way you can get out of going to the L.T. unit?"

"If there is, I haven't come up with it yet."

Kendra set down her booklet. "I don't think I can get by in here without you."

"Don't worry," Adam said. "Your mother will probably get you out eventually. I think if you have a family, you're okay here. I just don't have anyone to rescue me."

"That's sad," Kendra said. "Maybe once I get out, I could figure out a way to save you."

Adam smiled at her. When their eyes met, Kendra felt a tingle run down her spine.

"I'll think of something," she said. "I promise."

"That's sweet, but I doubt there's anything you can do." Adam's face fell. "There's nothing anyone can do. I'm all alone in this."

"No you're not. Could you try running away from here again?"

"You can bet I'll be looking for another opportunity, but I can't count on that. It's one chance in a million. Even when it seems like they're not watching us, they're watching us."

Kendra and Adam turned as they heard one of the other patients yell. Her name was Alicia and she was cursing up a storm at the staff.

"I don't want to talk to that fucking doctor! He's an asshole! I don't give a shit. Leave me the fuck alone!"

They couldn't hear the staff's response. They could see two psych aides follow the girl as she barreled into the *Livingroom.* She flopped down into the chair beside Kendra.

"Just leave me the hell alone!" Alicia's face was red.

One psych aide took a delicate step toward her. "Individual therapy is part of your treatment here. How are you going to get better if you don't participate in your own treatment?"

"Maybe I don't want to get better." Alicia said, arms folded across her chest.

"This kind of acting out behavior is not an option." A second psych aide looked back at a nurse, standing nearby. "Maybe she needs an injection?"

The nurse, Joe, shook his head. "She's not that agitated. She's just being a teenager. Right, Alicia?"

"Whatever."

"Listen," Joe said, "why don't you and I go back to your room and discuss what's bothering you?"

"I have nothing to say."

"Why does she have to talk if she doesn't want to?" Kendra asked.

"Yeah," Adam chimed in. "Quit bugging her."

Joe smiled. "I know it appears to all three of you that I'm being a pain, but as Alicia knows, she's got some big issues to deal with that she can't avid permanently. I'm really just trying to help her. What do you say, Alicia? I promise to be a good listener. It will make you feel better."

"Fine," Alicia said. "I'll talk to you, Joe, and only you but it won't make me feel better." She stood up and looked at Kendra and Adam. "Later, you guys. Thanks for sticking up for me."

"Any time," Adam said.

After Joe and Alicia left the alcove, Kendra leaned closer to Adam. "I guess if you cooperate, you get an easier ride here."

"That depends," Adam said, looking in Alicia's direction, "on what they want you to cooperate with."

Back on the adult unit, a female psych aide slipped quietly into Maddie's room. Gently shaking her shoulder, she whispered in her ear. "Madison. Excuse me. Madison? Wake up."

"What?" Maddie stirred and wiped at her eyes. "Was I asleep?"

"Yes," the woman said. "You have a phone call."

"Oh." Maddie sat up on her bed. "Where do I take it?"

"At the nursing desk."

"Who is it?"

"A Helen Sibley. She's on your approved list of callers."

Maddie was suddenly wide awake. She went over to the communal patient phone, permanently affixed to the nursing desk. Maddie was annoyed that any of the staff could overhear her.

She cupped the receiver and whispered. "Helen? It's Maddie. What's going on?"

"I'm in the front lobby." Helen was whispering too. "This is getting worse by the minute. It looks like they're not going to let me take Kendra out of the hospital tomorrow."

"Why not?"

"Dr. Aiken says she is still suicidal and he's extending her involuntary commitment indefinitely."

"Can you fight it?"

"Apparently it could take a week for me to get a court appearance to even begin to fight it legally. How are you doing? Have you learned anything yet?"

"Nothing concrete," Maddie said, glancing at the staff and lowering her voice. "I'm going to have to pick up the pace though."

"I don't mean to pressure you, but I agree. We're not going to get anywhere playing by their rules."

"Don't worry. I've got some ideas running through my head. I want to get myself out of here as quickly as I want to get Kendra out."

"Tonight would be good." Helen's voice cracked.

"Tonight it is." Maddie said, unsure she could deliver on that promise.

Maddie felt a tap on her shoulder. She whirled around to see a male psych aide pointing to his watch.

"Time's up."

"Time's up?" Maddie asked. "What do you mean 'time's up'?"

"Phone calls are limited to five minutes."

"Why on earth? Never mind." Maddie spoke back into the receiver. "Listen Helen, I've got to go. Can you stay put for a while?"

"The receptionist has made it pretty clear that they are going to kick me out of here after visiting hours."

"I'm so glad you'll at least get to see Kendra tonight. Tell you what. Keep your cell charged."

"I will." Helen said. "I'm at the Delft Motel about 10 miles away. I'm not going back to Philly without Kendra. And don't worry, one of my staff from the bookstore is taking care of Winston. I took him to my house and asked her to stay there."

The receiver was taken out of Maddie's hand by the psych aide. He spoke to Helen. "I'm sorry, Madison has to hang up now. You can call back at phone hours at 8 o'clock tonight if you wish." He hung up on her.

Maddie stared at him. "Unbelievable. You have no right."

"I'm sorry. Those are the rules and I did give you a warning."

Maddie was about to argue than thought better of it. As she went back to her room to lie down, she looked around at the other patients' rooms. They were all filled. That meant Mark was back on the unit. So much for her safety. She sniffled a little and wished she had Winston there to cuddle with. And maybe even protect her.

Victor had given up on any plans he had of spending any time at home today. After taking care of what he felt was necessary, he arranged a business dinner that was sure to put more funding into his new dream project.

He walked over to a closet door in his office. Opening it, he surveyed the three stylish suits he kept on hand in case of a last minute event. Choosing a dapper, black ensemble with matching silk tie, he held it up to his rugged form, staring at himself in the full length mirror on the inside of the closet door. Perfection.

Though his door was locked and no one entered without knocking, Victor changed behind a folding screen beside his closet. After he was completely redressed, he once again stared at himself in the mirror. Handsome devil. Attaching platinum cufflinks to his shirt, Victor thought back to a time when the best clothes he wore were hand-me-downs from his cousins. They never fit and the kids at school made fun of him. Closing his eyes, Victor was 12 years old again in his mind.

Sitting on one of the wooden stools at the kitchen counter, Victor had been trying to trap a scurrying cockroach with a piece of paint he'd peeled of the wall. The roach was trying to make it across the Formica drain board to the sink but he was too fast for the bug. Victor blocked his every turn and eventually trapped him within a circle of paint peelings. Scooping the roach onto a plate, he was about to get a carving knife from the drawer when Mom walked in the front door.

"Hi, Victor. Sorry I'm so late." She tore off her vinyl, leopard-print raincoat and threw it over the other kitchen stool. She released her hair from it's yellow, plastic clip. Brassy, blond curls cascaded around her shoulders. Mom walked to the stove and glance at her reflection in the kettle. "I need a touch up," she said, stroking her tresses. "My roots are almost as dark as your hair."

Victor bit the corner of his lip and shrugged his shoulders.

"We were short on cashiers today so I had to stay an extra couple of hours. At least it's more money, right?"

"Yeah, right," Victor said, crushing the cockroach with his

hand and dumping it into the trash can. He vigorously washed his hands in the sink. Mom tousled his hair as she whisked by him toward the cupboards.

"Mom? I need to show you something." He pulled a neatly folded piece of paper out of his back pocket.

"Can it wait?" she asked, pulling a box of cereal out of the cupboard. "I've got a date with Jim and I've got less than 30 minutes to get ready." She turned to her son. "You're all right with corn flakes for dinner tonight, aren't you? I promise I'll make us a real meal on the week end."

"Can it be just the two of us this time?" he asked, giving her his best puppy dog eyes.

Mom let the cereal box fall to the counter. She yanked open the utensil drawer. "Don't start in on Jim. I don't have time." Then, she sighed and smiled. "All right, just the two of us. Jim probably has to work late on Friday anyway. We'll do it then." Shaking her head, she said, "Those pretty eyes of yours always get to me."

Victor hated his eyes. They made him look like a freak. One eye was dark brown from Mom. The other, an ice blue like Dad's. His pale, white skin made them stand out even more. But Mom melted whenever their eyes met and he used that to his advantage.

"I need you to read this." He pushed the paper toward her.

"Leave it on the counter. I'll read it when I get home tonight."

Victor felt his body stiffen. "Tomorrow morning, you mean." He picked up his spoon and dug into his dinner.

"You're 12 years old. You're big enough to stay by yourself once in a while."

"The guy's a loser. You could do better," he said, crunching away.

"Enough. Jim is great. Not many single guys want to date a woman with a 12-year-old kid.

I'm not going to have this conversation again. I'm going to take a shower." She headed toward the bathroom. Over her shoulder, she said, "Finish your corn flakes."

"I don't want any damn cereal!" Victor threw the plastic bowl across the small kitchen. The spoon clattered on the linoleum and the soggy mess splattered on the wall, the fridge and the floor.

"Clean that up right now!" Mom threw a roll of paper towels at him and left the room.

As he was sopping up the last trails of smelly milk off the wall, the phone rang. Mom ran into the kitchen in her bathrobe, the one with the big daisies embroidered on it. It was a dirty, greyish color and torn in several places. Grandmas Aiken had given it to Mom the last time she visited from England. That was before Dad died.

Mom grabbed the receiver off the wall mounted phone. "Hello? This is Darlene Aiken." She listened for a long time. "I see," she finally said. "I'll take care of it."

Slamming the phone back on the hook, Mom whirled around toward her son. "Ditching school again?" Her lips were so tight that they made a straight line. "You were supposed to give me a note from Mrs. Jefferson."

"I tried to tell you!"

She held up her palm. "I don't want to hear any of your excuses."

"But I was in the biology lab," Victor said. "I lost track of time. It wasn't like I was doing something bad."

"Never mind. I'll deal with you in the morning. For the rest of tonight, you are grounded. You are to stay in this apartment and no one comes over. Is that understood?" Her face was red.

"Sure." Victor didn't have any plans for the guys to come by so he let her win this one. Besides, he didn't want to push it and have Mom cancel Friday's dinner date.

While she was showering, Victor smoothed the school form flat out on the counter. He picked a leaky pen out of a plastic cup, wiped the excess ink off on one of the soggy paper towels, and signed *Darlene Aiken* on the note from Mrs. Jefferson.

The next morning, Victor got up before Mom got in. He poured himself more stale cereal. There was nothing else in the place. He dropped the box when he heard pounding on the apartment door. It had to be Mom. He had put the bolt lock on after she left on her date. He watched the local news every night and knew the Point Breeze area wasn't the safest place in Philly.

"You're up early," Mom said as she came into the apartment. She was wearing the turquoise satin dress she wore the night before. It didn't look as pretty this morning. Her hair was messy and her makeup was smeared. She smelled like beer and cigarettes. Her eyes were bloodshot.

"Super," she said, entering the kitchen. "You got yourself some breakfast." She sat on the other stool, poured herself some cereal, and joined Victor, holding her spoon in a fist like Dad used to.

Victor stopped eating. "You hardly ever have breakfast, Mom. What's up?"

"I thought we could talk this morning." She gave a fake smile. Only her mouth smiled. Her eyes didn't light up like usual.

He gave a wary smile in return. "About what?"

"I've been thinking a lot about this." She shoveled more corn flakes into her mouth, avoiding his gaze.

"I'm not going to like this, am I?" Victor pushed his bowl away.

"I'm only thinking of what's best for all of us," she said, tapping her spoon on the counter.

"What is it, Mom? Just tell me."

"You're getting older. And bigger. Bigger than me. I'm a small woman. When you were little, I could handle your temper tantrums." She gave another feeble smile. "I just can't manage you anymore." She held her hands out, palms up. There were tears welling in her eyes.

"You mean last night?" Victor asked, holding one of her hands. "I'm sorry I flipped out. I didn't mean it. I won't do it again."

"It's not that simple," she said, slipping her fingers out of his grasp.

"What? You're afraid of me?"

"Well, yes. I mean, you could hurt someone one of these days."

"But I never have. I've never hurt you, Mom. I never would."

"I'm sorry. It was different when your Dad was alive. He could control you. He could hold you down. I can't. Not anymore."

"But I haven't lost it like that in a long time."

"But you could have last night."

"I just threw a plastic bowl!"

"But what if it was something more dangerous you were holding. What if you threw it at me?"

"What are you saying, Mom? What are you going to do?" Victor struggled to hold back the tears welling in his own eyes.

She slid off her stool, standing just out of his reach. "There's this place, about 70 miles out of Philly. It's in Lancaster County. It's like a farm. Or a camp."

"You want to send me to camp?" he asked. "We can't afford

that."

"This place is covered by our Medicaid. It's sort of like a hospital. They can help you with your temper."

Victor's jaw dropped open. "You're talking about a place for psychos? You want to lock me up? No way! I'm not nuts. I'll be good. I'll never yell or throw things ever again." He jumped off his stool and threw his arms around her neck. She gave him a weak hug in return. When he pulled back and flashed his puppy dog eyes, she looked away.

"It's not a place for psychos," she said. "It's called a Boys Ranch. Jim told me about it. It has a good reputation."

Victor pulled himself out of her loose grip and backed away. "Jim told you about it? Of course Jim told you about it! He's the one who wants me out of the way." His face felt hot and his hands started to sweat. "You care about that loser more than you care about me!"

"That's not true." She came towards him. "I think this is best for you."

"Yeah, right." Victor turned away. "Leave me alone."

Mom continued to approach him.

He moved further away. His voice was quiet. "Don't come near me."

"Oh, Victor, baby, don't be upset." She kept coming closer.

A dark haze filled Victor's head. "Don't touch me."

She kept coming though. "Don't be like this." Her hand touched his shoulder.

Victor wheeled around and shoved her as hard as he could. Mom flew across the room, fell to the floor and slid along the kitchen tiles. She came to a stop when her head smacked against the far wall. A few chips of paint showered around her.

Victor wanted to make sure she was all right but when he approached her she screamed.

"Jim! Help me!"

The front door flew open and Jim came barreling inside. He was a foot taller than Victor and husky. He could have easily held Victor in a bear hug like Dad used to. Victor would have calmed down. He was already calming down. Instead, Jim grabbed Victor's T-shirt up in his meaty hands and held him close to his face. He was breathing heavily and his freckled, balding forehead was sweaty.

"Back when I was a boy. My father would have beat the crap out of me for a lot less than this," Jim said. "We Irish know how to handle things." He slammed Victor against the wall. Jim's face was almost as red as his receding ring of hair.

"You want a fight?" Victor swung his right fist upward and cracked Jim in the jaw. He kicked the man's shins and punched him square in the nose.

Jim didn't take long to recover. Within seconds, he had Victor at a disadvantage and got his own punches in. Victor's early surprise lead was gone in a haze of pain, nausea and blood.

Victor stared at his ringing cell phone. He ignored it. Though it brought him back to the present, he was still filled with the anger of his boyhood. Checking himself out in the mirror on more time, he assured himself he was a powerful, successful adult. Someone of whom his mother would be proud.

CHAPTER 9

At 5:00 pm, a psych aide, with a nametag reading *Bailey*, directed Maddie to join the other seven patients in a line at the door. He told them all to stay in single file. No explanation was given as to where they were going. Maddie was staring at the back of a woman's head. It was Stacey, the skinny one from group therapy. Mark was in line but he was facing forward and not speaking. Three other psych aides joined them. The group was ushered out of the unit.

Maddie looked the staff over. At the lead was Bailey, short but stocky with a pinched face and angry eyes. The two other men were tall and muscular. They were younger, twenty-somethings. They seemed more relaxed, walking along each side of the patient queue. Bringing up the rear was a small woman named Marietta, who barked out orders military style. A quick glimpse at her earned Maddie a scolding about facing forward at all times. The two side psych aides snickered quietly. Maddie wasn't sure if they were laughing at Marietta or her.

Continuing down the serene hallway, Maddie noticed it was dotted with large ceramic vases filled with giant sunflowers. The walls were painted a dusty rose, which relieved Maddie. The bombardment of blue on her unit was becoming annoying. In addition to the walls, the staff wore blue scrubs, although various hues seemed permissible. Maddie suddenly became aware for the first time that she was wearing a navy sweat suit that was not her own. Gripped with panic, she tried to remember having changed out of her jeans and sweater when she was admitted. Yes. Amy had helped her change into a hospital gown. Of course, she didn't sleep in her clothes. But wait. When Dr. Aiken was talking to her, she'd been waring this new get-up. And same with group therapy. Someone, at some point, had changed her without her knowledge. She hoped it had been a female staff. Why on earth had it taken her this long to register? *Maybe that medication is having more of an effect on me than I realize,* she thought. That made her shiver.

As the group turned right, Maddie was looking at Sam, the patient behind her, when she bumped into a man clad in a calf-length lab coat. The man held Maddie's elbow gently as she regained her balance.

"Are you okay?" he asked. "I'm so sorry."

Maddie smiled up at him. He was tall, black, handsome. His nametag said, *Jesse – Lab Supervisor.*

"I'm fine. It was my fault. I wasn't looking where I was going."

"No harm done." Jesse flashed a winning smile.

"Let's move it out," Marietta said, hand on hips.

Maddie noticed that the group was waiting for her. She smiled at Jesse once more. He let go of her elbow and gave a slight wave. She rejoined the other patients. As they plodded along, Maddie felt compelled to go back and talk to Jesse. When she turned around, he was gone. It was that same feeling she'd had when she first met John. John Blankenship. Why was he never too far out of her thoughts? Probably because there was no replacement for him. Would she ever meet the right man? She needed to snap out of it. More important things were going on right now. Like Kendra's safety. Her own safety.

As the group bunched up at a doorway, she focused on the other patients instead. All clothed in navy sweats and matching slippers. Standard uniform here. Why didn't she notice that in group therapy? Was this place destroying her brain. It seemed to be doing a job on the others. Charles, who had seemed clam in the group session, was now angrily muttering to himself. It was Mark who looked calm this time. He was washed up and clean shaven. The staff must have done that for him. With the far-away look in his eyes, Maddie doubted his was paying any attention to immediate things like grooming. The other man, Ben, who had not spoken in group while she was there, had tears welling in his eyes. His shoulders were now slumped and his face appeared to be caving in on itself. Maddie had never seen anyone look that sad. In front of her, Stacey, other than a rail thin frame, showed no outward symptoms that Maddie could see. Good posture, pleasant facial expression. Then again, she was probably stereotyping. Was she expecting unkempt, out of control psychopaths? It was sad that she had such a vision in her mind. After all, didn't Kendra have a mental health condition? Her own goddaughter. Right now, she herself was supposed to be the face of depression. And the staff were buying it.

She checked out the remaining patients with a kinder eye. Julia was shuffling in place, constantly rubbing her hands together. Her jaw was in constant movement as if she were about to speak but no words came out. Amy had explained to Maddie that long term use of these medications could cause permanent symptoms like that. It was even more frightening to actually see it. And frightening that she suddenly remembered Amy's explanation. Her thoughts were coming and going in fits and spurts like that. As if her brain was blocking then releasing memories. She looked at Sam, the addict. He looked like a different person than the man she'd encountered in group. He had absolutely no facial expression. No smile. No frown. Almost robot-like. He didn't even move his arms when he walked. That wasn't anything Amy had told her about. It was odd that just a while ago these people had been sharing information about their personal lives and now no one was talking to each other. No one made eye contact.

Maddie started to worry about where they were headed when Bailey opened the door and they walked into an elegant dining hall.

"You have one hour to complete dinner," Marietta said.

"No talking to patients from other wards," Bailey added. "Food line starts over there," pointing to the other side of the large room. "We sit at table #3."

Maddie's group went to an area that was cordoned off by a black, velvet rope linked to plastic poles. They entered the food line by a large sign reading *Entrance.* They picked up plastic trays, plastic utensils, plastic cups and paper napkins. The kitchen workers were behind a metal trough and they handed each patient a sturdy, sectioned paper plate full of food delivered from several, large serving bins.

No one asked what the patients wanted. No one even spoke to them. But the food looked quite appetizing and smelled even better. Maddie was starving. She hadn't eaten in over 24 hours. They hadn't bothered to wake her for breakfast as promised. Or lunch for that matter.

Maddie dutifully moved to the beverage section. Juice or water were the only choices. No coffee. No tea. No soda. She filled her cup with water and followed the line toward the elegantly scripted *Exit* sign, where all four psych aides were now waiting.

"Over there," Bailey said, painting to the back of the room towards a black dining table with matching, padded chairs. It had a placard with #3 in the middle.

Maddie surveyed the room. It was decorated in black, grey and white. A faux, crystal chandelier hung from the ceiling. There was air filtering into the room from vents up there, making the ornate lamp sway ever so slightly, creating a pretty clinking sound. The carpet was dark grey, flecked with silver.

Plastic utensils aside, she felt like she was in a fancy restaurant.

Maddie sat down with the other adult patient in the hospital. She noticed Dr. Aiken enter the room, accompanied by a severe-looking woman in a pink power suit and matching pumps. They mingled at various tables already occupied by patients from the children's units.

While passing Maddie's table, the woman stopped to inhale the warm food's inviting scent. "It smells delicious, Dr. Aiken. What a tastefully designed eating area." She touched her fingertips to her tight cheek. "This entire facility is so beautifully adorned and landscaped. With the pool, the gym, and the children's playground, I almost feel like I'm at a resort and spa."

"That is the idea," Dr. Aiken said, giving a dazzling smile. "I am sure if you ask any of the patients, they will agree."

"That's not necessary. It's obvious you treat them so well. No wonder you are doing such excellent business. I wouldn't mind coming here myself for a couple of day of R and R." The woman laughed while she tucked a loose tendril of hair back into her chignon.

"Does that mean your company will continue its most generous support of my research and expansion?" Dr. Aiken asked, placing a hand on her shoulder.

"Definitely. The accountants will make the next deposit into your account on the 15th."

Maddie watched them walk away. She saw Dr. Aiken guide the woman by the elbow as they left the room. He held the door for her and Maddie could hear the woman's high pitched giggle as they went out.

Another group of patients entered through the door on the opposite side of the room. Teenagers. Dressed in the same standard sweat suits. All of the patients, even the young children, were dressed alike. Just different colors for different ages. Maddie wondered if their units were painted to match their outfits. She looked more closely at the group of teens and did a double take. There, in the center of the line, in dark green garb, was Kendra. She watched her proceed through the food line. Then, Maddie stood up, cup in hand.

"Sit down," Marietta said.

"I was just getting more water," Maddie said.

"You have to ask first," Bailey said. "You can't just do whatever you feel like."

Maddie took a deep breath and slowly said, "May I please get a refill of water?"

"Yes, you may," Bailey said, "but use a better tone of voice next time."

Maddie got her water and lingered at the end of the food line, awaiting Kendra's approach.

One of the younger psych aides came up to her. "You really do need to come back to your seat."

"But I see someone I know."

"You're not supposed to talk to the other patients."

"Even if I already know them?"

"Sorry. Those are the rules. That way no inappropriate relationships are formed."

While turning around, Maddie gazed intently at Kendra, willing her to look up. *Come on girl. Hurry up. Look at me.* The psych aide gently held Maddie's hand, directing her back to their table. Just before she fully turned away, Kendra looked up. Her eyes flew wide open and a smile spread over her face as she mouther the word, *Maddie!*

Maddie reluctantly returned to her table. She kept an eye on Kendra's location. Once they were both seated with their assigned groups, she had a clear view of the girl. After 15 minutes, she indicated to Kendra with her eyes and a sideways nod. At the same time, they both asked their staff for second helpings. Unfortunately, they were both escorted by a psych aide and couldn't make verbal contact.

At the end of the hour, all the groups in the room rose to leave. They carried their trays to an area marked *Tray Depository.* Multiple metal carts had sections in which to slide the trays. Maddie maneuvered herself near Kendra's group.

"Hurry it up," Marietta said to the patients.

Maddie bashed her tray into Kendra's, the contents of both falling to the floor.

"Pick that up, both of you," Marietta instructed.

As they bent down, Kendra whispered, "I can't believe you're in here, Maddie. What's wrong?"

"I came in as a patient so I could look for you. Your mother thinks that you might be in some sort of danger in here and I'm starting to agree with her. Are you okay?"

"I'd be a whole lot better if I got out of this crazy prison."

"Are you still thinking of killing yourself?"

"Hell, no. All I want to do is get out of here and go back to my normal life. If Mother did this to scare me, it worked."

"That's enough chatter," Bailey said. "How long does it take to pick up a tray?"

Maddie finished wiping the floor with napkins and slid her tray into a slot. "I'll see you soon," she whispered to Kendra.

"Promise?"

"I promise I will figure a way out for both of us."

Kendra looked as though she was about to cry. She slammed her try into a slot, whirled around and followed her group out of the room.

Maddie rejoined the adult patients. The four psych aides marched the eight patients out of the dining hall. Looking behind her, Maddie saw Kendra exiting through the door on the opposite side of the room.

After lying on her bed for half an hour, Maddie got up and approached one of the psych aides. He was quiet and had a pleasant look about him.

"Phil," she said, reading from his name badge. "Do you have any maps or diagrams of the facility. I like to know the layout of places. It's sort of a hobby."

"We might," Phil replied. "That sounds like a good way to pass the time. Let me look around."

"She doesn't need a map," Bailey interrupted. "You can see everything in this unit. If you need to go anywhere else, the staff will take you."

Phil shrugged his shoulders and sighed. "Sorry. He's the senior aide."

Maddie felt her jaw clench. She headed to the nursing desk.

"Where are you going?" Bailey asked. "You need to get back in your room."

"I have a headache. I'm going to ask the nurse for something."

"I can tell her for you."

"Actually, I'm having some cramps and other female problems that I need to talk to her about. Do you want me to go into more detail?"

"No thanks," Bailey said. "Go ahead and see the nurse."

Maddie approached June, the Registered Nurse on duty this evening, and whispered, "Do you have a map of the hospital? I always feel better when I have my bearings."

"Sorry," June said. "I don't think we do."

“I was also wondering if I could get something for a headache.”

June looked doubtful but asked, “Where exactly does it hurt?”

Maddie pointed to her forehead.

“I thought you had cramps,” Bailey said as he came behind the nursing station desk.

June was pulling up Maddie’s chart on the computer. Maddie saw June point to a section that was titled *Diagnosis.* She could only make out the second line. The Roman numeral II followed by the typed words, *Borderline Personality Disorder,* seemed to be what June was pointing at.

Bailey nodded to June. “I told you.”

June looked back at Maddie. “How about a cold pack? That usually helps most headaches.”

“Sounds good,” Maddie said. Inside she was fuming. She needed to find out what that diagnosis meant. She was pretty sure the staff had a negative connotation toward it. She wondered if it meant she was faking it.

June got a square shaped package and squeezed it until it popped. It was still intact as she handed it to Maddie who held the cold pack on her brow and returned to the comfortable bed. She struggled with her map dilemma, not coming up with any answers.

Then Amy walked into her room. “Hi Maddie. It’s just after 7 pm. I told you I’d be back.” She smiled brightly.

“Hi Amy. I’m glad to see you.” Maddie realized how very true this was.

“You look better this evening.” Amy said. “Are you feeling better?”

“That depends.”

"On what?"

"On whether or not you intend to give me those two shots in your hand."

Amy laughed. "I'm so sorry. No, these aren't for you. I thought I was going to have to use them for another patient but it turns out he was okay without them."

"Then put them away," Maddie said. "They scare me."

"They are just injections of lorazepam, a common sedative," Amy said, placing the pre-filled syringes into her scrub top pocket. "Do you feel better now?"

"Definitely." Maddie smiled. "Although I do have one question. What exactly is borderline personality disorder?"

"Think of it just as it is described, a disorder of personality development that can be caused by both neurological and environmental factors. The symptoms show up in terms of emotional issues, relationship problems, and sometimes employment issues because the person struggles with their sense of self-worth and their interpersonal interactions. Does that help at all?"

"Sort of."

"Anything else I can help you with before I go and get report?"

"Yes. I hate feeling lost when we leave the unit. Do you have a map of the hospital so I could have my bearings and feel more comfortable?"

"I'm sure there's one around her somewhere," Amy said. "I'll track down a copy and be right back."

Amy kept her word and Maddie spent the next hour pouring over the map of Aiken's Haven.

Back in her motel room, Helen Sibley was wearing down the

almost threadbare carpet with her constant pacing. Finally, her cell rang.

"Jake, is that you?"

"Yes, Helen, it's me," her lawyer said. "What's wrong?"

Helen sat on the faded, flowered bedspread and explained the whole saga to Jake. "Are they telling me the truth? Do I really have no legal recourse?"

There was a long silence on the phone. "I'm not an expert on the mental health laws, Helen, but from what I know, they seem to have their facts straight. Do you think they are falsely keeping Kendra in there now? You don't think she's suicidal anymore?"

"That's just it. I don't know. She was definitely suicidal on Friday when I admitted her. God only knows what she's feeling now. She must hate me."

Jake sighed. "That will be nothing new."

"You're not helping."

"Sorry. I just mean that's the least of your worries. When do you see her again?"

"I can visit her in half an hour. I want to have some good news to tell her. Even if she is still thinking of killing herself and even if I have to stay awake 24 hours a day to watch her, I want her out of there. I want to give her hope of that at least."

The attorney coughed. "I can't promise you quick action. I can go to the courts in the morning and request a hearing, but like Dr. Aiken told you, it will probably already be in the works and will be a week or so before we're called."

"There's nothing else you can do."

"I can advise you that you can't stay awake 24 hours a day to watch your daughter."

"Besides that."

"I won't know anything more until tomorrow morning. Just tell your daughter I'm working on it."

Helen stood up. "It's a good thing you're not the only one."

"Excuse me?" Jake said.

"I mean that I have someone else looking into things from another angle." She told him about the situation with Maddie.

"I wish you hadn't told me about this," he said.

"Why not?"

"Because, Helen, what your friend is doing has all sorts of legal ramifications. Not to mention, she could be putting herself in very grave danger."

"I know. I told her that, too. She insisted and who was I to argue? It's my child we're talking about."

"Maddie could be brought up on quite a few charges for this."

"You're not going to do anything?" Helen asked in a panic. "You're not going to try to stop her?" She bit her lower lip. "I never should have said a word."

"No," Jake said. "It would've been better if you'd left me in the dark about Maddie's involvement." A long pause was followed by a heavy sigh. "Helen, let's pretend that this part of the conversation never happened. Can you do that?"

Helen realized she'd been holding her breath. She let it out slowly and said, "What conversation?"

CHAPTER 10

At 9:00, Edgar, one of the night shift psych aides, turned out the lights in the eight rooms from a master panel at the desk. He dimmed the lighting in the nursing station, too. Then, he sat down, put his feet up on the desk and pulled out a muscle car magazine. Another psych aide, Billy followed suit with the local sports section. Amy was giving medication to the patients.

Maddie sat up when Amy entered her room. She used the dimmer switch on the wall to bring some faint light over the bed. She motioned for Maddie to lie down.

In a hushed tone, Maddie said, "I really don't want any more medicine."

"I know but I have to give you what the doctor ordered." She shrugged her shoulders and her face looked pained.

"Can't you just pretend you gave me the shot?"

Amy looked down at the tray of medicines she was holding. She looked back at Maddie. "I can't sign off that I gave you a medication when I didn't. I could lose my job and my license."

"I certainly won't tell anyone."

"You wouldn't have to. Dr. Aiken and Dr. Rutger will know just by looking at you."

"I'll fake it. Pretend I'm out of it."

"They'll be doing lab work on you soon to see how much of

the drug is in your system."

"Last night's injection turned me into a zombie. I don't ever want to feel that way again."

Amy sighed heavily.

"You're not like all the other staff here," Maddie said.

Amy didn't respond.

"You seem to be caring and compassionate. You're a good nurse."

"Thank you." Amy blushed.

"You know there's something wrong with this place, don't you?"

Amy looked at the floor.

Edgar popped his head into the room. "Everything okay in here?"

"Yes," Amy replied. "We're just doing some relaxation exercises to help Maddie settle down to sleep."

Edgar rolled his eyes. "Give her a butt shot and it'll be lights out in no time." He left the room.

"Quite a guy," Maddie said.

"He does have room for improvement."

"Why does someone like Edgar work in a hospital? Or someone like Bailey for that matter? They obviously don't care about helping people."

"The pay and benefits here are excellent. That's their motivation. They don't make waves. That's the hospital's motivation for keeping them."

"That's sad."

"Yes, it is," Amy admitted.

"Why do you work here?"

"I have to work somewhere. Besides, conditions are the same everywhere you go. You just have to work around the negative stuff and do some good where you can."

"It's a relief to know that there are some people who work here for reasons other than just money."

"There are a few of us." Amy smiled.

Maddie leaned forward and motioned Amy to lean in closer. "I have to tell you something because I need help and I think I can trust you." She lowered her voice even further. "I'm not really suicidal. I'm not even depressed. Aside from being a little neurotic, I'm not in need of psychiatric help at all." Maddie explained her true situation. She told her about Kendra and Helen. She described her own admission and what she'd learned so far.

"Can you help me at all? I'm making very slow progress. I'm not sure how much time I'll have in here or how much longer I can safely stay in here."

Amy was silent for a long time. When she did speak, her reply was firm. "There is one way I can help you." She grabbed Maddie's upper arm and held it in a tight grip. She looked back at the nursing station where the two psych aides were watching them. Then she turned back smiling as she jabbed the needle into Maddie's deltoid muscle.

Maddie was trembling. She wanted to pull her arm away but the nurse had too strong a hold on her. Amy depressed the plunger of the syringe. Maddie cringed. Her mind was racing with thoughts of what Amy and the rest of these evil people were going to do with her now that she'd blown her cover.

But Amy only injected half the contents of the syringe. She bent down close to Maddie's ear. "Maybe with only half a dose you'll be able to stay more alert and we won't be found out." She winked as she dropped the half-filled syringe into a small, red container labeled *Biohazardous Waste* that was on her med tray.

Maddie breather a huge sigh of relief. "I wasn't sure how you were going to react to my confession. I thought for a minute there I'd made a big mistake. I'm glad you understand."

"I do," Amy said. "I also understand that I'm putting my nursing license in jeopardy."

"Maybe your own personal safety, too?" Maddie asked.

"Maybe that, too."

"Can they tell from the lab tests that you only gave me part of the dose?"

"People absorb and process medications differently. As long as you show a gradual increase, we'll be okay. Unless..."

"Unless what?"

"Unless they feel your blood levels of the drug aren't high enough and they start raising your dosage."

"How soon would they start that?"

"Could be as soon as a couple of days."

"No problem," Maddie said. "I don't plan to be here that long. But how am I going to get off this unit so I can do some serious investigating?"

Edgar stood up and began hovering around the entrance to Maddie's room.

"I'll think of something," Amy whispered as she dimmed the lights and joined Edgar in the hall.

For the next few hours, Maddie lay quietly in her bed, fighting the sedating effects of the drug. It wasn't as much of a struggle this time. She watched the psych aides get comfortable behind the desk. Both of them dosed off while Amy checked each room and then paused outside of Maddie's.

"Edgar! Billy!" Amy looked at the nursing desk. "Wake up, please."

The two men shook their heads and looked around with [illegible]led, groggy expressions.

"I'm going to do my rounds on the Adult Long Term Unit. You both know you're not allowed to sleep on the job. I'd appreciate it if you stay alert while I'm gone."

Maddie could just make out Amy's wink to her. As she watched the nurse leave the unit, she wondered what the plan was. Had Amy left the unit door open? Maddie slipped slowly out of bed. Hovering in the shadows, she peered up at the desk. The psych aides both had their eyes closed. Edgar was outright snoring. She crawled on the floor toward the unit door, her heart pounding in her chest. When she pulled on the door handle, it was locked. She slumped back down to the floor. Then she felt the door push open. She scooted out of the way into the shadow behind the door and watched a housekeeper enter, wheeling in a bucket of water and a mop. She watched him head to the nursing station. The unit door was swinging shut but Maddie managed to squeeze through it before it could fully close.

In the hallway, she silently thanked Amy. She fought through the haze in her mind. She fought to recall the map. She remembered that the Lab was just down the hall to the left. That seemed like a good place to start snooping.

She was up to a crouching position when she felt eyes on her. Someone was watching her. She looked down one hallway, then another. She returned the gaze of her spy. Maddie stood up, smiled and gave a slight wave. From the entrance to the Long Term Adult Unit, Amy gave a quick wave then disappeared behind a door.

Maddie made her way slowly down the hall. She thought of how brave Amy was being. Also, she was smart. If Amy wasn't personally on the unit when Maddie escaped, the sleeping psych aides would take the fall.

She turned at the first left, walked down a short hallway and found herself staring at an oversized metal door. A plaque on the door read *Laboratory and Pharmacy* in black lettering. Maddie tried the handle to the door. It was locked. Out of the corner of her eye, she noticed some light further down the hallway to her left and she crawled toward it. The light was coming from a slat of glass in the middle of a plain, wooden door. Maddie slowly lifter her head and peeked through the window. She saw counters and sinks, test tubes and unidentifiable appliances. This was a second way into the lab. Someone came into her view. It was Jesse, the man she'd run into on the way to dinner. She watched him pick up some folders from a desk and she ducked as he headed toward the wooden door. She raced back down the hallway and turned the corner just in time. Craning her neck to get a look down the hall, she saw Jesse exit the building through a door adjacent to the wooden one. She caught a glimpse of the night sky as the door swung shut. She ran back down the hall and tried to open the steel door leading outside. It was locked. She tried the little door to the lab. Jesse had left it unlocked. Maddie smiled as she slipped inside.

The lights had been left on and she looked around. The laboratory was immense and immaculate. Maddie looked over the extensive equipment then headed to the desk Jesse had been at. The computer monitor was still glowing. He must have been in a hurry to leave. She peered at the monitor but couldn't make any sense of the text. It was a jumble of numbers, letters and symbols. She sat down in the leather office chair and started opening the desk drawers. Nothing helpful in there. She didn't know quite what she was looking for. Something about the medication. Some incriminating proof.

Maddie moved on to the towering filing cabinets beside the desk. She noticed the key still in the lock and pulled out one of the drawers. She lost herself looking through file after file. In the bottom drawer, she found a large box containing a collection of files. On the outside of the box was a computer generated label. *Protocol Drug #8 – Files #1 through #10.* Maddie pulled out the file marked #1, opening it slowly. She didn't read it, however. Instead, she turned toward a noise that she heard. A cough? No, a throat clearing. Jesse was standing in the doorway, staring at her.

Maddie was frozen. She couldn't move. She couldn't speak. She stared at Jesse. Jesse stared back.

"What are you doing in here?" he asked.

"What?" Maddie asked. "Where am I ?" She let her eyelids close halfway and her mouth hang open slightly.

"You're in my lab," Jesse said, "and I can't imagine that you have a good reason to be here."

"I'm sorry. Is this the lab? I thought I was in the dining hall. I was hungry. This medicine has me all confused."

"I'll bet. Why else would you be looking for the dining room at one o'clock in the morning? By the way, you forgot to slur your words and your jaw is not slack enough."

Maddie stood up, file still in hand. "Okay, you got me. I'm not that sedated. But I am taking medication and I'm actually trying to get some information on it. It's called Protocol Drug #8. I don't like taking something when I don't even know what it is."

Jesse walked slowly toward her. "I'm sure the doctors and nurses told you all you need to know about it."

"That's just it. They haven't really told me anything."

"I find that hard to believe."

"Ask any of the patients. You'll see that I'm right. That is when you can get a coherent answer out of them and if they're not too scared to talk."

"They really didn't give you information about it?"

"I swear. Barely a word." Maddie looked him straight in the eye. "You know, don't you."

"Know what?" Jesse look away.

"That there's something suspicious going on around here."

He shook his head. "The only thing I find suspicious is you." He smiled.

"I doubt that. Why else would you consider that what I'm saying might be true. Why else would you listen to the paranoid ramblings of a psychiatric patient who broke into your lab in the middle of the night?"

"Good point," Jesse said, giving a mirthless laugh. "So what's this melodrama all about? Why are you really here in the hospital then? Are you hiding from something or someone?" He paused. "Is it a legal problem?"

"Not even close," Maddie said. "I'm not the one with the secrets. I'm here to find them out." She took a deep breath. "I'm a freelance journalist."

"You're wasting your time then," Jesse said, his expression hard. "There's no story here."

"It's not just a scoop I'm after. Actually, that's secondary. I'm really here to look out for a fifteen-year-old girl. My godchild." Maddie told Jesse most of her story. She left out Amy's participation.

When she finished, Jesse motioned for her to sit on a swivel stool near one of the stainless steel counters. He sat on a second stool beside her. Picking a test tube out of a rack, Jesse stared at the clear fluid then poured it down the drain of a nearby sink.

"Is that it?" Maddie asked. "Is that Protocol Drug #8?"

"No. That was a failed trial for #8b2d4-s." He let the test tube fall into the sink. It broke into several pieces.

"What's the difference between that and #8?"

"At the moment, very little. Hopefully soon, it will have less side effects."

"So they are different stages of the same drug?"

"Yes. What you are taking is really version #8b2d4-t."

"Oh my God. Then there have been how many versions?"

"That's not abnormal for a new drug. It goes through many phases."

"I'm glad you're looking to decrease the side effects. I was beginning to think the goal around here was to turn people into vegetables. If I got a sample of what the current version does, then the first version must have been horrific."

Jesse's face tightened. He said nothing.

"Why are you still developing this if you think it's harmful. Why are the doctors prescribing a dangerous drug?"

Jesse scooted his stool so he was right next to Maddie. He took her hands in his. She was frightened. Had she misjudged him? She pulled her hands away and he let them go. When he spoke, Maddie calmed down.

Jesse said, "I felt an instant, special connection to you when we bumped into each other. I think you felt it too. Something drawing us together. I couldn't quite explain it so I read your chart. I read between the lines. It's hard to fake suicidal depression. I didn't get a borderline vibe from the notes despite what the diagnosis says. I knew you didn't belong here but I couldn't figure out your motive for signing in. I wasn't sure what to do about it. Then you show up in my lab adding fuel to my fears. I'm not sure about anything anymore."

"What are you talking about?" Maddie felt fearful again.

Jessie took the entire rack of half-filled test tubes and toppled it into the sink. The cracking glass startled Maddie. Jesse didn't flinch.

"I guess it's about time. I have to trust someone," he said. "Maybe you're the one. If you have the guts to put yourself at risk in a locked psychiatric facility to rescue your goddaughter, then maybe you have the guts to muddle through this madness."

"What do you mean? Tell me what's going on?"

"Are you ready for a long story?"

Maddie leaned her elbows on the counter, resting her chin in her hands. "Let me have it."

There was a long pause. Jesse cleared his throat. He remained quiet for several more minutes, trading his stool for a leather office chair. He rolled up the sleeves of his lab coat, leaned back and crossed his legs. Maddie moved to a second office chair beside him. Jesse got up and stared pacing. Maddie just watched him. Finally, he sat back down in the chair.

"Sometime tonight would be good. The psych aides might wake up and notice I'm missing."

"Good point," Jesse said. "Okay, here goes nothing. Dr. Victor Aiken and I met as juveniles. Juvenile delinquents. I was doing some petty theft at the time. Victor's story was a bit different. Anyway, we were both tossed into a boy's ranch. It was more like a detention home really. Both of our parents relinquished custody to the state. Victory arrived shortly after I did. Being the new kids created a bond between us. We looked out for each other. Mostly, I looked out for him. He wasn't like the rest of the guys. He was always being picked on because he was so smart and did so well in school."

"If he was so gifted, why didn't someone notice that and place him somewhere more nurturing and encouraging?"

Jesse uncrossed his legs, leaned forward in the chair and began rubbing his hand together. "It was different in those places back then. They acted like they were trying to help us but they were really just housing us until we turned 18. There was a lot of abuse going on. Verbal, physical, sexual. You get the picture?"

Maddie nodded. "Did Victor suffer a lot?"

"He made me promise never to talk about it. In fact, Victor and I swore we'd be friends for life and at the time, we took it very seriously, cut our hands, sealed it with blood. A couple of years later, Victor was taken in by a rich foster family. His brains were finally an asset to him. I thought I'd never hear from him again but he kept his word and stayed in touch with me."

Jesse continued, "Victor wrote to me on the first day of every month, telling me he had a plan for our futures but never said exactly what it was. He ended every letter saying he was right on course."

"Odd," Maddie said.

"That's Victor Aiken. Odd. The rich family ended up adopting him which is almost unheard of for a teenager. Mr. Russell put money in a trust that Victor would get at age 21. He sent him to private school, then college. Pre-med. Then medical school. Victor follow the path his new father had created for him to the letter. Until he chose to specialize, that it."

"Psychiatry wasn't a good choice?" Maddie asked.

"Mr. Russell had Victor pegged as a cardiothoracic surgeon. But when Victor was 21, he had his own money and his own agenda. Not even his surrogate father could stop him. They had a falling out over it and Victor never spoke to the man again."

"How sad."

"I thought it was selfish of Victor to cut off all ties," Jesse said, "but when Victor's mind is set on something, it's set. He started to distance himself from everyone for a while. Focused only on his studies."

"Did you try to talk to him?"

"I did. Victor didn't speak to me for three months. He may be brilliant but his social skills need serious fine-tuning. Finally, I reached out to him and apologized for whatever it was I did wrong. I was back in his good graces again. In fact, that's when he let me in on his grand plan. The first stage of it anyway."

"What was that?"

"After finishing his psychiatric residency and fellowship, he purchased land. Not just any land, though. He purchased the land on which Toloucan Boys Ranch had stood. He tore down the vacant building and had a new facility built."

"Aiken's Haven is sitting on the old site of your boys' ranch? That's eerie."

"It was symbolic for Victor. I can recall that day clearly in my mind."

"Perhaps it meant something to you, too?" Maddie asked.

"It definitely had an impact on me but not as intensely as it did for Victor."

"Tell me about it."

"Victor had invited me to the demolition. We were standing near the site with hard hats and protective glasses and ear protectors on. Everything was ready to go. I looked over at Victor. He had this strange grin on his face that I'd never seen before nor since."

"I cannot believe this day is finally here," Victor said.

Jesse said, "I'm going to enjoy seeing this place fall."

"It is a death," Victor said. "Also, a rebirth."

"What are you talking about?"

"You will see. Everyone will see."

The implosion started and the noise was deafening. Jesse watched Victor raise his arms up, throw his head back and then he laughed so hard and so loud that he could be heard above the thunder of the crumbling of Toloucan. When the din and dust started to settle, Victor did not move. Jesse was beginning to worry about him when he regained control of his laughing.

"Beautiful," Victor finally said. "So beautiful."

Afterward, they went out to dinner to celebrate. During the

meal, Victor steered the conversation toward education.

"You are wasting your talents," he told Jesse. "You need to pursue new horizons."

Jesse had a few beers in him and happily asked, "What do you recommend for me?"

"Do you have any interest in biology and chemistry?"

Jesse had no idea what his friend was talking about but he was in such a great mood, he said, "Sure. If that's where you think my talents lie."

"Then it's a done deal."

Two days later, they met at a local coffee bar. Jesse ordered an espresso. Victor had herbal tea.

"I have enrolled you at my alma mater," Victor said. "I have paid the entire undergraduate tuition up front so you are ready to start on your new career track with this coming semester."

"I barely made it out of high school," Jesse said. "I doubt if I'm up to the challenges of a college program."

Victor said, "That is because you didn't try. You are much smarter than you realize. I will help you if you need any assistance."

"I feel strange about you paying for this."

"Nonsense. It is my gift to you. An act of thanks. I will be insulted if you choose not to accept it."

It sounded better than the dead end jobs he'd been doing. Victor had already bought his way into an ivy league school. It was probably the only shot Jesse had at an elite education, given his grades.

"All right, Victor, I'll do it. But you have to let me repay you."

"There's no need," Victor said. "I'm doing this as much for myself as for you."

"You'll have to explain that one, buddy."

"My idea for the new facility I am about to build will provide psychiatric and behavioral treatment to children and adolescents. I have developed new forms of therapy. I want to create a medication to target uncontrolled rage. The mission of the facility will be to provide advance therapeutic treatment aimed at helping children grow out of their troubled pasts and move toward a healthy, happy future."

Jesse spent the rest of the afternoon listening to Victor describe the physical layout of the place, the treatment ideas, and his role in the new hospital.

Maddie sat back in her chair. "His plans were quite noble."

"I thought so too," Jesse said.

Maddie said, "His plans back then sound like the vision of a warm, caring person. Not at all like the distant, eccentric clinician that I met."

"Victor still has it in him. It's buried deep down, but it's in there."

Maddie and Jesse got up and stretched their legs, moving back to the stools.

"How did your education play a role in the birth of Aiken's Haven?" Maddie asked.

"I have a degree in biochemistry, specializing in pharmacokinetics," Jesse said. "I've just started a Master's program."

"Congratulations."

"Thanks. It's not quite the turn I thought my life was taking, however."

"What do you mean?"

"My main job here is research and development of Victor's miracle drug. I believe he started out with good intentions.

That's why I joined in." Jesse looked down at his feet. "Somewhere along the line, it turned ugly. Now I'm already so deeply involved, it's too late to back out."

"My brain may be a little foggy but if I'm getting this," Maddie said, pushing her stool a few inches away, "you are doing unethical experiments just to keep your job and save your own skin?"

"It's much more than that."

"I don't understand. Why can't you stop what you're doing and blow the whistle on him if he's endangering patients?"

"I would if it were that simple. It's not just myself I'm thinking of. There's a lot of people working here who owe Victor. They have a lot to lose. Victor's not the kind of man you cross."

"What do they owe him? Is he holding a gun to their heads? To yours?"

"That's one way to put it," Jesse said.

"You make it sound like lives would be in danger if you stopped the work," Maddie said.

"Do I?" Jesse reached out and took Maddie's hands. "With Victor that might not be so far from the truth."

"Then you need to do something not only to protect these patients but to protect your coworkers, too," Maddie said. "If you're involved, it's your responsibility to do the right thing."

"The right thing?"

"It's pretty clear to me what needs to be done. I don't care about any extenuating circumstances. The choice for you is obvious. So are you with me?"

"I don't know if we can do it," Jesse said.

"I know I can. I'm going to find out exactly what's going on in this place with or without your help." Maddie stood up.

Jesse followed suit. "You don't know who you're messing

with."

"But you do. So help me."

"Then you'll need the rest of the story. As I said, Victor let me in on the first part of his plan. I thought it was a great idea, tearing down that house of horrors and building a caring, nurturing hospital. He included units for all ages, even adults, but his main interest was always troubled teens."

"Because he was one."

"Right. My role was to develop a medication targeting brain neurotransmitters that would control the aggression and anger, prevent kids from being assaultive and, in Victor's misguided words, from attracting abuse. I think he was trying to cure his younger self."

"Seems like an admirable goal. That last part sounds odd though. Sort of blaming the victim there."

"I thought so too. I never thought anyone attracted abuse but that was his thinking and he never varied from it."

"Isn't it the abusers who are at fault. Don't they need help or punishment depending on the circumstances?"

"Victor doesn't quite see it that way. It would mean putting blame on his mother. He would never have done that until…"

"Until?"

"That's a detail for later. Too long of an off topic story for now. Anyway, we filled up Aiken's Haven with patients in no time and had innovative formats for therapy. We started to work on what Victor called an anti-aggression agent. Victor has made quite a name for himself. He's already started construction on facilities in New York and California. He expects to expand to all fifty states.

"Sounds like Victor's plan is unfolding nicely. What happened to derail things?"

"Victor's biological mother showed up. It was the first time he'd seen her since his intial days at Toloucan.

"That must have been an awkward moment."

"It was painful just to watch," Jesse said.

"You were there.?"

"She showed up here at the hospital. In the lab. I wanted to give them privacy but Victor insisted that I stay."

"A lot of nerve on her part," Maddie said. "Tell me what happened."

Victor and Jesse had been analyzing some MRI results in the lab. The receptionist had brought Darlene to the lab without calling first, assuming Dr. Aiken's mother would be welcome. Victor looked up immediately.

"Mom? Mom! Is it really you?"

"Yes, Victor, honey. It's me," Darlene said and rushed to his side.

There was a short pause as Victor stared at her, then he embraced her. They hugged for a long time.

"Look at you. A big, strong man now," Darlene said. "So smart and successful. I've been following your career."

"Really?" Victor asked, flashing a dazzling smile.

"Everything I can find. I have a scrap book of newspaper and online articles. I'm so proud of you. I've missed you terribly."

"I have missed you Mom. I knew you would find me someday." Victor hugged her again, tears in his cold eyes.

He let go of her and said, "I always knew you did not want to give me up."

"Of course I didn't, honey. It's just that I had no choice at the time."

Jesse said, "I'll just head over to the Pharmacy next door and give you two time together."

Victor shook his head at Jesse, released Darlene, and said, "Mom, this is Jesse. He is my Director of Pharmacological Research and Development and my best friend."

Jesse had never seen Victor in such an emotional state. He'd never heard him refer to him as his best friend before either. Jesse looked at mother and son. They were both beaming.

"Nice to meet you," he said, shaking Darlene's hand.

"Oh, give me a big hug," she said, entrapping Jesse in her arms. "If you're Victor's best friend, then you're part of the family."

Jesse hugged the woman, though it felt odd hugging this person who was a stranger to both himself and really to Victor.

"Right," Victor said. "Where are you living now, Mom?"

"Only about an hour away from here. Isn't that great?"

"Perfect. Are you working?"

"Yup. I'm a waitress at a truck stop. It's okay. It pays the bills. Well, most of them."

Victor looked concerned. "If you are having trouble, why not move in with me? There is lots of room in the main house or you could live in the guest house if you prefer. We have a lot to catch up on."

"My baby," Darlene said, touching his cheek. You're so sweet. I'd love that. I just have to talk to someone first. My husband." Darlene looked at the gold band on her ring finger.

"You got remarried? When?"

"Several years ago."

"When?" Victor took a step back from her. His voice was tight when he said, "Was it right after I went into Toloucan?"

"No. It was over a year after you went away."

"Who did you marry? It better not be that Jim guy."

"Well, my last name *is* Torrence now."

"Mom!"

"You know I've always loved him. He's not that bad of a guy. You just have to give him a chance."

"I do not. How could you marry him? He was an abusive drunk then and I am certain he still is. Besides, he is the one who made you give me away to the state."

Darlene said nothing.

Victor's face was reddening. For a moment, Jesse thought he might hit her.

"What does he do for a living?" Victor asked.

"He's not working right now," Darlene said. "He's between jobs.

"My guess is that he does not know you are here."

"Oh yes he does. In fact, he's the one who suggested it. He thought it was time you and I reunited. See, he does have a heart."

Victor walked over to Jesse. His face was rigid and his voice stern when he said, "Tell this woman to get out."

"You don't mean that," Jesse said.

"I mean every word." Victor stalked out of the lab.

Darlene just stood there.

"I'm sorry," Jesse said to her. "I guess that must have hurt."

"Yeah," Darlene said, a look of devastation on her face.

"Is there anything I can do?" Jesse asked.

"Maybe there is," Darlene said. "I need to make a call." She pulled out a cell phone. "Here's the plan. When Jim gets on the line, I'll tell him what happened. You can be my witness that I tried."

"Tried to do what?"

"To make amends with Victor. Wait," she said. "Hi Jim. I'm at Victor's hospital right now. Hold on." Speaking to Jesse she said, "You have to tell Jim that I tried to talk to Victor but he refused to talk to me." She shoved the cell phone at Jesse.

"Hello?" Jesse said.

"Who's this?" asked a drunken voice on the other end of the line.

"This is Jesse. Darlene wanted me to talk to you."

"Just ask her if she weaseled any bucks out of that rich brat of hers."

Jesse handed the cell phone back to Darlene. "He's not in the mood to talk right now."

"Great," she said, disconnecting. "What can I do to get Victor to talk to me again?"

"I think it's time you left," Jesse said.

Darlene shrugged. "Maybe an extra six pack will make Jim stay calm."

Jesse came out of his reverie. "Darlene left the hospital and I never saw her again. I didn't see Victor for a week."

"Where did he go?" Maddie asked.

"I'm not positive but I have a theory."

Jesse got up, unlocked a desk drawer with keys from his pocket and pulled out a slightly yellowed newspaper clipping from a lock box inside. He handed the article to Maddie. Skimming the introduction, Maddie paused at the next paragraph. She read it aloud.

The body had been in the lake for at least six months,

the coroner said. It was identified by dental records to be the corpse of 53-year-old James Henry Torrence, an unemployed male, originally from Philadelphia...

"My God! You think Victor killed him." Maddie glanced at the date of the story. "This was just two years ago."

"Yes," Jesse said. "The story came out six months after Darlene's visit. They still haven't caught the murderer."

"Why don't you go to the police with this?"

"With what? I have no tangible proof. Like I said, it's just a theory."

"Based on?"

"Based on the fact that Victor left as an angry man and returned as calm as I've ever seen him. When I asked him if he was all right, he said that he'd taken care of things. Everything was as it should be."

"Meaning?"

"He didn't elaborate," Jesse said, handing Maddie a second article. The date was six months prior to the finding of Jim's body.

"This one is from just after Darlene's visit?" she asked.

Jesse nodded.

"You have quite a scrap book going yourself." Again, Maddie read the article aloud.

Police are still searching for the whereabouts of 38-year-old Darlene Phyllis Torrence. It has not been determined whether her absence is of her own choosing or if foul play is involved.

The woman had taken her purse and identification with her.

Though police are still investigating, there are no signs of

forced entry or violence in her home. Previous names used

by the woman include Darlene Phyllis Aiken from a first

marriage and Darlene Phyllis Rosewood, her maiden name.

Anyone with information....

"He killed his own mother?"

"I doubt it," Jesse replied.

"What do you think happened to her? Do you think she got scared and ran away?"

"No. A month later, I was at a fund-raiser at Victor's estate. There were lights on in the guest house which was unusual. I'm the only one who ever stays there. Only his housekeeper lives on the grounds but she has her own living quarters."

"No one else has been in the guest house?"

"Only me. I would stay overnight sometimes. Once, I'd had a fire in my apartment and Victor let me live there until I found a new place to rent. After that, we didn't hang out much anymore and I haven't stayed overnight since. That was before his mother's visit to Aiken's Haven. Anyway, at the fund-raiser, I tried to get Victor's attention but he was busy chatting up his benefactors. I was curious about the light in the guest house so I went outside to check it out myself. Maybe his mother decided to move in with him after all. Maybe he actually had a lady friend."

"And?"

"And I never got near the guest house. If the two Dobermans hadn't stopped me, I would have walked through the faint blue glow of a laser beam surrounding it. He had the place surrounded with an alarm. Not to mention, his entire spread has state of the art security."

"So you learned nothing," Maddie said.

"Not quite. I saw a shadow cross the curtained window inside the house. It was the silhouette of a woman."

"Darlene?"

"I couldn't be sure. I still don't know. The barking dogs might have warned Victor. Maybe he saw me. He never said anything. But the guest house has been closed up every time I've been to parties there since and I've never been invited to hang out with him there, just the two of us, ever again."

CHAPTER 11

Kendra quickly slipped out of bed, got on her hands and knees and quietly crawled to the entrance of her room. She wanted to hear Alicia better. From the doorway, she could clearly hear the neighbor patient's labored breathing and Kendra wondered what was wrong. At the nursing station, the unit nurse, two psych aides and a nurse from another unit were all staring at the same piece of paper. As long as they weren't looking at her she was all right.

A tap on her shoulder made Kendra flinch with fear.

"It's just me," a boy quietly said.

"Adam," she whispered fiercely. "You almost gave me a heart attack. What if I'd yelled or something."

"Then we'd be screwed. But you didn't." He smiled.

Kendra smiled too. "Did Alicia's breathing wake you up?"

"Wasn't sleeping. But yeah, it sounds funny. Just like David's."

"That guy who died the night I was admitted, right? You think Alicia is dying, too?"

"I know she is."

"We've got to tell the nurses."

"They won't do anything," Adam said.

"How do you know?"

"Because they're the ones killing her. Just like they killed David. They'll kill us too, if we don't stay out of sight."

They watched the nurse and psych aides approach Alicia's door. A second nurse was on the telephone. She hung up and joined the other staff in the girl's room. Scooting along the floor, Adam and Kendra found a better vantage point to see into Alicia's room while staying out of view.

"See? They're going to help her after all. Why did you think they were going to kill her?" Kendra asked.

Adam shook his head. He wondered why anyone would trust an adult. They never believe you. His parents called him a pathological liar. He knew he made up stories to get out of trouble but that was for a good reason. He could control it. Even Dr. Aiken has told him that. It wasn't pathological if you could control it. Adam was surprised that another teenager wouldn't believe him, especially since he was telling the truth this time.

"Why are you being stupid about this, Kendra? It's for the same reason they offed David. Because he knew something."

"What?"

"I don't know. I'm still alive, aren't I?" Adam said. "But I bet Alicia does. Maybe she told them about David's breathing."

"Why would they kill her for that?"

"I don't know. I haven't totally figured it out yet but David was the one who told them about Shane Reynold's breathing problems. Shane died last week. Same way as David. The same way Alicia will tonight."

"Stop saying that," Kendra said.

"Just trying to prepare you."

"Alicia is just sick. Nothing bad is going to happen to her. We're in a hospital. They might be assholes here but they'll help a sick patient. They'll help someone who can't breathe right?"

"I wish that were true. I wish they were just assholes. But trust me, they are fucking evil," Adam said, putting his hands on Kendra's shoulders.

"Why are they putting those straps on her?" Kendra asked. She watched in horror as the staff put thick leather straps on each of Alicia's limbs and one across her chest. Lastly, they put one over her forehead. Each strap held her tightly to a rolling gurney.

"I saw them do that to David and Shane, too. I think it's so she won't fall off the rolling bed."

"Because she's shaking so bad. See, they are concerned about her."

"Yeah, right," Adam said. "Just wait. It gets worse."

They watched Alicia closely. Her arms and legs were trembling. Her fingers and toes were curling.

"Why are they just standing there?" Kendra asked. "They've got to help her." Kendra started to rise but Adam pulled her down and held her in a tight bear hug from behind.

"I told you they wouldn't save her. If you go over there, or say anything, it won't make any difference and the two of us are as good as dead."

"Really?" Kendra asked, tears running down her cheeks. "We've got to do something, though. We can't just sit here."

"Trust me," Adam said. "We can't do anything for Alicia now. We can only keep ourselves from falling into the same trap."

They continued to watch Alicia shake. Her breathing was noisy and fast.

"I hate this," they heard the unit nurse say.

"I know," said the second nurse.

"Isn't she too far gone anyway?" a psych aide asked.

"Wouldn't she be a vegetable even if you were foolish enough to try to save her?"

"No," the other psych aide said. "You have to be without oxygen for a certain amount of time, right?"

Both aides looked at the nurses. Neither nurse answered for a minute.

"We're following Dr. Aiken's orders," the unit nurse said.

"We have to let her go," the second nurse said.

Putting her face in her hands, the unit nurse said, "I just can't watch another one."

"There's got to be a better way to make a living," the second nurse said.

"Just try and quit this place," the unit nurse said. "You may as well be lying on that bed yourself."

Adam and Kendra moved out of the shadows to get a better look at Alicia. They were taking a chance but the staff still didn't notice them. All eyes were now trained on Alicia's failing form. Her eyes were closed. Her face was grimacing. She started trembling more ferociously. Her head was flailing side to side. White foam was bubbling from her mouth. Blood stared running out of her ears. Then, her body stiffened in a grotesque arch.

Kendra turned and buried her face in Adam's shoulder, crying silently. Adam felt sick to his stomach.

They heard someone say, "It's almost over."

Driving home from the restaurant, Victor smiled with satisfaction. Ms. Vivica Bennet had been impressed with the facility, his future plans and with him. He was glad they drove separate cars from the hospital. It avoided the awkward moment of what to do next. Victor had given Vivica a peck on the cheek and then a kiss on the lips, lingering just long enough to get her interest but not too long that it might be construed as an invitation. There was only one woman for him and she was already living with him.

Though he was pleased with how the evening has passed, he still felt wired, irritable. He was not sure what was bothering him, so he just let his mind roam as he took and aimless drive around the countryside.

He thoughts kept going to his mother, that cretin, Jim and that damned Toloucan. Despite trying to steer them away, the memories flooded full force into his consciousness.

It had taken almost an hour for them to pull into the driveway of Toloucan Boys Ranch. Victor stared at the place from the back seat. With it's gray, brick buildings surrounded by a tall fence which was topped with a coil of barbed wire, it looked more like a prison then a camp or a hospital. He removed the washcloth from his nose. It was no longer filled with ice anyway. As he leaned on the top of the front seat, Jim turned and glared at him, keeping his own palm pressed tightly against his jaw. There were dried droplets of blood still under Jim's nose. *I should have pretended to like him all along,* Victor thought. *I should have come up with a scheme to get rid of him. He beat me to it. Maybe there was still time.*

As they walked in the front door of the place, Jim had a painfully tight grip on his left biceps. On his right side, Mom was holding his hand. He felt nauseous but he wouldn't let himself throw up. He bit his lower lip to stop it from quivering.

A large, young woman met them in the lobby. "Darlene Aiken? Jim Torrence?" After receiving nods, she continued. "I'm Olivia Garvin. We've been expecting you. Follow me." She ignored Victor, turned and briskly lumbered away. They had to do a slow trot to keep up with the woman.

Victor realized that the woman said they were expecting them. Mom had been planning this. It wasn't a spur of the moment thing that she decided this morning. She'd been planning it at least since yesterday. Probably a lot earlier than that. Victor glared at Jim. It was his fault. He made Mom do this. She would never have done this to him alone. His own Dad would have never done this. Jim would pay. With his blood boiling, a curse was about to erupt from his lips when an idea hit him and he held his tongue.

They followed Olivia into a small office. She gestured for them to sit in the folding chairs across from a green metal desk. Victor tried to sit in the chair near the door but Jim pushed him to the side and took that seat. Mom sat by the window. He was trapped in the middle.

A gaunt Mexican man quietly entered the room. "Mrs. Aiken, Mr. Torrence, Victor," he said, "I'm Dr. Estevez." He shook each of their hands then sat in the only remaining chair. "We need to ask you a few questions and I'd like to start with Victor." He looked at Mom and Jim. "Would you two mind waiting in the lobby? Olivia will get you when we're ready for you."

Mom looked uncertainly at Jim. She wouldn't look at Victor at all. Jim shrugged his shoulders. His face was red. Finally, he got up and left the room. Mom scurried out after him.

Dr. Estevez pulled at one end of his thin mustache as he asked him a barrage of questions about his life at home and school. Victor gave him the answers he thought the man wanted to hear and followed the all with *sir*. The doctor seemed to like that. Olivia did not ask one question. She wouldn't look him in the eye. She was afraid of him.

Dr. Estevez smiled. "You did very well, Victor. You behaved very nicely for the interview. I appreciate that. Now we'll talk with your mother."

When Mom was brought back to the office it was not just her. Jim was with her. They made Victor go into the lobby this time and Olivia had to wait there with him. Victor listened at the door, knowing Olivia wouldn't have the nerve to stop him. She made a few gestures by clearing her throat and standing near him with her hands on her broad hips, but he ignored her. In fact, he glared at her for making it hard for him to eavesdrop. His expression grew even darker as he overheard the lies Jim was telling the doctor. He was accusing Victor of beating up Mom, saying he was dangerous. Victor burst through the office door.

"He's lying, sir!"

"You had your turn to talk already, young man." Dr. Estevez pointed at the door.

"But he's making stuff up. He just wants me out of the way so he can sponge off Mom. It's not right." Victor started to cry. "Don't listen to him." When he looked over at Mom she turned away and looked at the doctor. "Mom, please. Don't leave me here. Don't let that jerk send me away. Why would you choose that asshole over me?"

"That's enough," Dr. Estevez said.

"This is crazy. He's the one who should be locked up!" Victor pointed at Jim. "He's the one who beat me up." He lightly touched his nose. His hands were sweating and he wanted to pummel Jim. Instead, he grabbed a stapler from the desk and hurled it through the window.

The sound of shattering glass spurred everyone into action. Jim and Dr. Estevez grabbed Victor by the arms. Mom jumped behind her chair. Olivia dove for the phone.

"Male Call to Admitting!" she screamed. "Male Call to Admitting!"

Victor heard her words repeated over a loud speaker and within seconds, six, burly men were in the office. Jim and Dr. Estevez let go of Victor and they, along with Mom and Olivia, watched as these muscle men slammed him to the ground, shoving his face into the dank carpet.

"My nose!" Victor cried out. "You're hurting my nose. It's already busted."

"You should have thought of that before you broke that window over there," one of the gorilla men said. He was inches from Victor's face and his breath smelled rancid.

"Take him to the lockup," Dr. Estevez said. Tie him down. I'll be there shortly."

They picked Victor up from the floor. One man on each leg, one on each arm. Another guy wrapped his arm around Victor's waist. The other hand grabbed his crotch. The one with the foul breath had his head in a vice grip. Victor was facing the floor and was terrified they might drop him.

"Mom!" he yelled. "Help me!"

Out of the corner of his eyes, he could see Jim smiling as he held Mom back.

Victor stopped yelling. There was no one in the lockup room to hear him and the echo hurt his ears. The cell was dingy, cold and had no furniture. The floor was padded in hard plastic. Six large, metal rings were imbedded into it. He was tied to four of them. He pulled at the thick, brown, leather restraints on his arms. It was a useless gesture. He couldn't move them. They had slammed him spread eagle, flat on his back, onto the plastic. His legs were leashed, also. His socks and shoes had been removed and his pant legs pushed up. The worn insides of the leather cuffs chaffed the skin on his wrists and ankles. The back of his sweaty arms slid against the plastic flooring, rubbing them raw. Each restraint had a thick rope attached to it, the kind of rope he climbed in gym class. Each rope was tied to a metal ring. There was no way he could break free.

"Dr. Estevez wants you in five-point restraints before he

comes to talk to you," a muscle man said as he unlocked the door and entered the room. He wrapped a weight-lifter type belt around Victor's waist, through the two extra floor rings and buckle it at his left side. The man left without another word.

Victor noticed Dr. Estevez standing in the doorway. He watched as the doctor closed the steel door behind him, took a few steps forward and was standing right above his feet, staring at his crotch.

"How are you feeling now?" Dr. Estevez asked, twirling his tiny mustache.

"Better, sir," Victor lied. "Please let me out of these things."

"We'll see," he said. As he came around to stand on the right side. From Victor's vantage point, the doctor looked 10 feet tall.

"Have you learned anything from this little episode?" He touched Victor's side lightly with the toe of his shoe.

"Yes, sir. I will never lose my temper like that again."

"Why not?" Dr. Estevez pushed his foot harder into his ribs.

"Because someone could get hurt. I promise I'll be good."

The doctor removed his foot from Victor's rib cage and squatted down beside him. From this angle, he looked much less threatening.

"How do I know you will keep your promise?"

"We'll make a deal," Victor said.

Dr. Estevez smiled eerily. "What kind of a deal?"

"Name your price."

The doctor laughed loudly. "Okay. You agree to take the medicine I prescribe you, attend all classes and therapy sessions, and promise to cause no trouble to the staff while you're here. In exchange, I'll let you out of the restraints. Deal?"

"And out of this room?"

Dr. Estevez smiled. "And out of this room."

Victor looked up at him with the puppy dog eyes. "You've got a deal, sir."

As Dr. Estevez walked him across the compound toward a building he called *the cottage*, Victor looked the man over. He did not look back. Victor had heard of counseling and therapy. He went with Mom when she'd go to the free health clinic to see a shrink and get a tranquilizer prescription once a month. But this doctor was different than the one she saw. He was mean and tricky. Victor wondered what their therapy sessions would be like. The thought made him afraid as he touched his swollen nose and tender ribs.

They arrived at the brick structure. Dr. Estevez unlocked the metal door and held it open. As Victor passed through, he glanced at the sign above the door frame. *Cottage #4.* The door swung shut behind them and he heard a loud clank. A self-locking door. They walked down a beige hallway, the same beige color as his apartment at home. Victor tried not to think of home as he looked around. The long hall had numbered doors on each side. They entered the last door, which had no number on it, walking into what looked like a small living room. A man and a woman were seated on a sagging couch, drinking from coffee mugs.

"These are your cottage proctors, Mario and Adrianna Massimo." Dr. Estevez said. "They will be in charge of you while you're here."

Mario, a big, Italian man, stood up and looked Victor over. His tiny wife did not even glance up.

As Dr. Estevez turned to leave, Victor asked him, "When do I see you again?"

"Sometime this week."

"What do I do now?"

The doctor looked away from him and turned to the couple. "I'll leave him in your hands."

"Thanks, Dr. E.," Mario said. He was still standing. Adrianna hadn't moved, other than to sip from her mug.

Once Dr. Estevez left, Mario sneered at Victor. "Sit." He pointed at a rickety wooden chair beside the couch.

Victor sat where indicated, figuring the best way to find out the ins and outs was to cooperate with Mario for now.

"Vic, is it?" Mario took a swig from his coffee cup, cleared his throat loudly, waked behind him and gripped him by the back of the neck. "Well, Vic, I run a tight ship here." He pulled Victor's head back and pointed to his face. "You think you look tough with that shiner brewing and that busted nose? You planning on giving me any trouble?" He leaned in and Victor caught a whiff of alcohol.

"No, sir," Victor said, biting the inside of his cheek.

"Sir. Good. I like that. A sissy boy. We're going to get along just fine." He looked over at the woman. "What do you think, Adrianna?"

The woman shrugged her shoulders. She didn't break eye contact with her fashion magazine.

"What are the rules around here?" Victor asked, wanting to know how to play the game.

"The rules are what I say they are." Mario smirked and let go of Victor's neck, shoving his head forward in the process.

There was a loud commotion coming from the hallway.

"The brats are back from school," Mario said. "Come on."

He dragged Victor by the back of the shirt toward a group of teenage boys. They were talking, laughing and a few were pointing.

"Group room!" Mario growled.

The boys all turned to enter one of the rooms off the hallway. Victor went in behind them and Mario shoved him into a plastic chair. The other sat in the chairs, forming a circle. Mario stood at the doorway of the room, arms crossed over his broad chest, his hands shoved in his armpits. His facial expression had the tiniest hint of fear in it.

"This is Vic," Mario said. "Show him the ropes. You got half an hour before you get your butts back into class. Don't give me any trouble. Got it?"

The boys all mumbled agreements and Mario left the room, slamming the door shut behind him. A loud click sound as the door was locked.

"Hey, Vic," a freckle-faced boy said. "What did you do to get in here? Rob a gas station? Knock your sister up? What?"

"It's Victor, and I..."

"Fight! Fight!" Another boy was looking out the window. "Fight in the compound!"

All the boys ran to the window except one. He was black and lanky. He stared at Victor. "My name's Jesse," he said in a hushed tone. "I was the last new kid. Got here two months ago. It isn't so bad if you keep your mouth shut and go along with the others."

"What's up with that guy?" Victor said, nodding toward the one who had been about to confront him.

"That's Mitch. They put the worst of us in Cottage #4," Jesse said. Mitch mugged an old man then knifed him, left him to die. His real name is Mitchell but everyone here calls him Mitch. He punched one of the teachers in the face for getting it wrong. He's not as tough as he thinks he is but the other guys seem to do what he says."

"What about you?"

"Stole from a liquor store. Just a pint. Small stuff." He lowered his voice further. "Don't go asking these other guys what they're here for."

Victor nodded. "What about Mario and Adrianna?"

"Mario's on a power trip," Jesse said. "He likes to rough us up a bit but he doesn't do much harm. Just don't let him get you in a room alone and you'll be okay. Adrianna doesn't give a crap. They're just her for the free housing and the paycheck. Spend it all on booze and drugs."

"When do I get to see my Mom." Victor spoke in a barely audible whisper.

"Who knows. You're supposed to be able to see family or foster parents after a month but something always comes up. I haven't seen anyone have a family visit since I've been here."

As Mitch and the other boys started milling away from the window, Jesse said, "Fight's over. Here's the deal. We go to classes and groups but we don't like it. We hide the medicine under our tongues and spit it out in the bathroom. We hate everyone who works here. And if you didn't do anything radical to get in here, make something up."

Half an hour later, the boys were locked in a one-room portable with a dozen other kids, awaiting the arrival of the teacher. Mario had come into the group room while the others were hurling insults at Victor yet did nothing to stop them. He just ordered them to march over to the school. When they entered the classroom, Victor looked around. There were a bunch of wooden desks with green, metal chairs attached. Rickety shelves housed a bunch of torn textbooks. A globe that had been busted in half adorned the teacher's desk. In the back of the portable building was the only thing that looked halfway interesting. It was a makeshift science lab. Victor walked to it and picked up a test tube. Pushing aside a charred Bunsen burner, he read from a soiled piece of paper trapped underneath it. A simple experiment. They were years behind him.

"You like that stuff?" Mitch said as he approached, tucking his stringy hair behind his ears.

"No." Victor stared straight down into Mitch's green eyes. He was an inch shorter and his red hair made him look a lot less threatening than he was trying to be.

"Yes, you do. I can tell a geek when I see one. Hey guys, Vic is a mad scientist." He laughed a loud, maniacal laugh. "I think we'll call you Doc. Yeah, Doc, I like that."

Victor put the test tube back in its tray. Watching the other boys gather around, his hands started shaking and he was afraid he would drop it. "I don't know what your problem is Mitchell, but you better stay away from me."

Mitch got right up into Victor's face. "It's Mitch."

"It's Victor."

"Look, Doc, I'm the boss around here. Your name is Doc if I say it's Doc. I tell everyone what to do. Including you."

Victor said, "Trust me, none of you wants to mess with me."

"So," Mitch said, turning to his stunned audience, "Doc thinks he's tougher than me." He rolled up his sleeves. Mitch pointed to four of the boys. "You guys are going to help prove him wrong."

Victor started to back up as the guys approached but there was nowhere to go and within seconds they each had one of his limbs held firmly. Two of the boys were squatting on the floor with their arms wrapped around his legs. The other two had his arms in a tight squeeze against his own body. Victor tried not to cry. He did try to struggle. His head smacked the temple of the kid on the left who loosened his grip only long enough to slap Victor in the face.

"Stop it!" Mitch commanded. "I teach the lessons around

here. Jesse, go hold the back of his head."

Jesse hesitated for a second. He looked down at the floor and walked behind Victor, gripping his head gently in his hands as he positioned his head to one side. "Hang tough," he whispered, his voice almost drowned out to Victor by the growing cheers and shouts of the other boys.

Mitch stepped in front of Victor. A smile came to his lips. "So you think you're so tough, do you, Doc?" He laughed. "We'll see how tough you are." He laughed louder.

Victor took a deep breath and closed his eyes. As he opened them, he saw Mitch pulling back his fist and then pummeling it forward, right into the center of his chest.

CHAPTER 12

"Victor became a workaholic then?" Maddie asked, perched on her stool in the lab.

"He always was one," Jesse said. "He became intensely focused on the drug development. Obsessed with it. He was in this lab with me daily. And I suspect, some nights on his own. He wanted the drug perfected as soon as possible. He wouldn't follow the proper procedures that the FDA requires. He started the trials too soon."

"What do you mean?"

"There's a process, a specific step-by-step procedure to follow. You don't go to the next stage until you are 100% ready." Jesse took a long, deep breath. "We barely did enough animal testing before he was ready to start in on human subjects. I thought it was too soon."

"Did anything happen. Anything bad?"

"Not then. Not that I know of. We used low dosages and Victor reported back only minor side effects on the test cases. Nausea, trembling, muscle spasms. I tried to decrease all of those in the future modifications."

"So how has the response been to Protocol Drug #8?" Maddie asked.

"You're taking it. What do you think?"

"Well, I'm sort of taking it. I think it's horrible but I don't actually need it so I'm not sure I can give a fair judgment. What kind of responses have you heard?"

"That depends on who you talk to. Victor says it's perfected."

"You obviously don't agree."

"In the lab setting, yes. We were ready to move past animal studies but in a very limited way. I was only ready to begin the very first phase of human trials which involves a very small group of volunteer patients under very close scrutinized study. Victor's the one who went ahead with wide-scale prescription as if it's already been FDA approved." Jesse looked intensely at Maddie. "I've been hearing unpleasant rumors around the hospital."

"What kind of rumors?"

"There's been reports of some violent seizures."

"Did the nurses tell you this?"

"No. I overheard some psych aides talking. The employees here don't interact with me much."

"That's weird."

"It was for a while. Then, I learned from one of the aides that Victor had instructed all the staff here not to disturb me."

"So they were afraid not to follow his instructions or they believed you feel you're too important to talk to them?"

"Probably both. I rarely venture out of the lab anyway."

"Sounds lonely," Maddie said.

"I have a few friends outside of work," Jesse said.

"That's good," she said, "since I don't see too many people to trust around this place."

"Present company excluded," he said, smiling.

Maddie smiled back. "The seizures are what prompted you

to work on improving Protocol Drug #8 even further?"

As far as Victor knows, I'm done with it. He's given me a new assignment. I'm supposed to be working on a new antidepressant for adults. That's why I'm here in the middle of the night, working on my own time."

"You're trying to improve Protocol Drug #8 without Victor's knowledge?"

"I'm trying to retain the positive effects and eliminate the negative ones. I'm trying to follow Victor's original plan."

"He doesn't want the drug improved? Why not?"

"I'm still trying to figure that out."

"While still letting him test on patients? On me? On Kendra, my goddaughter?" Maddie said in a sharp tone?

"You're both relatively safe," Jesse said. "You're an adult and she just got here. It's only the long term kids I've heard about being prone to the adverse effects."

"Still, I never signed a consent to take the medication. They fake the signature here."

"They do?" Jesse said, looking up at Maddie.

"Don't act surprised."

"But I genuinely am. I hadn't found that piece to this ever-expanding puzzle yet."

Maddie examined Jesse's face. He did look surprised and disgusted.

"You're not in on all of this with Victor. Why don't you and the other concerned employees speak out against him?"

"Because he has all of us over a barrel." Jesse hung his head.

Maddie shook her head. "I still don't get that. Take that woman, Olivia, in Admitting. Why would she arrange to have other forms underneath the ones I signed so that my signature would seem to have been authorizing the others, basically forging my signature? Why would she do something so unethical just because Victor told her to?"

"Olivia," Jesse said. "Good choice. She's the perfect example. She worked at Toloucan when Victor and I were there. She was the one who admitted us when we were inmates, I mean residents, there."

"Quite a coincidence."

"Not at all. Olivia is cruel. She was then and she is now." Jesse got up from his stool and paced the floor. "She was also involved in the foster placement back then. If she didn't like a kid, she interfered. Got them hooked up with a bad family or blocked them from qualifying. With Victor it was for different reasons. She couldn't keep him from going into foster care. Mr. Russell adored Victor and he wasn't fostering for the money. He really wanted a son. That made Olivia mad.

Maddie remained on her stool and asked, "Was she mad to see Victor go?"

"Olivia had a crush on him. It was kind of sick. As a result, she blocked all of my own opportunities to go to a foster placement. She knew I was Victor's best friend and that might be her way to keep tabs on him. She read all my mail both to and from him. Even when Victor used a fake name. She told lies and got other boys to instigate fights that were blamed on me. That's what kept me stuck at Toloucan until I was 18."

"How awful for you," Maddie said, "but fortunate for Victor now since he has something to hold over her."

"She did a lot of despicable things. Some just malicious. Some illegal. I guess her motive in this is avoiding prison. At this point, she's got little to lose by falsifying consent forms."

"Aren't you furious with her? Don't you want to turn her in?"

"Yes and no. I can't change the past so I don't see how it will help me by going after her."

Maddie moved so she was on the edge of her seat. "Jesse, I think you're a good person at heart. It sounds like you feel like you're trapped. I have to ask, have any patients been permanently harmed by Protocol Drug #8?"

"I don't know for sure. I don't know anything for sure," Jesse said, "but I heard something a few days ago that a patient may have died following a grand mal seizure. He was taking the drug."

"Jesse! We've got to stop Victor. We've got to stop him tonight." Maddie stood up.

"What is it?"

"Kendra! She's only 15. She's on the medication and she's of the age where the side effects can hurt her. Just because you've only heard of long term kids being harmed doesn't mean she won't be the first short term patient hurt or worse. We've got to find her. We've got to get her out of here. In fact, we have to get all of the patients out of here." She started for the door.

"Maddie, you're a patient here. No one is going to let you release all the patients, let alone even one."

"But you aren't, Jesse. You work here. So let's do it together."

"Even if it were possible, it wouldn't stop him."

"What do you mean. We report him to the authorities right now," she said. "He'll do prison time for sure. Hopefully, life with no parole so he can't hurt anyone else."

"You really don't know Victor. He'd get out of it. Victor has kept his own hands clean while implicating others. He's also cultivated political connections. We couldn't touch him. Besides, not one of the employees here would risk backing us up."

Maddie thought for a moment. "I know one who might. First things first, though. Let's get Kendra out of her unit before she gets even one more dose of that dangerous drug."

"Right," Jesse said. "You said she's 15. How long has she been here?"

"A few days."

"She could be on either Adolescent A.C.U. #2 or #3."

"I think her mother said she was in 3 when we talked on the phone but I can't remember. My brain is still a little foggy. Can't you just look her up in the computer?"

"Victor has everything monitored. It would tip our hand. Believe me, it's safer doing it the hard way. Follow me."

"I know the way," Maddie said, realizing her mind was clearer than she thought. "I memorized the map of the hospital."

"Resourceful woman," Jesse winked at her.

Maddie felt herself blush as she followed him out of the lab. They furtively navigated the hallway toward the teenagers' units.

Maddie whispered, "How are we going to get her out?"

"Leave that part to me," Jesse said. "Should we go numerically?"

"You're the boss."

"A.C.U. #2 it is. Wait here. I'll only be a second."

Jesse punched some buttons on a keypad and the door clicked open. He approached the nursing station.

"Allison? I'm doing some testing for Dr. Aiken that requires me to bring the patient to the lab."

"Don't you usually do sleep studies on the unit?"

"Usually but we're doing something new. My equipment stays in the lab."

"Who's the patient?" Allison stared at Jesse.

"Kendra Sibley."

The nurse checked her computer. "I should call Dr. Aiken

first," she said, typing and clicking at a rapid rate. "I don't see any orders for this."

"If he didn't trust me, he wouldn't have me as his right hand man."

Allison glared at him. "She's not on my unit. She's next door. #3."

"Thank you. I appreciate your help."

"As long as it's not my patient."

Jesse left A.C.U. #2, rejoined Maddie and they moved silently down the carpeted hallway. Jesse went inside and gave the nurse, Marguerite, the same story as he'd given Allison. Jesse had seen Marguerite around. She was hard to miss with her long, black hair and striking, ice blue eyes. He didn't know her personally though. He had expected trouble from Allison. He wasn't sure how Marguerite would react to his ruse. He braced himself for opposition.

"Kendra's in room 304. Right over there." Marguerite tilted her head and smiled up at Jesse. "She's pretty out of it. I'll help you get her into a wheelchair."

"Thanks," Jesse said. "I'd appreciate that."

Once they'd wheeled her to the door, Marguerite stopped. She positioned herself so she was blocking the exit.

"Is there a problem?" Jesse asked, wondering if Allison had called her and given her a head's up.

"I was wondering," Marguerite said, tossing her dark hair over her shoulder, if you needed any help getting her to the lab. I'd be happy to go with you. The aides can watch the other patients for a few minutes."

"Thanks for the offer but Dr. Aiken wants this project to be very hush-hush. You know how he can be."

Marguerite nodded. "I sure do."

"By the way," Jesse said, "he also wants all of Kendra's meds put on hold until further notice."

"All of them?"

"It's part of the new project."

"Okay. I'll just call him for orders."

"No need to bother him. Dr. Aiken said you could write it as a telephone order and he'll sign it in the morning."

"Well, it's not good nursing practice, but I'll do it just this once since *you* asked me to."

Marguerite looked Jesse up and down as she moved out of his way. He was handsome. Probably had a great income. She needed a distraction in her life. No, not a distraction. A husband. Her kids needed a father. She was tired. She took a notepad and pen from a pocket in her scrubs and wrote quickly, handing the note to Jesse.

"That's my cell number. Call me if you want to get together sometime."

"Um, thanks."

"Just call the unit if you need help wheeling Kendra back from the lab."

"I'll be fine. This is going to take a couple of hours."

As Jesse left the unit, wheeling a sedated Kendra, he crumpled the paper into a ball and shoved it into his lab coat pocket, knowing he wouldn't call. Marguerite was a beautiful woman but he sensed a certain desperation about her that he didn't like. It reminded him of Cleo. It took a whole year and a temporary restraining order to get her out of his life. He laughed as he tried to tell himself he wasn't looking for a relationship. He knew his heart was already focused on someone.

Maddie ran toward Jesse and Kendra.

"Thank God you got her out of there. She looks completely

knocked out."

"Yes, she does. Remember, this is just a temporary kidnapping. We'll have to take her back in a couple of hours or the staff will become suspicious."

"She's not going back in there."

"It's okay. I had them hold all her medications."

"I don't care. She's staying with me."

"Then we have just a few hours to wrap this caper up, assuming no one on your unit notices you're missing."

"Not a problem," Maddie said, tapping her temple. "I'm already working on it."

They pushed Kendra down the deserted hallway, the squeak of the wheelchair making the only sound. They were about to turn the corner to head back to the lab when two psych aides almost walked right into them.

"Hey! Watch where you're going," the male psych aide said.

"Sorry," Jesse said, pushing the wheelchair faster. "Just going to do some testing."

Maddie stayed close to his side, linking her arm under his. She didn't look at the pair.

"Do you need some help?" asked the female psych aide. "It can be hard to manage two patients at a time."

"No, I've got it. This one's pretty sedated." He nodded at Maddie. "The one in the chair will be out for hours."

"If you're sure," the man said smiling.

"I'm sure. Go on and take you're break."

The man and woman smiled at each other. The woman blushed and giggled softly. They continued on their way, hand in hand. Maddie, Jesse and Kendra continued the other way down the hall.

Suddenly, Kendra opened her eyes and asked in a mildly slurred voice, "Is the coast clear now?"

"Kendra!" Maddie said, a little too loudly. "You're awake. Are you okay?"

Jesse came around to the front of the wheelchair and crouched down. Kendra looked up at her godmother for guidance.

"This is Jesse," Maddie said. "It's safe. He's helping us."

"How can you be awake?" Jesse asked. "You should still be out cold on the dose of Protocol Drug #8 you're on. Not to mention the sleeping pill they gave you."

Kendra sat up straighter in the wheelchair. "If you look really out of it they only give you half a dose or sometimes they skip a dose. I cheek the pills when I can, too. Otherwise I'd be like some of the other kids here – totally spaced out." She rubbed her eyes. "What kind of medicine is this anyway?"

Jesse said, "It's designed to-"

"It's like a really strong sleeping pill," Maddie said. "It's too strong for you to be taking."

"I was right. I told Mother I shouldn't be taking it." Kendra yawned loudly.

Jesse stood up and said, "We better get into my lab before someone sees us."

He went ahead and held the door open for them while Maddie wheeled Kendra to the temporary safety of the laboratory. They were about to help Kendra to one of the comfortable chairs when they heard a toilet flush.

Jesse looked toward the far wall. The door to the bathroom was opening.

"Is it him?" Maddie whispered. "Is it Dr. Aiken?"

"Shhh. Sit beside Kendra and act sleepy," Jesse said. "I'll

think of something."

They watched in silence as a grey-haired man in blue coveralls stepped out of the bathroom, wheeling an industrial bucket and mop. He turned and saw the young women staring at him like deer caught in the headlights.

Jesse smiled. "HI there, Barney. You have the graveyard shift this week?"

"Uh-huh," Barney said, walking toward the trio. "You doing some kind of experiment in here? I'll be glad to help if you need."

"Thanks," Jesse said, "but I don't need any help. This is a very secretive project. We don't want this getting out to the unit staff. I know I can trust you not to say anything. Dr. Aiken can trust you, right?"

Barney put his hand on his heart and held his mop at his side. "I won't say a word."

"Don't worry about cleaning the rest of the lab tonight. You can just head on out."

Barney said, "You won't tell that I didn't finish the job?"

"Not a chance," Jesse said. "In fact, I'll be glad to tell your boss what a good job you're doing and how dependable you are."

"Hey, thanks," Barney said, wheeling his tools of the trade toward the exit.

"That was close," Maddie said as the lab door swung shut.

"We were lucky," Jesse said, "but our luck won't hold out forever."

They were all seated in office chairs now. Kendra's eyes were only half opened.

"Are you going to be able to stay awake to help us," Maddie asked.

"I'm all right," Kendra said. "Just groggy again. It comes and goes. Though I'm not sure what I can do to help."

Jesse pulled his chair closer to her, leaned forward and said, "You can start by telling us exactly what's been happening to you here. Start from when you were first brought onto A.C.U. #3."

"It didn't go so bad at first." Kendra's words came out slowly. "They gave me a tour of the unit and showed me my room. I was a bit freaked when I saw it had no door. They said they have to keep an eye on us. Other than that, the place looked great."

"Then it's set up just like my unit," Maddie said.

"At least the bathroom has a door," Kendra continued, "even if it doesn't lock."

"What happened next?" Jesse asked.

"They gave me some pills and I slept for ages. That was fine by me. I didn't ever want to wake up."

"Are you still having thoughts of killing yourself?" Maddie asked.

"No way. I swear. It's just the opposite now. After what I've seen and heard, I feel like I'm fighting for my life. I don't want any medicine. I don't want to have one of those awful seizures like those other kids." Kendra's eyes opened wide. "I saw Alicia die." She started to sob.

"Then it is true," Jesse said, cringing. "There's been at least one fatality." He put his head in his hands.

Maddie cradled Kendra in her arms. "I'm so sorry you had to witness that. Don't worry, Kendra. We're going to figure out exactly what's going on. We're going to get you out of here. We're all going to get out of here."

"Can't you just let us out?" Kendra asked Jesse.

"I could," he said, "but I don't think you'd be safe that way."

"What do you mean?" Kendra's muscles stiffened.

"Just trust us," Maddie said. "It's for our own good not to leave right this second. We've got to do it the right way so that we are totally in the clear."

"What else can you tell us, Kendra?" Jesse asked.

"Well, Mother came to visit me the second evening I was here and she wanted to talk to Dr. Aiken. They wouldn't let her. She was worried about the gel and wire thing they did to me."

Maddie said, "Helen told me about that. Something about measuring brain wave activity. An EEG."

Jesse said, "Right. An EEG does measure brain wave activity. It doesn't do anything to the patient. Don't worry, Kendra. That didn't harm you. Anything else?"

"In the morning, they were giving shots to all of us. One boy started screaming. They held him down and he was struggling to get away. Four more psych aides came onto the unit and they held him so he couldn't move while the nurse gave him a shot in his butt. When it was my turn, I told them I didn't want a shot. I said I'd take a pill. I was really polite about it. The nurse said I had to take it or they'd hold me down, too. Are they allowed to do that?"

"Only under certain circumstances," Jesse said. "If a patient is out of control. If they might hurt themselves or other people."

"But I wasn't doing anything. Just asking them not to shoot me full of drugs."

"The same thing happened to me," Maddie said. "So you got that shot?"

"Yes. I was really pissed about it."

"How come you seemed so alert in the dining hall?"

"I caught on fast. I overheard one of the nurses telling a psych aide that she was going to hold the next injection on another patient, Adam, because he looked overly sedated. I acted like I was totally out of it when they came to check me. They tried to wake me up. They smacked my hands, ran something along my foot and stuck a flashlight in my eyes. It just about killed me not to react. But they bought it. I got out of the next shot. After dinner a doctor came to see me."

"Dr. Aiken?" Maddie asked.

"No. I'd remember him. He has those creepy mismatched eyes. It was someone else. He woke me up. I think he might have known I was faking it. He told me he was lowering the dose of my medicine. The nurse came in the room with a shot but it was only half full this time."

"So did you sleep through the night?" Jesse asked.

"I was sleeping off and on until I heard Alicia." Kendra welled up with tears. She told them the details of the girl's seizure. "Afterwards, she was stiff. They wheeled her out on the stretcher. I've never seen someone die before."

Maddie hugged Kendra tightly. "That's not going to happen to you."

Jesse said, "Are you sure she was dead?"

Both females gave him a hard stare.

"How could you even ask that?" Maddie demanded.

"Well, most people don't die from a seizure. Even grand mal seizures. Even status epilepticus is treatable."

"I don't know what you're talking about but I know she was dead," Kendra said, sniffling.

"What makes you so sure," Jesse asked. He received a jab in the ribs from Maddie.

"Yesterday they took me and Adam to a group therapy session with the long term kids."

"Why the two of you?" Maddie asked.

"The other kids were too out of it. On the long term unit,

Adam told me that Alicia was definitely dead. He said they took her to the morgue in the basement."

"Is there a morgue here?" Maddie asked.

"Not that I'm aware of," Jesse said. "Then again, I'm learning new things every minute."

"There were two other patients who died. David had his massive seizure on the day I was admitted. Adam told me about Shane who died the week before. Adam thinks they're killing them on purpose because they know something."

"Adam's quite a source of information," Maddie said.

"Don't even think about it," Jesse said. "Sneaking one patient out was difficult enough."

"All right. Maybe we can come back and talk to him later," Maddie said. "Anything else, Kendra?"

"Dr. Aiken came in to see me at bedtime. He said I'll be moving to Long Term in the morning and I have to stay there a month. I don't want to go there. The kids there are strange.

"Strange how?"

"They're awake, but they talk in weird voices. Like robots. Their faces are frozen. They don't smile or frown. Well, I know why they don't smile. Shit, maybe their aliens."

"I doubt it," Maddie said, smiling. "Haven't you noticed these patients, Jesse?"

"I don't have a lot of patient contact. I'm pretty isolated here," he said. "Kendra, did they all sound the same? Monotone?"

"Yes," Kendra said. "Except for one kid. He talked normally and looked normal, too."

"Is his name Clarence?"

"Yeah! How did you know?"

"One of Victor's rare successes. Using his definition of success, that is. Clarence, I have met. He has dodged all the side effects of Protocol Drug #8. He's calm, well behaved and he can't wait to get back to school. He was a D and F student who skipped classes, smoked pot and beat up his younger brother on a daily basis. Victor has been raving about how he has cured Clarence."

"Adam says that once you go to an L.T. unit you never get out, unless you're like Clarence," Kendra said. "Most kids are there for ages and the staff make them have seizures until they die. He said there's a cemetery out back."

Maddie jumped up. "That's it. I'm calling the police now."

"Wait," Jesse said. "We don't know if the stories about a morgue and a cemetery are true or just the overactive imagination of a bored teenage boy trying to impress a pretty, young girl."

"We're not talking about typical pick-up lines or exaggerated heroics here. Three dead teens, units full of zombies, people being experimented on without their consent. I think we have enough to go on," Maddie said.

"I agree that we have enough circumstantial evidence to go on but I don't want to act irrationally. We'll be of no help to anyone if we get caught with no hard evidence. The authorities won't take it seriously and that will leave us at Victor's mercy. Is that something either one of you is prepared to face?"

"Fine. I'll hold off for the moment," Maddie said. "But the second we have something tangible, I'm calling 911. We are going to put a stop to this maniac before one more innocent person is harmed."

CHAPTER 13

"We're going to need more help to accomplish this," Maddie said.

"Who else can we trust?" Jesse asked.

"Adam?" Kendra suggested.

"No, we need an insider. A staff member. I know just the person." Maddie told them about Amy. "It's worth taking the chance to see if she'll help us."

Jesse stood up and went to a phone on a counter beside the sink. He called over to Amy's unit and asked her to come to the lab immediately. When Amy arrived, she saw both Maddie and Kendra standing beside Jesse.

"Madison," she said. "What are you doing in the lab? How did you get off the unit? Thanks for finding her. I don't think we need to report this as an escape attempt since she didn't leave the building. Do you agree, Jesse?"

Jesse, Maddie and Kendra laughed.

"It's okay," Maddie said. "Jesse's on our side. And this is Kendra, my goddaughter." Maddie caught Amy up on all the new information.

Afterwards, Amy slumped into a chair. "I can't believe it," Amy said, sobbing quietly. "Or maybe I just didn't want to believe it. I really thought Shane's death was unavoidable. Dr. Aiken had prepared us for that outcome. Shane has suffered from a seizure disorder since early childhood and adding Protocol Drug #8 to his medications made chances of a seizure all that much higher, even though he was on anticonvulsant medication. Both Dr. Aiken and the state case worker thought the benefits of taking it outweighed the negatives since Shane was so severely troubled." Amy shook her head. "I had a feeling something was up but I didn't do anything about looking into it."

"Here's your chance," Maddie said. "Can you tell us anything else?"

"A lot of psychiatric patients also have seizure disorders. The medications they take can lower their seizure threshold and make them more prone to having one. But generally, these are minor to moderate seizures that can be easily managed and treated. When the severe seizures started with the administration of Protocol Drug #8, the staff were upset. Dr. Aiken held a nursing meeting. We wanted to treat them with IV medication, a typical procedure for severe seizures. He said we were dealing with catastrophic cases now, that if we tried to revive them they would have very little brain function left and no quality of life whatsoever. He said it was humane to let them go. He wrote DNR orders. Do not resuscitate. It sounded a little more ethical the way he explained it. Less so after a girl died last night."

"Alicia," Kendra said quietly, reaching out to hold Amy's hand.

Jesse nodded. "What will happen to Alicia's body now?"

The psych aides take the patient to an exam room and the nurse takes care of preparing the body," Amu said. "From there, Dr. Aiken takes care of things. He contacts the family and makes the arrangements."

"No one else calls the parents or guardians first?" Maddie asked.

"Oh no. That's a doctor's job and Dr. Aiken prefers to handle that himself."

"What funeral home does he use?" Jesse asked.

"I have no idea," Amy said. "Probably whatever one the family requests. Does it matter?"

"It could be important information to our case," Jesse said. "What have the funerals been like?"

"There's a rule that staff cannot attend patients' funerals so they don't give us any further information about the details. We don't get told about what happens to patients after discharge either. It's part of Dr. Aiken's strict definition of the therapeutic relationship. We're here to work with the patients, not become friends with them or their families. I always wonder. It's hard not knowing how people are doing after they leave here but maybe it's for the best. It prevents us from getting to attached to people while they're here, knowing they're going to leave. Especially the children."

"I'm curious," Maddie said. "Wouldn't even one death in a hospital being highly publicized? There's been at least three here."

"Dr. Aiken manages to keep them quiet," Amy said.

"The staff don't talk?" Maddie asked.

"Among ourselves we do. All employees sign a strict confidentiality agreement. We can't discuss anything about the facility, it's practices or the patients outside of these walls. Not with anyone. If we do, there are legal repercussions on top of losing your job. When I was first recruited down here, I thought the place was beautiful. A setting where real healing could take place. Once I got here, I realized it's run more like a...well, not quite like a prison. More like a secret government project or something. I've always heard that about the U.S government."

"Could that be it?" Maddie asked Jesse. "Is Victor a pawn himself involved in a government experiment?

Jesse snickered. "I doubt that. Victor is a willing participant in whatever is happening here."

"Has a family ever filed a lawsuit for wrongful death of a patient?" Maddie asked.

"Not that I've heard of," Amy said.

Jesse shook his head.

"I have a question," Kendra said. "Does anyone ever get the hell out of here and go back to a normal life?"

"Sure," Amy said. "I've discharged adults and kids back to their families. There are also some runaways but I don't suppose they run to any sort of normal life."

"Runaways" Jesse fanned his arms out. "I've never hear of that. This place is a fortress."

"Do you live under a rock, Jesse? Or rather work under one?" Maddie asked. "There's a lot going on in your own place of work that you are totally unaware of."

"Don't attack him," Amy told her. "Ever heard of the Masons?"

"Sure. Aren't they that secret organization with mysterious information that they won't share with the rest of the world? They do a lot of good for the community though, too."

"Uh huh. Trying to find out things in Aiken's Haven is like trying to find out the secrets of the Masons. Except I don't think Dr. Aiken is doing any good for the community."

"Not anymore," Jesse said. "Tell us about the runaways."

"I could understand a few escapes. These kids are pretty smart and have time on their hands. Maybe a patient catches an open door while someone's exiting. That sort of thing. But there's actually a lot of patient's on the A.W.O.L. list. More than I would have expected. I pulled it up by accident once when I was trying to pull up a patient's history and physical. I'm not sure how I did it and I'm not sure I could do it again."

"This sounds fishy," Maddie said.

"It sure does," Jesse said. "Amy, do you think you could try to get into that A.W.O.L file again?"

"I guess it can't hurt to try." Amy went over to a computer terminal on the lab counter and started typing away on the keyboard.

Maddie glance at Jesse and said, "Isn't this dangerous? You mentioned before that Dr. Aiken can access who logs onto the computer and what they look at."

"At this point," Jesse said, "I have to admit that's the least of out worries. He'll be finding out what we're up to one way or another. It's just a matter of time."

Jesse, Maddie and Kendra huddled around Amy as she keyed in various numbers and letters.

"I think I've managed to screw up the same way I did last time," Amy said.

"Meaning?" Maddie asked.

"Meaning," Amy said, "That I've got it."

The monitor flashed then showed the words, *Access Denied. Enter Password.*

"What? There wasn't a password on it before," Amy said.

"Guess he learned from your last visit to the site," Jesse said.

The group suggested a number of passwords but none of them seemed right. Amy was afraid to try anything in the event a wrong attempt would kick her out.

Jesse frowned, stared up at the ceiling, then quietly said, "I know what it is. Type in D-A-R-L-E-N-E."

"Who's Darlene?" Kendra asked.

"Victor's mother," Jesse said.

"He's not going to use something so obvious," Maddie said.

Suddenly the screen came to life. Rows and rows of numbers, names and dates.

"Then again, maybe an obsession with your mother drives you to do dumb things," Maddie said. She took in the contents of the screen. "Look at the custody column."

"Almost all the A.W.O.L. patients are in the state's custody," Amy said. "They probably have more reason to run away."

"What's this last row? A-1, A-2. What does that mean?" Jesse asked.

Kendra let out a strangled cry. "Look at the heading."

"Plot," Jesse said.

"Oh my God," Maddie said. "Adam was right."

"Right about what?" Amy asked.

"Plot," Kendra said in a whisper, "means cemetery plot. Adam told me there was a cemetery on the grounds."

"This is way too simple," Jesse said. "Why would Victor be so careless with data like this?"

"He wasn't careless," Maddie said. "We broke into his records. Besides, he's such a narcissistic megalomaniac, he probably doesn't think he's doing anything wrong."

"Look who's the psychiatrist now," Jesse said.

"She's right about the diagnosis," Amy said.

"He's also got all of us so scared or threatened, he probably thinks no one can touch him," Jesse said.

Amy was scrolling down the list when she gasped. "Christopher Talbot. Plot C-8."

"What about him?" Jesse asked.

It was hard to hear Amy with her hand over her mouth. "I was surprised to hear he'd run away. He just wasn't the type. Christopher was quiet, depressed and followed the rules to the letter. Are you absolutely sure this list means what you say it does?"

"I'm afraid so," Maddie said. "This A.W.O.L. list is actually a list of patients who died from receiving Protocol Drug #8."

A tear rolled down Amy's cheek. Kendra was sniffling. Maddie bit her lower lip. Jesse once again let his head fall into his hands in shame.

Then Jesse, looked up at the computer screen. He scrolled down the list of names. "This thing scrolls down for several screens. I can't believe there's been that many deaths and we haven't heard about it." He shook his head. "It's impossible. You're all jumping to conclusions."

Maddie looked at the monitor. "Some of these are from years ago. Are you sure the, what did you call them, catastrophic seizures only started with Protocol Drug #8? Maybe Victor did human testing with earlier versions, or with other drugs too?"

"I would have known about it," Jesse said.

"Like you knew about everything else going on around here?" Maddie said.

"Ouch," Jesse said. "You do have a point though. Someone somewhere at some time would have noticed all these missing children."

"Do you know how many missing children are listed with state and federal agencies at any given time? This is probably nothing, Maddie said.

"But all from one place? It would draw attention," Jesse said.

"Attention from who? Not their parents. They don't have any. Not their state workers who no longer have to follow their case and are overworked with huge caseloads."

Jesse nodded an agreement. "Sad but true. What about insurance reviews or outcome studies?"

Amy said, "State kids would be covered by state assistance. It's a lump sum payment. No insurance reviews. Dr. Aiken handles all the outcome studies himself. I'm surprised that man even has time to sleep."

"I'm not sure he does," Jesse said. "Is it possible he's reporting false findings in his research studies publications?"

"If he's capable of murdering children, and yes, that's what it is, I think a few false research papers wouldn't tear at his conscience. If he has one," Maddie said, as she got up and started pacing. "I don't know how he's kept a lid on this for so long but you're in denial if you don't think we've hit the jackpot here in terms of incriminating evidence."

"We can't provide enough proof to warrant a police investigation," Jesse said.

"I doubt we'll have any trouble once we tell them to dig around for a graveyard full of kids falsely listed as runaways. We'll get your proof," Maddie said. "I think we need one more assistant to pull it off. Who else in this place can we trust? Any ideas?"

"I have one," Jesse said.

He directed the group to gather on the other side of the lab where the section of lights was turned off. He picked up the phone and dialed the nursing statin on Adolescent A.C.U. #3.

"Marguerite," he said. "It's Jesse from the lab. I was hoping you'd answer."

Jesse could almost hear her smile as she said, "I knew you'd be calling. Need help in the lab after all?"

"I do. Can you come over?"

Within minutes, Marguerite was stepping into the lab, running her fingers through her silky hair. Her lips were pouty, her eyes dancing.

"I'm glad you came," Jesse said.

"Me, too." Marguerite flashed a seductive smile.

"I was hoping you could help me with something." Jesse gazed into her eyes.

"Anything," she said, batting her eyelids.

"Before I fill you in, I need to let you know there's other people involved."

"Other people?" Marguerite took a step backward. "I'm not into that kind of thing."

"I mean there are other people helping me with this project. It would be easier if we explained it to you as a group."

Marguerite looked around the lab. Jesse flipped the switch to the back lighting, instantly exposing the three other women.

"Kendra?" Marguerite asked. "Amy? What's going on? Who's that?" She nodded to Maddie.

Amy filled Marguerite in on all the details. Marguerite took it all in without a word, without a question. She looked at each one of them.

"So will you help us?" Jesse asked.

"I don't think so. I don't know how I could help anyway." Marguerite started to walk out of the lab.

"Wait!" Kendra said. Everyone turned to look at her. She had been silent for so long now. "Marguerite, do you really want to see me end up dead?"

"Of course not," Marguerite said. "This all sounds a little far-fetched to me. Alicia had a seizure disorder. With the medication mixed in, it turned fatal. That's what happened. It's sad but it couldn't have been prevented."

Amy said, "That's what I've been telling myself for a while but it's not true. Alicia could still be alive. Same with Shane and..."

"Stop it," Marguerite said. "I don't want to hear any more of this."

"What are you going to do. Go back to the unit? Pretend you don't know about any of this? Are you comfortable injecting patients with potentially lethal medication?"

"No. This was an isolated, rare incident. I think you're all blowing this out of proportion. I can't risk losing my job on some crazy theory. I have two children to support on my own. I don't want to get involved."

"You're already involved," Maddie said. "So is every person who works here. The way things are going, no one around here will have a job much longer. No one should have a job here much longer."

"It's just that...."

"You're scared," Maddie said. "We're all scared. But there's no turning back now."

"It's not just that."

"You've got a lot to lose," Amy chimed in. "I realize that. But what about Kendra and the other patients. Their lives are at risk."

"Well...."

"I promise to give you an easy task," Maddie said, "and I'll take the blame for anything you do."

Jesse said, "Maddie, I think this would be a good time to fill us in on your plan of how we are going to collect the evidence tonight. We don't have much time."

Standing around the stainless steel counters, Maddie outlined her idea and gave everyone a particular assignment.

"Let's get moving," Jesse said. "Maddie and Kendra need to get back to their units."

"What if we don't get all this done by change of shift at seven a.m.?" Marguerite asked. "Who will protect you two?"

"It won't take that long," Maddie said.

"What if it does?" Jesse said.

"Not all of the morning nurses are full time staff. We have two call-in nurses on schedule in the morning. I'll phone one of the call-in day nurses and tell her that the Director of Nursing said to cancel her shift," Amy said. "When she doesn't show up, I'll offer to stay overtime."

"What if they call another nurse in?" Maddie asked.

"It's hard to get anyone at the last minute. They'll be so happy that I offered to cover, they won't care that it's overtime pay for me."

"That buys us more time if we need it," Jesse said. "unless Victor catches onto us first."

"Hopefully, we won't need any more time," Maddie said. "Just in case, Amy, can you make it so you are covering Kendra's unit?"

"What about you?" Kendra asked Maddie.

"I can take care of myself," Maddie said. "Besides, if we hurry, we'll be done long before the day shift come on."

Jesse and Marguerite wheeled Kendra back to her unit. Amy and Maddie walked back toward theirs. As Amy opened the door to the unit, Maddie hung onto her arm and began shuffling awkwardly. The two psych aides immediately stood up.

"What's going on?" Edgar said, throwing his hand of cards down on the desk.

"What do you mean?" Amy replied, inching Maddie toward her room.

"Where did she go?" Billy asked while peeking at his partner's hand.

"Yeah, how did she get off the unit?" Edgar asked.

"Very funny," Amy said.

The men looked at each other quizzically.

"Remember," Amy said, helping Maddie into bed. "I told you I was taking her for another walk. The muscle cramps in her legs are worsening. They're a side effect of her medication. Any of this ring a bell? Hello?"

The psych aides said nothing.

"What," Amy said, "were you two asleep on the job when I was talking to you?"

"Oh now I remember," Edgar said. "You did tell us." He winked at Billy.

Billy nodded. "Sure. Leg cramps."

"Good," Amy said. "Now let me get this patient tucked in."

CHAPTER 14

Amy enclosed herself in the tiny medication room located between two of the patient rooms. She opened the top portion of the Dutch door so she could keep an eye on Edgar and Billy to ensure they weren't eavesdropping. Amy pulled a small, red binder down from a shelf. The front of it read, *Nursing Staff Phone Numbers – Confidential.* She turned on the computer and pulled up the centralized schedule for the upcoming day shift. There were two call-in nurses listed. One was listed working on a Long Term unit and one was listed working on Adolescent A.C.U. #3. Amy looked up the second nurse's number and dialed. After three rings, a sleepy voice answered.

"Hi, Jenny. It's Amy from Aiken's Haven. Sorry for calling so early. I know you're schedule to work this morning but the D.O.N. asked me to call and cancel you for today. We're over-staffed."

"But I need to work," Jenny said, sounding more awake. "I've hardly worked this week. Isn't there another call-in nurse you could cancel. It must be someone else's turn."

"Everyone else if full time on day shift. You're the only one that can be taken off the roster." Amy cringed, feeling bad for lying to the woman.

"I heard we got busy this weekend."

"Unexpected discharges. Sorry," Amy said.

Jenny sighed. "I really need to work."

"Hold on a minute, Jenny. Someone's trying to tell me something."

Amy blocked the receiver, giving herself a minute to think. Then, she went back on the line. "Jenny, you don't have to worry. I guess I misunderstood the D.O.N. It's a paid day off you're getting."

"Is this some kind of a joke?"

"Not at all. It's part of a new morale improvement plan. If the hospital has to cancel a call-in staff within four hours of the starting time, you still get paid for the shift."

"Really? I haven't heard about this."

"They just started it this week."

"Has anyone been called off like this yet?"

"Nope. You're the first lucky one. Now go back to sleep and enjoy your day."

"Okay, I guess. Seems too good to be true."

It is, Amy thought, but instead she said, "Bye Jenny," and hung up before the other nurse could voice any other protests.

Amy felt guilty about deceiving her colleague, especially since she was playing around with her income and reputation. However, if things went as planned, no one would be earning wages form this place beyond this morning.

Jesse looked at the A.W.O.L. list on the computer screen. He pressed the print icon and waited. Nothing happened. He tried again and got no response. He tried ctrl + P. Copy, paste. Nothing. Jesse sighed heavily and rubbed his eyes. Sitting back in his chair, he stared at the list until the letters and numbers fused together in his vision. Then he smiled and began furiously pecking at the keyboard. Victor had blocked the capacity to print this material but Jesse knew a way to deal with that. It was simple now that he had Victor's password. He compiled the data in a new format, adding in his own data, which enabled him to print it. Cross-referencing his files with the A.W.O.L list, he found that all the patients noted as missing had taken some version of Protocol Drug #8. Jesse closed his eyes.

"I've been developing a death serum."

On Adolescent A.C.U. #2, the nurse, Allison was still pondering what Jesse was really up to. It was bothering her. She told her psych aides that she was taking a short break over on the next unit. Marguerite watched Allison come onto the unit. Jesse had warned her to keep up her guard.

"Hi," Allison said, "Do you have a minute to talk?"

"Sure. It's a quiet night," Marguerite said.

"Never say the Q word," Allison joked.

"Oops," Marguerite said, laughing. "Too late. Have a seat." She pointed to a chair in the nursing station.

"Not out here," Allison said, glancing at the psych aides who were typing their patient rounding notes into desktop computers. "In the medication room. This is confidential."

The two nurses squeezed into the tiny room and Allison explained her concern about Jesse's actions.

"It seems a little odd. Do you think I should call Dr. Aiken?" Allison asked.

"What for?" Marguerite asked, trying to sound nonchalant.

"It seems like he's up to something," Allison said. "I don't know exactly how to explain it."

"Don't you think he was acting strange. He came over to your unit after mine, right?"

"Right. But no, I didn't think he was acting strange." Marguerite tried hard to maintain eye contact.

"I still think I should make the call."

Marguerite patted Allison's shoulder. "Think about it. What are you going to do? Wake up the Medical Director and C.E.O. of the hospital and tell him you think that his right hand man, who is also his best friend, just might be up to something but you're not sure."

"I guess that does sound pretty lame."

"I wouldn't want to be on the other end of that conversation with Dr. Aiken. Especially in the middle of the night. When you woke him up."

"I see you're point. But I still feel like I should do something."

"Why don't you just pass it on to the day nurse relieving you and she can follow up on it."

"I'm not sure," Allison said. "I'm not really comfortable leaving it until morning."

"Has anything else happened besides this one incident?"

"No," Allison said, looking square at Marguerite.

"I haven't noticed anything either. I tell you what. I'll call the other nurses on duty and see if they have any suspicious events going on. I'll let you know if I hear anything."

"I can call them," Allison said.

"You can," Marguerite said, "but since I'm assigned as Hospital Charge Nurse tonight, it might be better coming from me. It might sound weird coming from you."

"True. Should I fill out an incident report?" Allison asked.

"Good idea," Marguerite said. "Do a paper one. That way we can keep it confidential. It doesn't have to go through the hospital computer system and everyone doesn't have to know about it. We don't want to make Dr. Aiken mad. But this way, we've got it documented in writing. Just hand it in to me at the end of the shift."

"That's a smart idea," Allison said. "Thanks. I better head back to my unit now. Call me if the other nurses say anything."

"Promise," Marguerite said, letting out a slow breath as she watched Allison leave the unit.

Back on her own unit, Allison sat at the nursing desk, staring a patient's chart on the computer monitor, not reading a word.

"What's wrong?" one of the psych aides asked, scooting her chair closer to the nurse.

"Nothing," Allison said.

"We've worked together for a year. I think I know when something's bothering you."

"I'm just not sure about something, Lavonne."

"Maybe talking it out will help," Lavonne said.

Tony, the other psych aide looked up from his monitor. "Girl talk huh? I'm out of here. Is it okay if I take a break?"

"Fine," Allison said, swiveling her chair toward Lavonne. She shared her concerns about Jesse and her urge to call Dr. Aiken.

"If you call the doc, won't you be bypassing the proper chain of command?" Lavonne asked.

"Marguerite is the Hospital Charge Nurse tonight. I reported it to her but she doesn't seem worried at all about it. I don't think she's going to do anything about it."

"Well, it sounds like you've done your duty," Lavonne said. "It's up to her to follow through or not."

"What if no one reports it and something terrible happens?"

"What's going to happen?"

"I don't know. I just have a bad feeling."

"Girl, you're paranoid. You worry too much."

"No. Something's not right. I feel it. I just can't pinpoint what's wrong."

"You don't have to. It's Marguerite's responsibility now. You stress way too much."

"I guess," Allison said.

"Pass the buck, that's my motto," Lavonne said. "Once you report something to the higher ups, it's on them to deal with it. You're free and clear. Let it go. Move on."

"I still feel obligated to do something."

"Why do you want to make trouble for yourself?" Lavonne asked. "It isn't going to win you any points by going over Marguerite's head, not to mention the attending doctor's. Did you think of that?"

"That's true," Allison admitted. "But I have to do what's right to protect the patients, don't I? Isn't it my responsibility to make sure the patients are safe?"

"Yes," Lavonne said, "and could you protect the rest of the world while you're at it?"

Allison laughed. "I'm going overboard again?"

Lavonne smiled. "A little. Marguerite will follow up on it. It's probably nothing. Just take care of the patients here on the unit and stop worrying yourself to death."

"You're probably right," Allison said. "I guess I'll go prepare the morning medications."

In her medication room, Allison locked herself in and sat down on the one stool. It was still nagging at her. Marguerite was right. Lavonne was right. Allison stood up and looked at the large unit that housed the patient medications. Instead of sorting the doses into the patient bins, however, she found herself picking up the phone receiver. From memory, she dialed Dr. Aiken's cell number.

Victor got comfortable in his brown, leather recliner and looked at the blaze he'd just created in the stone fireplace in his living room. He loved to watch the flames delicately lick the timber, eating away at it with such a beautifully destructive hunger. He was glad the day was over. Too many thought s of the past had plagued him. Tomorrow, he's concentrate on the future. Smiling, he thought of his new facilities. He really had made something special and his empire was only beginning. And he'd done it all himself. Sure his adoptive father had helped financially but Victor was certain he'd have managed on his own just the same. Unable to stop himself, thoughts of his placement in foster care filled his mind.

Victor had been so sick of Toloucan Boys Ranch by the time he was finally dragged back into the same office he'd been in when he was first admitted to the crazy place. He walked over to the window. They had long ago replaced the glass he'd broken with the stapler. Now it had metal bars across it. Inside and out. Just like the bars in their cottage. Olivia Garvin's stubby fingers were wrapped around the phone. She was breathing loudly and looked ready to explode. Victor was amazed she still worked there. He thought Mario and Adrianna were the only lifers.

Olivia's face was quite red. As she hung up the phone, she was out of breath. "This is ridiculous," she said, glaring at Victor.

"What is? Am I going home?" Victor already knew in his heart that was not why he'd been called there. He had only seen Mom twice in all his time there and she hadn't called since his first week there.

"Going home?" Olivia laughed loudly, her double chin bouncing up and down. "I don't think so. You're going into foster care."

"Foster care? With who? Why?"

"Why is a good question," Olivia said. "After all the trouble you've caused, I don't know why anyone would want you."

"Does my Mom know?"

"She signed over custody of you to the state months ago. We aren't required to notify her."

"But did you?" Victor wanted to punch Olivia in the face.

"I doubt she'd care." Olivia picked up a stack of folders from her desk. "Your foster father will be picking you up within the hour. We've got some paper work to do before he gets here."

"In an hour? Why didn't anyone tell me about this? Who are these people? Why did they pick me? Can I call my Mom?"

"Mr. and Mrs. Wade Russell. Typical WASPs. Very rich. You don't deserve them." Olivia did not look Victor in the eye.

"It was your nickname, *Doc,* that got Mr. Russell's attention. He wanted to take in a smart, teenaged boy. He asked to look at your report cards. I told him you probably cheated to get those marks. He wanted you anyway. Mr. Russell has two daughters. Guess he thinks you'll be the son he never had. Boy, will he be disappointed."

Victor clenched his fists but kept his arms down at his sides. Thinking about escaping this place helped him calm down. He remained still and silent in his chair.

Olivia took a brief phone call. "Mr. Russell is here. Sit up straight." She shook her head. "With that healed over broken nose and those silly eyes, you're not much to look at. Try to look smart. That's what's going to get us rid of you. Hopefully for good. Unless you screw it up and they ship you back here. We should have a no return policy. I know I'll be seeing you back here very soon." She sounded almost hopeful.

Victor clenched his jaw shut as she clomped out of the room

to meet Mr. Russell in the lobby. When they returned, Mr. Russell shook Victor's hand as Olivia introduced them. He had a firm grip. Everything about Mr. Russell looked strong. Piercing grey eyes, jet black hair and a muscular build on his six-foot frame.

The paperwork didn't take as long as Olivia had made it sound. By 10:00 that morning, Victor was leaving Toloucan for good. He hoped. Olivia made it clear to Mr. Russell that he could bring Victor back at any time if things did not work out. Victor felt like a used car.

As he walked with this man who was now his foster father toward his large, foreign car, Victor was determined to make the situation work to his favor. He wasn't sure what he was getting into but it had to be better than the hellhole he was leaving.

Mr. Russell opened the front passenger door and Victor slid quickly onto the luxurious, crushed velvet seat. It felt like sitting in a living room recliner. He had sat on nothing but hard, plastic chairs for what seemed like an eternity. He didn't know exactly what type of car this was, but he knew it was European and he knew wealth when he saw it. The fancy car, the expensive suit, the gold cuff links. Olivia was right. Mr. Wade Russell had money. Maybe he was about to have money, too. If he didn't like it at the Russell's, he had picked up some tips from the other guys at Toloucan. He could fence stolen goods easy enough. Hell, he'd be living in the same house as the stuff so stealing would be the simple part. With enough cash, he could hitchhike to Philly or maybe New York and get a place of his own. A crummy place. But it would be his own.

They rode in silence for the first five minutes while Victor was planning his future getaway. Then it occurred to him that he might have it better staying at the Russell's. He'd have the best of everything. Of course, that wouldn't matter if Mr. Russell turned out to be just a high class version of Mario. Victor needed to find out this man's reason for choosing him.

"Sir? I appreciate you taking me into your home." Victor hoped he sounded sincere.

You are very welcome," Mr. Russell said in his deep voice. He looked over and smiled. "Or do you prefer *Doc?* I hear that is what your friends call you."

"Either is fine." Victor hated the nickname. It reminded him of all the times his brains got him beaten up. Except for his schoolwork, he'd tried to dumb it down when hanging out with the other guys. It was going to be good to be able to be smart out loud again.

"I hope you find our home satisfactory," Mr. Russell said. "I asked my wife to have a decorator fix up one of the guest rooms for you so it would feel like your own."

"Thank you." The man seemed nice but Victor still didn't know why he was chosen. "Sir? May I ask you a question?"

A chuckle escaped Mr. Russell's lips. "Why yes, my boy, what is it?"

"If it's not too personal, what made you and your wife want a foster child?" Victor stared out of the front windshield at the rolling hills and waited for the answer.

"Since you are the one we picked, I would say it is a fair question." Mr. Russell adjusted himself in his seat. He kept one hand on the steering wheel and put his other arm over the passenger seat headrest. "My wife and I have two beautiful daughters. Britany is 17 and Cassandra is 12. You are almost 15, correct? That will put you in the middle. We wanted more children but we cannot have any. We decided to look at adoption but my wife was not comfortable with a newborn. When I mentioned foster care, she agreed to a child closer in age to my girls. Does that answer your question?" He brought his arm back over, lowered his visor and reached over to lower Victor's as well.

"Yes, sir." But it didn't fully. He needed to know why he specifically was chose. "You and your wife wanted a boy this time?"

"I sure did," Mr. Russell said. "Do not get me wrong. I love my girls. But it would be nice to have another man around the house." He gave Victor a playful jab to the arm.

So it was he, not his wife, who wanted Victor. "What kind of boy were you looking for?"

"Someone just like you," Mr. Russell said. "Smart, handsome, rugged."

"What made you go to Toloucan, sir? What made you pick me out of all the others?"

"You are direct, my boy. I admire that." He smiled but kept his eyes on the road. "I will let you in on a secret. I was not always where I am today, President of Russell Industires, Inc., with a big house in the country and lots of material possessions. I grew up in a place similar to Toloucan. An orphanage actually."

Victory stared at him. "Really?" It was all he could manage.

"Yes, really. Then someone recognized my intellect and gave me a change to make something of myself. Just like I am giving you a chance."

"Sort of returning the favor."

"You are a sharp boy. But this is not a handout. Even though I received a helping hand, I worked hard to get where I am. I had the brains and the drive. I just needed the opportunity."

"So you're going to give me the opportunity now."

"Yes," Mr. Russel said, glancing over at Victor. "I hope you will make the most of it."

Around noon, after driving northwest the entire way, they pulled into a paved driveway, lined with majestic pine trees. Mr. Russell opened and closed the iron gates behind them with a handheld device from within the car. Victor couldn't see much of the heavily forested yard, but he noticed a white, brick wall extending from the sides of the gate that appeared to surround the property. As the foliage cleared and they pulled up to the house, he could see this was much more than just a nice place in the country. They drove onto the cobblestone turnaround and came to a stop in front of a white, marble staircase. As Mr. Russell got out of the car, so did Victor. After taking Victor's one suitcase out of the truck and handing it to him, a man in a black uniform came over, got in the driver's seat and drove toward a four car garage a few hundred yards away.

Mr. Russell put a hand on Victor's shoulder. He was about six inches taller. "Ready to go in?" he asked.

Victor looked up at him. "As ready as I'll ever be."

They marched up the stairs and through the double glass doors, trimmed in brass, that fronted the house.

"Whoa," Victor said, then clasped his hand to his mouth. "I mean, you have a lovely place here, sir."

Mr. Russell laughed heartily. "It is comfortable."

The front foyer was white marble from floor to ceiling. On either side were white marble hallways leading to unseen rooms. In front of them was a spectacular staircase, also in white marble and also trimmed in brass. Victor figured he could get several hundred bucks a piece on the lion heads topping the pillars at the end of the stairway. As he was adding up the value of the items he could see and imagining the value of the items he couldn't, a beautiful girl came into his vision, gracefully navigating the stairs.

"This is my daughter, Brittany. Brittany, this is Victor." Mr. Russel met the girl at the bottom of the stairs with a kiss on the cheek. "Or call him Doc. That is his nickname."

"Whatever," Brittany said in a flat tone, after making the briefest nod of her head.

"Brittany is starting college in the fall," Mr. Russell said, a proud smile on his face.

"You must be excited about that," Victor said, setting down his suitcase.

"Yeah," Brittany replied, studying her pink nail polish. "Real excited."

"Have you decided what you want to major in yet, my dear?" Mr. Russell asked.

"Father, I told you, I just want to have some fun my first year. I'll figure out something. Gees. Get off my case."

Mr. Russell's smile was fading but it returned quickly as a young girl bounded down the staircase. "This is Cassandra, my younger daughter. Cassandra, this is Victor."

"His nickname's Doc," Brittany said, rolling her eyes.

The girl caught her sister's look and imitated it, then looked back at Victor. "What's wrong with your eyes?"

"Cassandra," Mr. Russell's tone was stern.

"But they look funny, Daddy. They're two different colors."

"That is not polite, Sweetie," Mr. Russell said, then turned to Victor. "Cassandra is at the Hillcrest School right now but she will be attending junior high at Blakely in September."

Mr. Russell listed these schools as if Victor should know them. He nodded in what he thought was an approving manner.

"I'm on the Dean's list," Cassandra said.

"Congratulations. You must really like school," Victor said.

"Father," Brittany said. "I need your credit card. I've got some shopping to do."

"Can I come?" Cassandra asked.

"I guess." Brittany forced a loud yawn.

"Do you two not want to stay and help your foster brother

settle in?' Mr. Russell asked.

"I have to go shopping. It's an emergency." She glanced at Victor, looking him up and down, then looked at her sister.

"Yeah," Cassandra said. "It's an emergency."

"All right but be back by six. I want us all to have a family dinner."

"Yes, Father." Brittany kissed him on the cheek as she took the credit card from his hand. He returned a kiss to Brittany's cheek. She cut her eyes at Victor as she let her hot pink cardigan fall from her shoulders, exposing a matching tank top and a flash of skin.

"Sure, Daddy," Cassandra said. "Bye, Doc. See you at dinner."

"Come on, Cassandra," Brittany said. "I'm not waiting all day for you."

Victor watched the girls leave through the ornate, front doors. At least the younger daughter seemed okay with him being there. The older one might try to put an end to his stay. He wasn't sure what he thought of her but she was pretty. If Mrs. Russell liked him then he'd be okay. As if thinking of her wished her into being, a woman floated down the stairs. Mrs. Russell was dressed in a silk dress, her hair swept up in a French twist and her neck and ears adorned with pearls.

"Catherine," Mr. Russell said. "This is Victor."

"Pleased to meet you, ma'am," Victor said, giving the slightest of bows.

She nodded with a puzzled expression on her face. "I thought you weren't coming until next Saturday."

"No," Mr. Russell said, sighing heavily. "I told you it was today."

Mrs. Russell said, "I'm so sorry. I got the dates mixed up. I hope you'll be comfortable here. Lindy can help you settle in. I believe she's finished setting up your room." She adjusted her necklace. "I do hate to be rude but I'd forgotten you were coming and I have a fund raiser I absolutely must attend. It's for charity. You'll both forgive me, won't you?" She gave her husband a weak smile.

"I understand, ma'am," Victor said.

"How sweet," she said. "Wade can show you around." She turned to her husband. "I'll be back by six. Seven at the latest."

"Should we bother to hold dinner for you?" Mr. Russell was frowning.

She gave a light shake to her head.

However, seeing that Victor wasn't offended, Mr. Russell said, "All right, honey. See you later." He kissed his wife on the cheek with remarkable similarity to the way he'd kissed Brittany.

Mrs. Russel hurried out through the front doors. She didn't seem to care if Victor was there or not. Not for him or against him. Mr. Russell was his only ally.

"I guess it is just you and me," Mr. Russell said, placing his hand back on Victor's shoulder. He picked up Victor's suitcase. "Would you like a tour of your new home?"

"That would be great, sir."

The tour ended in Mr. Russell's study, an antique filled room paneled in dark mahogany. As Mr. Russell sat behind his expansive desk, he motioned for Victor to sit in one of the burgundy linen chars in front of it. Victor was eyeing the well-stocked bookshelves behind him when a maid entered the room. She was dressed in a pale blue uniform with a white apron tied around her waist.

"Excuse me, sir," the maid said in a strong German accent. "I have some refreshments." She rested a silver tray lightly on the desk and handed Mr. Russell a cup of steaming coffee. She gave Victor a glass of soda.

"Thank you, Lindy. That will be all. Please close the door on your way out."

"Yes sir," Lindy replied, delicately bowing her head.

Mr. Russell took a sip of his coffee then placed the mug on a silver, initialed coaster on his desk. Victor repeated those actions with his soda.

The prospect of living in a mansion like this was making the idea of running away much less attractive. Living in a roach-infested apartment, or more realistically, in the streets had nothing on the soft double bed beneath the bay window in his new room.

"So tell me, my boy. What do you think of your humble new home?"

"It's incredible. I mean, it is incredible." Victor wanted to be just like Mr. Russell and he was going to start by speaking properly, the was Mr. Russell did.

"Your room is satisfactory?"

"It's...it is amazing." A smile came to Victor's face as he thought of the new TV, stereo system and computer that Mr. Russell had supplied. Things he had to share with others for a long time. "It is very generous, sir."

"I am glad you are pleased. The next topic we need to discuss is your education. I have enrolled you in the Blakely School, of course. They extend from junior high through high school. Based on your academic records and aptitude test, the Dean wants to move you ahead and start you in your senior year in September."

"They are skipping me ahead to 12th grade?" Victor could not keep the smile off his face.

"They know brilliance when they see it and they reward hard work. That is why all my children go to Blakely."

"That is where Cassandra will be going?"

"Yes. It will be nice to have you two at the same school."

Victor doubted Cassandra would feel the same way after her older sister got through with her.
"Yes, I am so glad we will be attending together." It didn't really matter what those girls thought though. As long as he got the education he needed for what he planned to do. It sounded like Mr. Russell was on board with that.

"After your year at Blakely, I thought we might look at Harvard, Yale, Vassar, and Princeton. We will have to prepare your applications in the fall. I am a Yale man, myself. Any idea where you want to go or what you want to do?"

This was going better than even he could have hoped. "I know what I don't want to do, sir." Victor was going to take full advantage to the opportunity before him. Any thoughts of running away, robbing the place or letting anyone interfere vanished.

"That is a start," Mr. Russell said, chuckling. "To tell you the truth, I have always wished I had been better at the sciences. I might have become a doctor." Mr. Russell's eyes bored into Victor's. "Have you ever thought of going to medical school?"

The truth was out. Victor was to fulfill his foster father's unrealized dream of becoming a doctor. Obviously, Brittany was not going to cooperate with his grand scheme and Cassandra was too young to pressure yet. Besides, they were girls. Mr. Russell needed a male to live his life through.

"Medical school," Victor said, making tears well up in his eyes. "What a coincidence. It has always been my dream."

Victor suddenly shuddered. The fire had almost gone out. Lamenting the past again. Losing track of time. He had to get control over that. It only stalled his progress. Getting out of his recliner and stoking the fire, Victor vowed to stay focused on the present.

Once he had the fire going, he heard the faint buzz of his cell phone. Checking the display, he saw that it was a hospital number. He didn't answer it. Silently cursing to himself, Victor went to one of his five bathrooms to splash water on his face. Delicately patting it dray with a towel, he felt a little more refreshed. He went back to the living room to return the call.

CHAPTER 15

Jesse was startled by the ringing of the phone. He punched the speaker button, hoping it was one of the team reporting good news.

"Lab."

"Jesse," a booming voice said. "I thought I would catch you hard at work."

"Victor?" Jesse said, sitting up straight in his chair and picking up the hand set. "What's up?"

"That is what I was about to ask you."

After a brief silence, Jesse said, "I'm not sure what you mean."

"I wasn't aware we had scheduled any overnight testing," Victor said.

Allison must have called him, Jesse thought. Either that or someone on their team was a traitor.

"We hadn't," Jesse said. "I couldn't sleep so I thought I'd get some work done. I've been screening some candidate to help speed things up."

"I appreciate your effort," Victor said. "Though I have to question your selection."

"Kendra Sibley."

"Yes," Victor said. "She does not exactly fit the profile for expandeded studies."

"In some ways she does. She's the right age and has most of the psychiatric symptoms required," Jesse said.

"She does not have a strong history of aggressive behavior."

A shiver ran down Jesse's spine. "I thought she'd make a good comparison candidate."

"I do not want her included in the testing in any way and I would prefer if you left the selection process to me, the way we always do."

"I'm sorry, Victor. I didn't mean to step over the line. I'll get some more work done on the adult antidepressant project instead."

There was a crackle on the line and Jesse temporarily lost Victor's voice.

"I missed what you said, Victor. Something's wrong with the line."

"That was from my end. I just drove under an old stone bridge."

"You're calling from your car?"

"Yes. I am on my way in. We can talk further when I get there."

The connection was broken. Jesse listened to the dial tone, hung up the hand set and picked it up again, frantically punching in numbers.

"Marguerite," he said when she answered his call. "Can you get off your unit right now?"

"One of my psych aides is on break," she said. "I can't leave only one aide on the unit."

"Get the other aide back. Victor is on his way in."

"Dios mio! I knew I shouldn't have been a part of this. I bet Allison called Dr. Aiken after all. Pinche puta! I tried to convince her not to."

"Allison talked to you about it?"

"Yes, she's a freaking worry-wart, goody two-shoes. I'm sorry. I tried my best."

"Don't worry. You're doing a great job. Now you've got to get into the Admissions Office before he gets here."

"Me? Why me?"

"I have other jobs for everyone else."

"But what if he catches me?"

"He called me. He's coming in to see me," Jesse said. "He'll head straight to the lab."

"Maybe I shouldn't do this."

"Marguerite, it's too late to back out now. I promise I'll call you if Victor heads toward Admissions. If the phone rings in there, just get out. No one calls that office at night. Can you do that?"

"All right," she said, her voice quivering. "I guess that makes sense."

Marguerite hung up the phone and dialed one of the long term units, getting her psych aide on the line.

"Sorry, Henry, but I need to cut your break short."

"I've still got 15 minutes left," Henry said, clearly shoving food into his mouth at the same time.

"I know, but I have to help Amy on the Adult A.C.U. with a medication problem and it's urgent. You can take another full break when I get back."

"Right. Bet I won't get a chance to take one later."

"Then you can leave 30 minutes early, okay?" Marguerite was ready to smack Henry with the phone receiver.

"All right," Henry said. "I'm on my way back."

"Thank you." Marguerite hung up the phone and walked over to the unit door, tapping her foot as she waited.

Maddie could see Amy talking on the phone and glancing in her direction. After hanging up, Amy circled the unit, checking on each patient, then stopped at Maddie's room.

"What's going on?" Maddie whispered.

"Jesse just called. Dr. Aiken's on his way in and he's suspicious. Jesse covered as best he could and said he was switching to adult research for the rest of the night since Dr. Aiken has little interest in adults."

"Gee, nice to know the medical director doesn't care about a good portion of his patient population." Maddie smirked. "Anyway, who tipped Victor off?"

"I'm not sure. It might have been Marguerite," Amy said.

"She was pretty uncomfortable with this," Maddie agreed. "Maybe we made a mistake trusting her."

"Maybe it was Allison, the nurse on Adolescent A.C.U. #2," Amy said.

"Jesse was worried about her," Maddie said, sitting up in bed. "Either way, we better move fast. Can you get me back into the lab?"

"I guess. Why?"

"I've got an idea. I'll explain it to both you and Jesse when we get there."

Waking Edgar and distracting Billy from his cell phone game, Amy told them she needed to take Maddie for another walk to work out the muscle cramps. Both psych aides shrugged and went back to their previous endeavors.

Jogging to the lab, Maddie said, "I can't believe those guys don't get fired."

"I told you, they show up and don't ask any questions," Amy said. "Those seem to be the preferred qualifications for employment here. I have already given up complaining about it. It's not going to change and it only gets me into hot water."

"Why would Dr. Aiken want employees who sleep all shift? Isn't that dangerous to the reputation of the hospital and the safety of the patients?"

"Those aren't Dr. Aiken's primary concerns. Employees who are asleep don't see what's going on," Amy said. "It also gives him justification to threaten to fire them at any time.

"Does he have anything on you?"

"Not until tonight." Amy smiled.

Entering the lab, they watched Jesse leap up from his chair. "I thought you were Victor," he said.

"Good thing it wasn't him," Maddie said. "You look guilty as sin."

'I was trying to think of how to look busy when Victor arrives."

Maddie said, "That's why I'm here."

Marguerite made her way through the halls, past the Reception area and stopped in front of the door to the Admissions Office. She pulled on a pair of latex gloves and tried the doorknob. It was locked. Pulling a credit card out of her pocket, Marguerite tried to override the lock. On the old movies she watched, it looked so easy. Doors weren't made that way anymore. If they ever were. She had no success.

Marguerite walked back into the Reception area and picked up the phone. Calling around to the units, she located the housekeeper on one of the Long Term Units.

"Barney? This is Marguerite. I need you to open the Admissions Office for me."

"Who's the nurse in charge tonight? Don't they have a key?" Barney asked.

"I am but I think Olivia wants to limit the number of keys floating around. She doesn't leave one for us. You're the only one who has a key. Could you help me out? Pretty please." She rolled her r's to make it sound sexy.

"Well, for you, I guess I can," Barney said. "I guess I'm the only one they trust around here."

Within minutes Barney was opening the door and Marguerite stepped into the office. Barney flicked on the light switch and surveyed the room.

"What are you looking for?" he asked. "Maybe I could help you?" He smiled at her and raised his eyebrows.

"I would love that," Marguerite said, "but it's confidential patient information. A new admission is coming in and they want me to coordinate it."

Barney stood by the door.

"You don't have to wait," Marguerite said. "I'm going to read through the information in here so I may be a little while."

"Are you sure?" Barney looked disappointed.

"Yes. Thank you so much. I really appreciate your help." No rolled r's this time.

"Okay," Barney said. "Just give me a holler when you're ready to lock up again."

As he left the office, Marguerite let out a long sigh. "Now to find those forged consent forms," she said aloud.

She scanned the room and decided to start with the row of filing cabinets of the left. Every single one of them was locked. Heading to the row on the back wall, she found those inaccessible, too. Trying the drawers of all the desks was her next step, but everything was safe and secure. Taking a letter opener from the largest of the desks, she headed over to the smallest of them, crouched down and tried to break the lock on the top, right-hand drawer. Aside from bending the letter opener, she made no progress.

Marguerite stood up, wondering what to do next, when she saw a shadow go by the door. Heading out to inspect the situation, she walked right into Olivia Garvin.

"Olivia! What are you doing here at four in the morning?"

"Funny, Marguerite, I was just about to ask you the same thing."

Marguerite surreptitiously slid the mutilated letter opener into her scrub top pocket. "I got a call on a possible admission," she lied. "I thought I'd check if there was any documentation started on him."

"Uh-huh." Olivia crossed her arms over her chest. "How did you get in here?"

"Barney, the housekeeper, let me in. It's not his fault. I told him to."

"Did you find what you were looking for?"

"Actually no. There's nothing out on the desks. I'd already checked the computer from my unit. I was just about to leave."

"Who's the admission?" Olivia asked.

"Excuse me?"

"What's the name of the person that is possibly being admitted? Who were you looking for information on? Wouldn't I know where to look?"

"Yes, of course. It's an adult patient," Marguerite said, wiping at her brow. "A Mr. Nelson. Joe Nelson."

"Doesn't ring a bell. Who's referring him?"

"Um...it was another hospital. A social worker. I forget her name. I wrote it down. The paper I wrote it on is on my unit."

"That's fine." Olivia closed the office door. She paused beside Marguerite and stuck her hand in the woman's scrub top pocket. Pulling out the damaged letter opener, she shook her head and looked as if she were about to cry.

"Victor gave this to me," Olivia said, caressing it.

Marguerite said nothing. She watched Olivia walk into the office and take some keys out of her purse, unlocking one of the filing cabinets. Olivia flipped through several files while Marguerite hovered over her.

"Has Mr. Nelson been here before?" Olivia asked.

"I don't know. I was just checking," Marguerite said.

Olivia gave her a doubtful look as she went over to one of the computers. "When were they wanting to send him over?"

"It's still just a possibility. We don't know if he's coming in for sure," Marguerite said. "Olivia, you don't start work until eight. Let me worry about it until them. It's my job right now. If he come in, I'll call the Admissions Nurse-on-call to handle it." She turned to leave.

"One last question," Olivia said. "Why are you wearing gloves? We certainly keep this office clean."

Marguerite looked at her latex coved hands. "I was cleaning up the med room on my unit earlier. Guess I forgot to take them off."

Olivia nodded.

Marguerite approached the door. "By the way, Olivia, you never said what brings you in this early."

"No, I didn't."

Marguerite stood there for a moment. She gripped the door handle and tried to turn it. It wouldn't budge. "It must be the gloves," she said, taking them off. She wiped the powder residue off her hands with her scrub top and tried the doorknob again. It still wouldn't move. She looked back at Olivia.

With a grin on her face, Olivia held up a small gadget. She clicked it twice. Marguerite heard the door unlock then relock. Olivia punched in some text on her cell phone then sat back and waited. Within seconds, her phone range. Olivia slowly answered it.

"Thanks for calling back Dr. Aiken. I'm in my office and I think you should come over here as soon as possible."

Victor disconnected from Olivia and turned off his computer monitor in his office. He figured Olivia could handle whatever the supposed emergency was that she texted him about for a short while. It could not be more important than what he was about to deal with. He decided to head to the lab.

Maddie was lying on a gurney. Amy was putting conductive gel on Maddie's scalp in the areas where she would attach the electrodes. Jesse was wheeling the electroencephalogram toward the gurney.

"I don't like this at all," Jesse said.

"Neither do I," Amy said, "but I have to agree it's the only way to have witnesses to your conversation with Dr. Aiken.

"Try to get him to say something incriminating," Maddie added. "How fast can you set this thing up? I doubt we have much time left."

"We have a few minutes. We have to make everything look legit," Jesse said. "Victor has an eye for detail."

"Which one?" Maddie said. "The brown one? No, it's that piercing blue one."

Amy shook her head. Jesse snickered and said, "Amy, you'd

better go hide in my bathroom now. I can handle the rest of this."

"Okay," Amy said, attaching the last electrode to Maddie's head. "What do I do if Dr. Aiken has to use the bathroom?"

"He probably won't," Jesse said. "He only uses the private bathroom in his office. The only thing I can imagine is that he'll want to wash his hands but he would use one of the sinks out here."

"Let's hope he has strong kidneys." Amy headed to her hiding spot, leaving the door open a crack.

"I'm going to start the EEG now," Jesse said, turning on the machine.

As the contraption started to buzz, Victor walked silently into the room.

"Hello," he said.

Jesse jumped slightly. He placed a hand on Maddie's shoulder and as she looked up at him, he blinked his eyes. Maddie closed hers.

"What are you up to?" Victor said, heading to the nearest sink.

"Just a baseline sleep EEG on one of the adult patients," Jesse said, trying to concentrate of the brain wave patterns on the graph in front of him.

Victor dried his hands with a clump of paper towels, shut the taps off with them, then tossed the used towels in the trash.

"Is this one of our candidates for the new antidepressant?" Victor asked, moving to the other side of the gurney. "I see that it is. Madison Blythe Blankenship. One that I recognize by sight. Is she already fully sedated?"

"She's been completely out for 15 minutes," Jesse said. He stared at the graph as Victor came to stand beside him.

Maddie tried to stay as still as possible, keeping her breathing even. It felt like hours to her before the men spoke again.

"Looks normal so far," Jesse said.

"Yes," Victor said. "What is your reason for running an EEG on her?"

"Like I said, a baseline."

"Didn't we do a regular EEG on the day of admission, per protocol?"

"It had subtle abnormalities. It was done by a 4th year medical student. I wasn't sure if it was just artifact or if there was something going on. I wanted to do another more thorough sleep EEG to be sure."

"Such subtle abnormalities can be triggered by a small tumor or a lesion," Victor said with a smile. "We could do an intracranial EEG."

Jesse gulped. "I'm sure the first one was just artifact. Look how normal this is reading. I hardly think exploratory neurosurgery is called for. Besides, I would do an MRI or CT scan first if I thought something was going on."

Victor laughed. "I agree. I was just testing you."

Jesse sighed heavily. He felt Maddie's shoulder relax under his grip. "Didn't you say you wanted to talk about Kendra Sibley?"

"Actually," Victor said, "I want to talk about you. You are right, though. I do want to know why you went behind my back and selected Ms. Sibley as a test case," Victor said.

"I wasn't going behind your back," Jesse said. "I intended to discuss it with you when you came in this morning."

"I am here. I would like an explanation."

"As I told you on the phone, I couldn't sleep so I thought I'd get some work done and help speed up our research and development."

"Assuming things need to be moved along, why did you choose that particular girl?"

"I thought I explained this? She is on Protocol Drug #8. I assumed you wanted her to be part of the program somehow."

"I see," Victor said. "Why did you assume, as you mentioned, that she would be a comparison candidate as opposed to a study case."

Jesse felt something on his thigh, looked down and saw Maddie's fingers nudging him. He took a deep breath.

"Because she's not a state case."

"Go on."

"Almost all of the patients who are maintained long term on Protocol Drug #8 and identified as study cases are teenagers in the custody of the state."

"Anything else you would like to tell me?" Victor moved toward the computer at Jesse's workstation.

"I'm not sure what you mean."

Victor pushed the space bar on Jesse's keyboard and his computer monitor came out of its standby mode.

"The A.W.O.L. list. It looks like you have been doing some investigating," Victor said.

Jesse looked down at Maddie and squeezed her hand tightly. Maddie opened her eyes the width of a sliver and looked at him. He looked frightened.

"I just want to remind you," Victor said, "that you are part of this organization and you are more involved in the R & D of this drug than even I am."

"I'm not sure what you're point is," Jesse said, his hands trembling.

Victor smiled. "You are an accomplice in my work. A partner. You are in just as deep as me, if not deeper."

"So you're admitting you're doing something wrong?" Jesse's dry mouth made it difficult to talk.

"I said no such thing. I did not invent this drug. You did."

"It was your idea. You know everything about it."

Victor shook his head. "Not really. I just had a wonderful idea. That is why I have you. You are a biochemist. You are the expert that brought my idea to fruition. If there was something wrong or dangerous about the drug, you should have told me."

Jesse stared at Victor in disbelief. "You were involved in every step. You dictated the chemical properties of the medication, what neurotransmitters you wanted targeted. I just mixed your recipe. You chose how we adjusted it. You chose who received the drug and at what dosages. You chose the timing of the trials. When we started on human subjects."

"Perhaps. However, I did not personally give the drug to anyone. The nurses did that. Yes, I ordered it. But if they saw it was having side effects, they should have informed me." Victor held out his hands.

Jesse stared at his lifelong pal in complete shock. "Victor, we've been friends a long time. I watched your back at Toloucan. I was your only loyal friend through all these years. I appreciate everything you've done for me but this is it. I can't stick by you on this one. Not for the sake of the friendship or for gratitude. You've gone too far. People have died. Kids have died. Innocent kids. It has to stop. It has to stop now."

"I am surprised, Jesse. I believed that you were indeed my one true friend. I see now that you are just the same as everyone else. Falsely accusing me, plotting to destroy me. It is a good thing I kept my eye on you. I knew you would eventually betray me. Those closest to me always have."

"Victor, I know you started out meaning well. You wanted to help troubled kids, just like we were. I know Toloucan motivated you to improve the situation of these kids. It was a noble idea but now you've sacrificed lives in the name of what? Quick results? A string of hospitals with your name on them? It's not about your ego or your brilliance. You've completely lost touch with the path that brought you here in the first place. I can't support you in this. I can't cover it up."

"You do not have to," Victor said. "I have done nothing wrong."

"What? How can you say that?" Jesse asked. "There are bodies of children that were experimented on buried on this property!"

"I am the C.E.O., Clinical Director and Lead Medical Faculty of this teaching facility and I am developing additional hospitals across the country. I cannot be expected to know every move that is made in each facility. Nor can I be held personally responsible. I will take action, however. The corporation of Aiken's Haven might take a beating and dissolve but I've developed my new clinics under a different name, using separate funding sources. Rosewood Retreats will flourish."

"Rosewood Retreats?" Where did that name come from? Don't you want your name in the title?"

"It's from my mother."

"Darlene Aiken Torrence?"

"Darlene Rosewood. Her maiden name."

"But you hate your mother."

Victor shrugged his shoulders.

"Why are you telling me this?" Jesse asked. "Aren't you afraid I'll reveal the correlation?"

"No one will listen to you," Victor said calmly. "How reliable is an inmate of the state correctional facility? Or if the FDA has their say you may be lucky enough to get a Federal stint. Your past history of juvenile delinquency and denials of foster care will support the fact that you are untrustworthy."

Jesse felt like he'd been stabbed in the heart. "What are you talking about?"

"Prison. Prison is where they will put you after the authorities learn that, unbeknownst to me, you were developing and distributing a lethal concoction. You killed every one of those patients, Jesse. Not me. You did it."

Victor's cell phone went off, startling everyone in the room. Victor looked at the display and decided it was time to check on Olivia.

"Admissions is calling. I will be back, Jesse. There is no use trying to run or hide from the truth."

CHAPTER 16

Once Victor had walked out of the lab, Amy crept out of her hiding place. Maddie propped he head up on her elbow.

"He really is crazy," Maddie said. "Hearing him talk just confirmed it."

"I didn't know he was that far gone," Amy said. "What do we do now?"

Maddie and Amy looked at Jesse. Jesse said nothing.

"You're not taking that madman's babble seriously?" Maddie asked.

"He had a point. I did essentially create the drug."

"No! Do not let Victor talk you into taking blame. He's the conductor of this band."

"But if I hadn't followed his directions those kids might still be alive," Jesse said.

"Wrong!" Maddie said. "You weren't even aware of the deaths until tonight. You weren't even fully aware of any serious side effects. Victor made sure of that. I know you had suspicions but you weren't even sure there was foul play until I pulled you into this."

Maddie tried to sit up but the electrodes pulled at her scalp. Amy rushed over and started taking them off.

"We'll get Maddie back to the unit," Amy said. "I'll come

back so you'll have a witness when Dr. Aiken returns."

"Leave them on. I'm staying here," Maddie said. "I wouldn't miss Victor's next tirade for anything."

"I don't think it matters anymore," Jesse said. "Besides, I just thought of another problem. Victor was called from Admissions. Marguerite is in there looking for the falsified consent forms."

"Oh no," Amy said. "Maybe she got caught by someone."

Maddie said, "Or maybe she's about to get caught."

"Or maybe," Jesse said, "she wasn't on our side to begin with."

"You think Marguerite alerted Dr. Aiken?" Amy asked.

"It's a possibility," Jesse asked. "Who else would be in Admissions at this hour?" His breath caught in his throat. "If there is a chance she's with us then I've just put another person in the line of fire." He started to leave the lab. "You two get back to your unit.

"Jesse," Maddie said. "Be careful."

"I'm a murderer, Maddie. Nothing worse than that can happen to me."

He left before either of the women could say a word.

Victor put his hand on the doorknob to the Admissions office and let out a grunt as he ran face first into the door.

"Sorry," Olivia called out, cringing.

Victor heard a click and tried the door again.

"Are you all right, Doctor?"

"Yes, yes," he said, irritably. "What is going on in here?"

"It's a good thing you called me to come in Dr. Aiken. I found this nurse ransacking the office."

Victor looked at Olivia who was holding a gun trained on a pale, trembling nurse.

"Marguerite, is it not?"

"Yes, sir."

"What are you doing here?"

In a trembling voice, she replied, "As I told Olivia, I'm the Hospital Charge Nurse tonight and I was looking for past records on a potential readmission."

"A nonexistent person from a nonexistent caller," Olivia said, glaring at Marguerite.

"Is anything missing in here?" Victor asked.

"Not that I can tell but I haven't had a chance to do a thorough search," Olivia said.

Victor walked to one of the desks and tapped a keyboard, causing the screensaver on the computer to vanish. He flashed through several displays then stopped.

"Interesting," he said. "I see all the calls logged for the night. They are logged by category. There does not seem to be any admission calls logged on your shift."

"It came in around 3 o'clock," Marguerite said. "Maybe there's a computer glitch."

Victor nodded to Olivia. Olivia moved closer to Marguerite, her gun never wavering from its target.

"Perhaps you would like to take this opportunity to tell me the truth," Victor said.

Marguerite said, "I've told you the truth."

"Stop it!" Olivia shoved the barrel of the gun against Marguerite's temple. Marguerite started to cry.

"Calm down, Olivia," Victor said. "I just wanted to see whose side she is on. I already know what is going on."

"You do?" Olivia asked.

"Yes," he said. "Now it is time we all take a walk. There is some unfinished business in the lab."

Jogging down the hall, Jesse was kicking himself for bringing Marguerite in on the plan, wondering whether she'd betrayed them or he placed her in danger. Either way, it was his place to do something. As he turned the corner, he ran right into Victor, Olivia and Marguerite.

"Watch where you're going!" Olivia pulled her foot out from under Jesse's.

"Sorry," he said, recoiling from Olivia's verbal assault. "I didn't see you there."

"Obviously," she hissed at him.

Victor said, "Where are you going Jesse?"

"I was going to Admissions to talk with you."

Victor gave a creepy smile. "Perhaps you were more concerned about rescuing your coconspirator?" He glared at Marguerite.

Sensing that Marguerite was in serious trouble, Jesse said, "Why don't we all go back into the Admissions Office and talk about this?"

"I think not. There has already been enough activity in there for one night," Victor said.

"Don't blame Marguerite for it. I put her up to it."

Marguerite's eyes widened. She shook her head ever so slightly but enough that Jesse caught her meaning.

"Put her up to what? Why was she ransacking my office?" Olivia snapped.

Jesse shrugged, letting his breath out slowly. "I asked her to get consent forms on all the candidates in the drug study."

Marguerite stared at him in shock.

"Your need for them would be what?" Victor asked.

"I'm compiling complete records on all patients involved in the study since we are so close to a finished product."

Olivia said, "You're such a liar."

Victor replied, "No, he is not. I believe him."

Olivia stared at her boss. "You do?"

Even Jesse and Marguerite stared at him.

"Yes. I think our nurse here was trying to get consent records. I think he is compiling those records. I just think the purpose for obtaining them is different. Am I right Jesse?"

Jesse said, "Why don't we all go into the office and talk this thing through?"

"I don't think so," Victor said. "We are going back to the lab."

"Why don't we let Marguerite go back to her unit. She's done nothing wrong," Jesse said. "That way you and I can talk, Victor."

"She's not going anywhere," Olivia said.

Jesse watched Olivia move away from Marguerite's side just enough to expose the gun in her hand. She waved the gun in the direction of the lab. Jesse and Marguerite silently obeyed her nonverbal orders.

As the group rounded the corner, they all saw Maddie and Amy exiting the lab, a stack of papers clutched in Amy's hands.

"Going somewhere?" Victor called out.

Amy linked her arm under Maddie's elbow. "Just helping this patient back to the unit."

"She looks perfectly capable of walking on her own," Victor said. "The two of you can join the rest of us in the lab."

"I really should get this patient back in bed and get back to my unit, Dr. Aiken."

"I suspect, Amy Bunton, that you have already spent plenty of time off your unit tonight. A few more minutes will not matter."

Olivia flashed her gun. "You better do as he says."

Amy and Maddie were taken aback. They quickly retraced their steps back into the lab, followed by Jesse, Marguerite, Victor and Olivia bringing up the rear.

As they passed the first stainless steel counter, Amy opened a drawer and grabbed two syringes filled with a thick, clear liquid and slid them quickly into her scrub top pocket. Everyone was focused on the gun. Everyone except Olivia. She was focused on Victor.

Jesse saw an opening. Oliva was holding the Glock with only one hand and it was a little too big for her stubby little hands. He whirled around and body checked her, knocking the weapon free. He dove and picked it up, training it on both Victor and Olivia.

"Oh my God! Victor! Protect me," Olivia said as she moved to his side and grabbed his arm.

Victor brushed her off like a gnat. He moved toward the door. "You are on your own."

"Where do you think you're going," Jesse said.

"You are not going to use that thing," Victor said.

"I'm going to hold the both of you here until the authorities arrive," Jesse said. "Marguerite, could you call 911?"

Olivia looked puzzled, "Why are you calling the police?"

"We know what Dr. Aiken has been up to," Maddie said. "The

death serum, the morgue, the cemetery. We know it all."

"They know?" Olivia said, horrified.

"I am fine with the authorities coming. The people who are going to be implicated in this situation are all in this room." He pointed at Jesse, Amy, Marguerite and Olivia.

"Why are you pointing at me?" Olivia complained.

"You are the one who has been forging consent forms."

"On your instructions."

"I did not know a thing about it until today. We all choose our own actions. You, Olivia, chose to commit fraud. These nurses chose to commit murder and Jesse," Victor wheeled around to look him in the eye, "it is you who chose to create the murder weapon."

Everyone was staring at Victor. A tear ran down Olivia's face as she looked at Victor. He turned to leave.

"Don't leave, Victor," Jesse said.

"You are not going to add another homicide to your list of crimes." Victor's voice was strong and steady. "You would not be able to live with yourself.

"What have I got to lose?" Jesse said. "According to you, I'll be spending the rest of my life in prison. At least with you gone, no more children will be harmed."

Behind him, Amy pulled out the two pre-filled syringes from her pocket and handed one to Maddie, giving her a two second, visual lesson on how to use it. The two women rushed the doctor. Victor felt a stinging pain in his right upper arm and his left thigh, right through his clothes. Amy and Maddie had jabbed the needles in and pushed the contents of the syringe in. When Victor pulled away, Maddie's needle tip broke off, staying in his thigh. She stared at her damaged, empty syringe. Amy pulled her away.

"It's okay," Amy said, holding her own empty, intact injection. "We both got the medicine in."

Olivia ran forward, putting her hands out toward Victor. He grunted and pushed her away.

"What have you done to him?" Olivia cried.

"What do you care?" Maddie said. "He's letting you take the fall."

"Is he going to die?" Olivia looked around panicked. "Can you help him?"

"He's not going to die," Amy said.

"There will be no more killings," Maddie said.

Amy turned to Victor. "We gave you eight milligrams of lorazepam so I suggest you don't go anywhere." She turned to Olivia. "It won't kill him but it will keep him sedated long enough for the police to get here and investigate." She turned to Jesse." It's not going to kick in for about 5 to 10 minutes and it could take another 15 to 20 to sedate him, so keep the gun on him until we're sure."

"Isn't holding a loaded gun on him enough?" Olivia asked. "You had to overdose him, too." She was crying.

"Keep it up," Maddie said, "and you're next."

"You're crazy," Oliva said.

"I guess I'm in the right place then," Maddie replied.

Amy said, "We better call the police."

Marguerite said, "I'm already on it."

Amy and Maddie stood at Victor's sides. His eyelids were heavy and his knees were weakening. They eased him into a chair.

"What happened, Victor?" Maddie asked. "You started this hospital with wonderful intentions. When did that change?"

"It hasn't changed," Victor said, his words slurring slightly.

"I'm sure you've help some kids along the way," Maddie said, "but why did you allow those other patients to die? Why did you tell your nurses not to save them?"

"They are better off," Victor said, leaning to his left side.

Amy and Maddie propped him up.

"Better off dead?" Amy asked.

"Yes," Victor said, his eyes fluttering, his breathing slow and even. "If I cannot save them with the drug then..."

"Then what?" Maddie asked, giving Victor a gentle nudge. "If you can't save them with the drug then what?"

"Then I cannot help them at all. They will have to suffer through life the way I suffered. Alone. Miserable. Unloved."

"You think putting them out of their misery is better than letting them live and deal with their aggression and issues? Have you ever heard of therapy?"

Victor let out a snore.

"He's a lightweight, isn't he?" Maddie said.

"I'm surprised it's kicking in so fast," Amy said. "It is a very high dose, though."

"After Toloucan, Victor has never taken any medication," Jesse said. "His body isn't used to it."

"A doctor who won't take medicine. Huh." Maddie said.

"Should we have used a lower dose," Jesse asked.

"No," Amy said. "He will just sleep longer and deeper. We need to keep an eye on his vital signs. Especially his breathing. He should be fine. Physically, that is."

"There sending two homicide detectives over," Marguerite said, rejoining the group, "and a squad car is on its way."

They stood there watching Victor's body sink down into the chair. Olivia was down at his feet, clinging to him and sobbing.

“Olivia,” Amy said, “he’ll be all right.”

“No, he won’t,” she said. “You’ve ruined him!”

Victor’s breathing remained slow and even. Maddie turned to tell Jesse that things looked safe but instead, she was shocked into momentary silence. Then, she found her voice.

“Jesse, no!” she yelled.

Amy whirled around. “Jesse! What are you doing?”

Marguerite screamed. “Dios mio!”

Jesse wasn’t pointing the gun at Victor or Olivia. He has the weapon pointed directly at his own head.

“Put it down!” Maddie cried, movie toward him.

“Don’t come near me,” Jesse said, tears streaming down his cheeks. “I don’t want to hurt anyone else.”

“Why are you doing this?”

“Victor is right. I am responsible for putting every single one of those kids into those graves. How can I live with that?”

“Victor is playing mind games with us,” Maddie replied. “He’s twisting to facts to protect himself.”

“I can’t deny my role in this.”

“Your role was to develop a medication to help troubled teens. You never intended to hurt anyone. You didn’t know how twisted Victor was. No one did. Victor is the devil here, not you.”

It doesn’t matter what my intentions were or what I was aware of,” Jesse said. “The results are still the same. Children are still dead.”

“You didn’t know that. Not for sure,” Maddie said. “Not until tonight.”

“I should have investigated more quickly when I started feeling uncomfortable. Maybe Alicia would still be alive.”

Maddie motioned for Amy and Marguerite to join her. She whispered to them and then they both took a step toward Jesse, crowding him.

"What are you doing?" he asked.

"If you're going to kill yourself then you're going to have to kill us, too," Amy said.

"What?" Jesse tried to step back from them.

The three women stepped forward.

"That's right," Marguerite said. "We gave the medication to the patients. We're as much to blame as you are."

"In fact," Amy said, "we're more directly responsible than you are so we should go first." She reached for the Glock.

"Don't you think they should die, too, Jesse?" Maddie asked.

"Of course not."

"Why not?"

"They're not to blame. They were just doing their jobs. They had no way of knowing what Victor was up to."

"Exactly," Maddie said. "So take your own advice."

Maddie reached up and slowly moved the gun away from Jesse's temple. She pried the gun from his clenched fingers and handed it to Amy. Maddie put her arms around him. A few seconds later, Jesse returned the hug.

"Don't ever scare me like that again," Maddie said.

"I'm sorry," Jesse said, wiping at his eyes.

Maddie let her hand run along Jesse's cheek. He ran his hand down her hair. They shared a sad smile.

Marguerite coughed lightly. "I hate to interrupt but it looks like Olivia isn't as hot for the doctor as she seemed."

The other three looked around to see Victor, now snoring loudly, still slumped in the chair. Olivia was nowhere in sight.

"Maybe she was an innocent player, too," Amy said.

"Maybe," Jesse said, putting his arm around Maddie. "A victim of her feelings for Victor.

"She was really in love with him?" Amy asked.

Jesse said, "She'd do anything for him."

"Almost anything," Marguerite said. "Except take the fall."

A siren screamed outside. It was getting louder by the minute.

"I have a question," Maddie said. "Is that how you see someone in love, Jesse? As a victim?"

"In Olivia's case, definitely. As for other people..."

Maddie smiled, stood on her toes, and kissed him.

EPILOGUE

ONE MONTH LATER

Maddie walked around the rustic living room, admiring the old fashioned furnishings. She walked to the stone fireplace and used the poker to rearrange the wood logs, creating a stronger flame. She listened to the sap simmering in the heat.

Jesse walked into the room, handing her a mug and kissed her on the cheek.

"Cappuccino made just the way you like it."

"You're spoiling me."

"Yes, I am and I intend to keep on doing it."

Jesse tossed some oversized pillows on the floor in front of the fire. He threw down a heavy blanket, picked up his own matching mug from a bare wooden table and motioned for Maddie to sit. From the kitchen they heard grunting noises. Maddie laughed.

"Yes, Winston, you can join us," Jesse said, rolling his eyes. "I don't know if I'm ever going to get used to this crazy mutt of yours."

Winston lumbered out of the kitchen and came into the living room. At first, he rutted around in the blanket trying to make a space for himself. Then, he gave up and crept underneath a wooden side table.

"Comfortable Winston?" Jesse asked.

The bulldog snorted.

Maddie smiled. "Did you make this table he's tucked under? I like the carving detail on the legs?"

"I did," Jesse said, "thanks. If I'm going to change career directions, I figured I'd jump right into it."

"Carpentry is a big switch from biochemistry."

"Not really. They're both about putting pieces together to create something."

"When did you become such a skilled woodworker?"

"It was what I originally planned to go into. I did really well in shop class at Toloucan."

"At least that place was good for something."

They sipped their coffee and stared into the flickering fire. Jesse leaned over and kissed Maddie on the lips.

"Who would have thought," Maddie said, smiling, "that something so wonderful could have come out of something so horrible."

"Don't remind me," Jesse said. "I'm relieved I was cleared of any charges but I'm not looking forward to testifying at the trial."

"I know but with Victor behind bars, I think we can all rest a little easier."

"Victor will get out."

"I can't picture the eminent Dr. Aiken digging through concrete with a spoon."

"Not that way." Jesse laughed. "His lawyers will find a loophole. Or he'll find it for them. That is if he is even convicted at all."

"I can't believe Darlene is refusing to testify."

"Maybe being held prisoner in your son's mansion isn't so

bad. Once that Jim Torrence was out of the picture, he had her all to himself. That's all he ever wanted. He still adores her despite everything. She has a free ride."

"Will they be able to link him to Jim's murder?"

"I doubt it. I told them what I know but it's pretty weak. At this point, I don't think they're even looking into it."

"You think Victor will want revenge on those of us who do testify?"

"I'm sure of it," Jesse said. "I'm just not sure how he'll dole it out."

"That scares me."

"Me too, but I'm not going to live under Victor's threats anymore."

"I'm so proud of you."

They cuddled and kissed again. Winston came out from under his table and snuggled against Maddie's leg.

"I didn't realize I was going to have to share you," Jesse said, laughing.

"I still can't get over Olivia being given immunity to testify," Maddie said.

"As Amy said, she was one of Victor's unwitting victims."

Maddie rolled her eyes. "More like one of his henchmen."

They both laughed mirthlessly.

"I'm going to miss Amy," Maddie said.

"Where in Canada is she going again?"

"Her family is in Halifax, Nova Scotia. She plans to go back to school to get her Master's degree in counseling so she can open a private practice. She'll be good at it. In fact, I may be in need of her services to deal with everything that's happened."

"You'll be fine. We both will," Jesse said. "It's Marguerite I'm concerned about."

"I know. Amy said the shock of the situation made her condition worse. Then she stopped her medication and got so depressed."

"I still can't believe she's been struggling with manic-depression all this time."

"Hey, the proper terminology is bipolar disorder and people with mental illnesses can function perfectly well when they get proper treatment," Maddie said.

"I know, I know, you don't have to tell me," Jesse said. "But it sounds like you are cultivating a new article in your brain."

Maddie laughed. "Maybe. But I've written so much on Aiken's Haven, I need a break. And I want to see Amy before she leaves and check in on Marguerite. I need to see Helen and Kendra again soon, too."

"How's Kendra doing?"

"Good. I called Helen yesterday. Kendra's seeing Dr. Park, the psychologist regularly and taking an antidepressant. An FDA approved, well researched medication. She even started back to school last week. Helen says she's back to her old self again."

"Having Adam around probably helps, too. Where is he going to stay once his visit at the Sibley's is over? Will he go into foster care?"

"He'll be in foster care but he doesn't have to go anywhere," Maddie said, smiling.

"Meaning?" Jesse looked at her quizzically.

"Helen is taking Adam in as a foster child. She's already started the adoption process. Kendra's always wanted a big brother."

"That will be good for all of them," Jesse said. "Why don't we have everyone over for a dinner party once Marguerite is feeling better?"

"Great idea," Maddie said. "It has to be before Amy leave town."

"Before you leave, too."

They both feel silent. The fire burned intensely and Maddie's cheeks felt hot.

"I know you're upset about my moving to New York but having my own column in a major newspaper has always been a dream of mine. It's something I can't pass up."

"I know," Jesse said. "I think it's a great opportunity for you. I'm not asking you to pass it up."

"Then what are you asking me to do?"

Jesse reached into his pocket, took out a small, red, velvet box and opened it. Maddie gasped. In front of her was a brilliant diamond in a delicate, tiffany setting. Also in front of her was the man she wanted to spend the rest of her life with.

"Will you marry me?" Jesse whispered, slipping the ring on her finger.

"That," Maddie said, "is something I can do."

THE END

Made in the USA
Coppell, TX
08 December 2019

12576269R00150